Just Beyond
the Clouds

**Center Point
Large Print**

**This Large Print Book carries the
Seal of Approval of N.A.V.H.**

Just Beyond the Clouds

KAREN KINGSBURY

CENTER POINT PUBLISHING
THORNDIKE, MAINE

This Center Point Large Print edition
is published in the year 2008 by arrangement with
Center Street, a division of Hachette Book Group USA.

Copyright © 2007 by Karen Kingsbury.

The text of this Large Print edition is unabridged. In other
aspects, this book may vary from the original edition.
Printed in the United States of America.
Set in 16-point Times New Roman type.

ISBN: 978-1-60285-107-8

Library of Congress Cataloging-in-Publication Data

Kingsbury, Karen.
    Just beyond the clouds / Karen Kingsbury.--Center Point large print ed.
      p. cm.
    ISBN 978-1-60285-107-8 (lib. bdg. : alk. paper)
      1. Widowers--Fiction. 2. Down syndrome--Patients--Fiction. 3. Women teachers--Fiction.
    4. Large type books. I. Title.

PS3561.I4873J87 2008
813'.54--dc22

2007032528

Donald, my prince charming.

We've reached a new year, another season in life, and still I cannot imagine this ride without you. Our kids are flourishing, and so much of that is because of you, because of your commitment to me and to them. You are the spiritual leader, the man of my dreams who makes this whole crazy, wonderful adventure possible. I thank God for you every day. I am amazed at the way you blend love and laughter, tenderness and tough standards to bring out the best in our boys. Thanks for loving me, for being my best friend, and for finding "date moments" amidst even the most maniacal or mundane times. My favorite times are with you by my side. I love you always, forever.

Kelsey, my precious daughter.

You are seventeen, and somehow that sounds more serious than the other ages. As if we jumped four years over the past twelve months. Seventeen brings with it the screeching brakes on a childhood that has gone along full speed until now. Seventeen? Seventeen years since I held you in the nursery, feeling a sort of love I'd never felt before. Seventeen sounds like bunches of lasts all lined up ready to take the stage and college counselors making plans to take my little girl from here and home into a brand-new big world. Seventeen tells me it won't be much longer. Especially as you near the end of your junior year. Sometimes I find myself barely able to exhale. The ride is so fast at this point that I can only try not to blink, so I won't miss a minute of it. I see you growing and unfolding like the most beautiful springtime flower, becoming interested in current events and formulating godly viewpoints that are yours alone. The same is true in dance, where you are simply breathtaking onstage. I believe in you, honey. Keep your eyes on Jesus and the path will be easy to follow. Don't ever stop dancing. I love you.

Tyler, my beautiful song.

Can it be that you are fourteen and helping me bring down the dishes from the top shelf? Just yesterday people would call and confuse you with Kelsey. Now they confuse you with your dad—in more ways than one. You are on the bridge, dear son, making the transition between Neverland and Tomorrowland and becoming a strong, godly young man in the process. Keep giving Jesus your very best, and always remember that you're in a battle. In today's world, Ty, you need His armor every day, every minute. Don't forget . . . when you're up there onstage, no matter how bright the lights, I'll be watching from the front row, cheering you on. I love you.

Sean, my wonder boy.

Your sweet nature continues to be a bright light in our home. It seems a lifetime ago that we first brought you—our precious son—home from Haiti. It's been my great joy to watch you grow and develop this past year, learning more about reading and writing and, of course, animals. You're a walking encyclopedia of animal facts, and that, too, brings a smile to my face. Recently a cold passed through the family, and you handled it better than any of us. Smiling through your fever, eyes shining even when you felt your worst. Sometimes I try to imagine if everyone everywhere had your outlook—what a sunny place the world would be. Your hugs are something I look forward to, Sean. Keep close to Jesus. I love you.

Josh, my tender tough guy.

You continue to excel at everything you do, but my favorite time is late at night when I poke my head into your room and see that—once again—your nose is buried in your Bible. You really get it, Josh. I loved hearing you talk about baptism the other day, how you feel ready to make that decision, that commitment to Jesus. At almost twelve, I can only say that every choice you make for Christ will take you closer to the plans He has for your life. That by being strong in the Lord, first and foremost, you'll be strong at everything else. Keep winning for Him, dear son. You make me so proud. I love you.

EJ, my chosen one.

You amaze me, Emmanuel Jean! The other day you told me that you pray often, and I asked you what about. "I thank God a lot," you told me. "I thank Him for my health and my life and my home." Your normally dancing eyes grew serious. "And for letting me be adopted into the right family." I still feel the sting of tears when I imagine you praying that way. I'm glad God let you be adopted into the right family, too. One of my secret pleasures is watching you and Daddy becoming so close. I'll glance over at the family room during a playoff basketball game on TV, and there you'll be, snuggled up close to him, his arm around your shoulders. As long as Daddy's your hero, you have nothing to worry about. You couldn't have a better role model. I know that Jesus is leading the way and that you are excited to learn the plans He has for you. But for you, this year will always stand out as a turning point. Congratulations, honey! I love you.

Austin, my miracle child.

Can my little boy be nine years old? Even when you're twenty-nine you'll be my youngest, my baby. I guess that's how it is with the last child, but there's no denying what my eyes tell me. You're not little any-more. Even so, I love that—once in a while—you wake up and scurry down the hall to our room so you can sleep in the middle. Sound asleep I still see the blond-haired infant who lay in intensive care, barely breathing, awaiting emergency heart surgery. I'm grateful for your health, precious son, grateful God gave you back to us at the end of that long-ago day. Your heart remains the most amazing part of you, not only physically, miraculously, but because you have such kindness and compassion for people. One minute tough boy hunting frogs and snakes out back, pre-tending you're an Army Ranger, then getting teary-eyed when Horton the Elephant nearly loses his dust speck full of little Who people. Be safe, baby boy. I love you.

And to God Almighty, the Author of life, who has—for now—blessed me with these.

Acknowledgments

This book couldn't have come together without the help of many people. First, a special thanks to my friends at Hachette Book Group USA, who continue to believe in my books, and my ministry of Life-Changing Fiction™. Thank you!

Also thanks to my amazing agent, Rick Christian, president of Alive Communications. I am more amazed as every day passes at your sincere integrity, your brilliant talent, and your commitment to the Lord and to getting my Life-Changing Fiction out to readers all over the world. You are a strong man of God, Rick. You care for my career as if you were personally responsible for the souls God touches through these books. Thank you for looking out for my personal time—the hours I have with my husband and kids most of all. I couldn't do this without you.

As always, this book wouldn't be possible without the help of my husband and kids, who will eat just about anything when I'm on deadline and who understand and love me anyway. I thank God that I'm still able to spend more time with you than with my pretend people—as Austin calls them. Thanks for understanding the sometimes crazy life I lead and for always being my greatest support.

Thanks to my mother and assistant, Anne Kingsbury, for her great sensitivity and love for my readers. You are a reflection of my own heart, Mom, or maybe

I'm a reflection of yours. Either way we are a great team, and I appreciate you more than you know. I'm grateful also for my dad, Ted Kingsbury, who is and always has been my greatest encourager. I remember when I was a little girl, Dad, and you would say, "One day, honey, everyone will read your books and know your work." Thank you for believing in me long before anyone else ever did. Thanks also to my sisters, who help out with my business when the workload is too large to see around. I appreciate you!

Especially thanks to Tricia Kingsbury, my sister who runs a large part of my business life. God brought you to me, Tricia, when things in my office were insanely crazy, and I'll be grateful for always. You are my sister, my friend, and now my assistant. It doesn't get any better than that. Don't ever leave, okay? And to Olga Kalachik, whose hard work helping me prepare for events allows me to operate a significant part of my business from my home. The personal touch you both bring to my ministry is precious to me, priceless to me . . . Thank you with all my heart.

And thanks to my friends and family, especially my sister Sue, who is a new addition to my staff, and to Shannon Kane and Melissa Kane, my nieces, who helped me with major projects this past year. Thanks to Ann and Sylvia, and to all of you who pray for me and my family. We couldn't do this without you. Thanks to all of you who continue to surround me with love and prayer and support. I could list you by name, but you know who you are. Thank you for believing in me and for seeing who I really am. A true friend stands by through the changing seasons of life and cheers you on not for your successes but for staying true to what matters most. You are the ones who know me that way, and I'm grateful for every one of you.

Of course, the greatest thanks goes to God Almighty, the most wonderful Author of all—the Author of life. The gift is Yours. I pray I might have the incredible opportunity and responsibility to use it for You all the days of my life.

Forever in Fiction™

A special thanks to Al and Sandee Kirkwood who won the Forever in Fiction™ auction at the YWCA benefit in Washington State. The Kirkwoods chose to honor their daughter, Kelley Sue Gaylor, by naming her Forever in Fiction™.

Kelley Gaylor is thirty-nine, married to Dean, her husband of sixteen years. They have three children: Allie, twelve; Matt, ten; and Joey, five. One of Kelley's many blessings is the fact that both sets of their parents live close by, and that the entire family gets together often.

Kelley enjoys vacationing with her family at Black Butte Ranch in Central Oregon and spending time with the people she loves. She is the oldest of three siblings and spends much of her free time watching her kids play sports, or biking, skiing, and doing weekly Bible studies. She helps out at her children's school and loves her reading time.

In addition, Kelley does charity work for children and started a group called "For the Children," which provides basic clothing to kids at four schools. Her parents have a thoroughbred racing and breeding business in Washington, and Kelley has had the privilege of attending the Kentucky Derby and the Belmont Stakes. She is a good listener and is liked by everyone who knows her.

You'll notice that Kelley Gaylor's character is a volunteer in *Just Beyond the Clouds*. She works with handicapped people and helps them find their greatest potential. I chose to name this character after Kelley because it was closest to how Kelley is viewed by the people who love her—giving, generous, attentive, and caring.

Al and Sandee Kirkwood, I pray that Kelley is honored by your gift, and by her placement in *Just Beyond the Clouds*, and that you will always see a bit of Kelley when you read her name in the pages of this novel, where she will be Forever in Fiction™.

For those of you who are not familiar with Forever in Fiction™, it is my way of involving you, the readers, in my stories, while raising money for charities. To date, this item has raised more than one hundred thousand dollars at charity auctions across the country. If you are interested in having a Forever in Fiction™ package donated to your auction, contact my assistant at Kingsburydesk@aol.com. Please write *Forever in Fiction* in the subject line. Please note that I am able to donate only a limited number of these each year. For that reason I have set a fairly high minimum bid on this package. That way the maximum funds are raised for charities.

Just Beyond
the Clouds

Chapter One

The eighteen adult students at the front of the classroom were a happy, ragtag group, mostly short and squatty, with sturdy necks and squinty eyes. All but two wore thick glasses. Their voices mingled in a loud cacophony of raucous laughter, genuine confusion, and boisterous verbal expression.

"Teacher!" The one named Gus took a step forward, lowered his brow, and pointed to the student beside him. "*He* wants the bus to the *Canadian* Rockies." Gus rolled his eyes. He gestured dramatically toward the window. "The buses out *there* go to the *Colorado* Rockies." He tossed both his hands in the air. "Could you tell him, Teacher?"

"Gus is right." Twenty-six-year-old Elle Dalton—teacher, mentor, encourager, friend—looked out the window. "Those are the *Colorado* Rockies. But our trip tomorrow isn't to the mountains." She smiled at the young men. "We're going to the Rocky Mountain Plaza. Rocky Mountain is just the name."

"Right." Daisy stood up and put her hands on her hips. She knew the Mountain Metropolitan Transit system better than anyone at the center. Daisy wagged her thumb at Gus. "I told you that. Shopping tomorrow. Not mountain climbing."

"Yes." Elle stood a few feet back and studied her students. She'd been over this two dozen times today already. But that was typical for a Thursday.

"Everyone take out your cheat sheets."

In a slow sort of chain reaction, the students reached into their jeans pockets or in some cases their socks or waistbands for a folded piece of paper. After a minute or so, the entire group had them out and they began reciting the information—all at different times and with different levels of speaking ability.

"Wait"—she held up her hand—"let's listen." Elle knew the routine by heart. She approached the line and waited until she had their attention. "Everyone follow along with me." She walked slowly down the row of students. "Bus Route Number Ten will take us from the center at Cheyenne Boulevard and Nevada Avenue south past Meadows Road, left on Academy Boulevard to the shops."

"Academy Boulevard?" Carl Joseph stepped out of line, his forehead creased with worry. Carl Joseph was new to the center. He'd been coming for three months. His ability to become independent was questionable. "Is that in Colorado Springs or somewhere else?"

"It's here, Carl Joseph." Daisy patted his shoulder. "Right here in the Springs."

"Right." Elle grinned. Daisy could teach the class. "The whole bus trip will take about fifteen minutes."

He nodded, but he didn't look more sure of himself. "Okay. Okay, Teacher. If you say so, okay." He stepped back in line.

And so it went for the next half hour. Elle broke down the directions. The color of the bus—orange— and how much time they'd have to climb aboard and how long it would take to make the drive down to Academy Boulevard, and how many stops would happen between getting on and getting off the bus.

For many of them the lesson was a review. They tackled a different route every week, memorizing it, drawing it out, play-acting it, and finally incorporating it into a field trip on Friday. When they reached the end of the thirty most common bus routes, they'd start again at the beginning. But Elle's students had Down Syndrome, so most of them experienced varying degrees of short-term memory loss. Reviewing the bus routes could never happen often enough.

At the thirty-minute mark attention spans among the group were fading fast. Elle held out her hands. "Break time." She looked out the window again. It was a late April morning, and sunshine streamed in from a bright blue sky. "Fifteen minutes . . . outdoors today."

"Yippee!" Tammy, a student with long brown braids, jumped and did a half spin. "Outdoor break!"

"Ughh! I hate outdoors!" Sid scowled and punched at the air. At thirty, he was the oldest student at the center. "Hate, hate, hate."

"Don't be a hater." Gus shook a finger at the complaining student. "Ping-Pong is good for outdoors."

"Tag, you're it!" Brian tapped Gus on the shoulder and ran out the door laughing. Brian was a redhead who'd been coming to the center since Elle took over two years before. He was the happiest student by far. As he ran he yelled: "We could play tag and everyone could play tag!"

"Yeah!"

"I hate tag." Sid crossed his arms and stuck out his lower lip. "Hate, hate, hate."

The students headed for the door, all of them talking at once. Straggling behind and lost in their own world were Carl Joseph and Daisy. He was pointing outside. "No rain today, Daisy. Just big bright sunshine. That's thanks to God, right?"

"Right." She looked up at him with adoring eyes. "God gets the thanks."

"I thought so." He laughed from deep in his throat and clapped his hands five quick times. "I thought God gets the thanks."

Elle smiled and went to the back room. She poured herself a cup of dark coffee and returned to her desk. Her job at the center had everything to do with Delores Daisy Dalton. Her favorite student, her little sister. Her project. How different life was for Daisy here in the Springs. Two years ago Daisy had spent all her life with their mother an hour east of Denver in Lindon, Colorado—population 120.

The oldest of the Dalton daughters was only nine when their big strapping father left home one morning for his office job in Denver and never made it back. A patch of black ice on a back country road took his life, and he was dead before the first police officer made it to the scene. There was life insurance money and a settlement against the drunk driver who hit him— enough to allow their mother to stay home, to continue schooling them in their small wood-paneled living room. Enough so, that life wouldn't change in any way other than the most obvious and painful.

Because their daddy had loved his girls with everything he had.

Time flew, and one by one the Dalton girls left home and moved to Denver to attend the University of Colorado. Elle was no exception. She pursued a teaching credential and then her master's. But Daisy was the youngest, and when she turned nineteen one thing was certain.

If she stayed in Lindon, Daisy was out of options. And that wouldn't do, because their mother had never dreamed less for Daisy than for the other Dalton girls. Never mind what the doctors and textbooks of that day said about Down Syndrome. From an early age their mom believed Daisy was capable of great things. She believed in mainstreaming and immersion, which meant if the math lesson was about counting money, Daisy learned to count. If it was time to clean the kitchen, Daisy was taught how to run a dishwasher.

When the short bus for handicapped students drove by, it didn't stop at the Dalton house.

"You girls will show Daisy what to do, how to act and think and behave," their mom said. "How else will she learn?"

As it turned out, their mother's thinking was innovative and cutting-edge. When Elle earned her master's degree in special education, mainstreaming was all the rage. People with learning disabilities could do more than anyone ever expected as long as they were surrounded by role models.

When she was offered the director position at the Independent Learning Center—or ILC as everyone called it—Elle formed an idea and presented it to her mother. They could sell the house in Lindon and the three of them could buy a place in the Springs. Elle would run the center, Daisy would be a student, and their mother could find work outside the home.

Sentimental feelings for the old farmhouse made their mom hesitate, but only for a minute. Life was not a house, and family was not limited to a certain place. The move happened quickly, and from her first day at the center Daisy blossomed. Her friendship with Carl Joseph was further proof.

Elle sipped her coffee, stood, and made her way to the window. She sat on the sill and watched her students. A center like this one would've been unheard of fifteen years ago. Back when most of her students were born, their parents had few options. Half the kids were institutionalized, shipped off to a facility with little or no expectation for achievement. The others were sent to special education classes, with none of the stimulation needed for advancement.

Elle took another sip of coffee. The ILC was good not just for her students—most of whom came five days a week, six hours a day. It gave her a purpose, a place where no one asked about the ring she wasn't wearing anymore. She glanced at her watch, stood, and headed for the door. Some days her work at the center not only gave her a reason to move forward, it gave her a reason to live.

She opened the door. "Break's over. In your seats in two minutes."

"Teacher, one point!" Gus waved his Ping-Pong paddle in the air. With his other hand he grabbed the table. "One more point. Please!"

"Okay." Elle stifled a smile. Gus was adorable, the student who could best articulate his feelings. "Finish the game, and get right in."

The transition took five minutes, but after that everyone was seated and facing her. The center took up a large space, with areas designated for various activities. The bus routes were practiced in a carpeted alcove with a large blackboard on one wall and several benches framing the area. Another corner included a kitchen and three kitchen tables with chairs. Social skills, cooking, and appropriate eating behavior were taught there.

The next session was speech and communication. The learning area was again carpeted, and students sat on sofas and padded chairs—simulating a living room setting. The idea was to get the students comfortable in everyday living situations, learning how to read social cues and interact correctly with others.

Elle looked at her students. "Who would like to share first?"

Daisy's hand was up before Elle finished her question. "Me, Teacher!" Daisy got a kick out of calling Elle "Teacher." Daisy tipped her head back and laughed, then looked at Carl Joseph for approval. "Right? We're ready, right?"

"Uh . . ." Carl Joseph pushed his glasses up the bridge of his nose. He seemed confused, but his eyes lit up as he connected with Daisy. His words came slow and thick and much too loud. "Right, Daisy. Right you are."

"Shhh." Daisy held her finger to her lips. Her eyebrows rose high on her forehead. "We can hear you, CJ." There was no disapproval in her tone. Just a reminder, the way any two friends might encourage each other.

Carl Joseph hunched his shoulders, his expression guilty. He covered his mouth and giggled. "Okay." He dropped his voice to a dramatic whisper. "I'm quiet now, Daisy."

The others were losing interest. Elle motioned to the spot beside her on the carpet. "Daisy and Carl Joseph, come up and show us."

"Yeah." Sid scowled and punched at the air again. He was the most moody of the students, and today he was in classic form. "All right already. Get it over with."

Undaunted, Daisy stood and took Carl Joseph's hand. His cheeks were red, but when he focused on Daisy, he seemed to find the strength to take the spot beside her at the front area of the class. Daisy left him standing there while she went to the nearby CD player and pushed a few buttons. The space filled with the sounds of Glenn Miller's "In the Mood."

Daisy held out her hand and Carl Joseph took it. After only a slight hesitation, the two launched into a simple swing dance routine. Carl Joseph counted the entire time—not always on beat—and Daisy twirled and moved to the rhythm, her smile filling her face.

Elle's eyes grew damp as she watched them. Neither friendship nor love had ever been this easy for her. But this . . . this was how love should look, the simple innocence of caring that shone between these two. The way Carl Joseph tenderly held Daisy's hands, and how he led her through the moves, gently guiding her.

Today's date hadn't escaped her. It would've been her fourth wedding anniversary. She rubbed the bare place on her ring finger and bit her lip. How many years would pass before the date lost significance?

Then, midtwirl, Carl Joseph accidentally tripped Daisy. She fell forward, but before she could hit the ground, Carl Joseph caught her in his arms and helped her find her balance again.

"You okay, Daisy? Okay?" He dusted off her shoulder and her hair, and though she had never hit the ground, he brushed off her cheek.

"I'm fine." Daisy had years of dance experience. It was how their mother made sure Daisy got her exercise. No question the slight trip-step hadn't hurt her. But she balanced against Carl Joseph's arm and allowed him to dote on her all the same. After a long moment, she and Carl Joseph began again, laughing with delight as they circled in front of the class.

The music's effect was contagious. Gus stood and

waved his hands over his head, swaying his hips from one side to the other. Even Sid pointed at a few of the other students and managed the slightest grin.

When the song ended, Daisy and Carl Joseph were out of breath. They held hands and did a dramatic bow. Four students rushed to their feet, clapping as if they'd just witnessed something on a Broadway stage. Daisy waved her hands at them. "Wait . . . one more thing!"

Elle stepped back. A situation like this one was good for Daisy. She had spent all her life around able-bodied people, people blessed with social graces. She wasn't skilled at trying to command a group of people with Down Syndrome.

"Hey . . ." She waved her arms again.

The other students danced merrily about, clapping their hands and laughing. Even Sid was on his feet.

"I said . . . wait!" Daisy's happy countenance started to change.

But before she could melt down, Carl Joseph stepped up. "Sit down!" his voice boomed across the room.

Instantly the students shut their mouths. Most of them dropped slowly to their seats. Sid and Gus stayed standing, but neither of them said another word.

"Thanks, CJ." Daisy looked at him, her hero. She turned to the others. "We have one more thing."

"Yeah." Carl Joseph chortled loudly and then caught himself and covered his mouth again.

Daisy nodded at him. "I go first, okay?"

"Okay." The loud whisper was back.

"Here it is." Daisy looked at Elle and grinned. Then she held out both hands toward her classmates. "M-I-C . . ."

Carl Joseph saluted. "See you real soon."

"K-E-Y . . ."

"Why?" He put his hands on his hips and then pointed at Gus. " 'Cause we like you."

Then he linked arms with Daisy and together they finished the chant. "M-O-U-S-E."

Sid tossed his hands in the air. "Yeah, but did you go to Disneyworld yet or what?"

"Not yet." Daisy grinned at Carl Joseph. "One day very, very soon."

The two of them sat down as Gus jumped to his feet and scrambled to the front.

"Gus . . . you want to go next?" Elle moved in closer.

"Yes." He said it more like a question, and instantly he returned to his seat. "Sorry, Teacher." He raised his hand.

"Gus?"

"Can I go now?"

"Yes."

The training continued for the better part of an hour. Each student was progressing toward some form of independent living—either in a group home or in a supervised setting with daily monitoring. Already twelve graduates had moved on to find independence.

They attended twice-weekly night sessions so that they could hold jobs during the daytime.

Elle leaned against the wall and watched Gus begin a dramatic story about playing a game of chess with Brian, a redhead who at sixteen was the youngest student. After Gus had received a standing ovation for his story, they heard a poem by Tammy, the girl with long braids—Sonnet Number 43 by Elizabeth Barrett Browning.

When the girl struggled with one line, Carl Joseph stood and went to her side. He pointed at the paper and put his arm around her shoulders. "You can do it," he whispered to her. "Go on."

Daisy raised an eyebrow but she didn't say anything.

Tammy was shaking when she finally found her place and continued. Her next few sentences were painfully slow, but she didn't give up. Carl Joseph wouldn't let her. When the poem was finished, Carl Joseph led her back to her spot on the sofa, then returned to his own.

Finally Sid told them about a movie his dad had taken him to see, something with dark caves and missing animals and a king whose kingdom had turned against him. The plot was too difficult to follow, but somehow Sid managed a question-and-answer time at the end.

They worked on table manners next, and before Elle had time to look at the clock, it was three and parents were arriving to pick up their students.

Elle spotted Daisy and Carl Joseph near the window waiting for his mother. She went to them and patted her sister on the back. "Nice dance today."

"Thanks." Daisy grinned. "Carl Joseph has good news."

"You do?" Elle looked at the young man. There was an ocean of kindness in his eyes. "What's your good news, Carl Joseph?"

"My brother." He flashed a gap-toothed smile. "Brother's coming home tomorrow."

"Oh." Elle put her hand on Carl Joseph's shoulder. He'd talked about his brother before. The guy was older than Carl Joseph, and he rode bulls. Or maybe he used to ride bulls. Elle wasn't sure. Whatever he did, the way Carl Joseph talked about him he might as well have worn a cape and a big S on his chest. She smiled. "How wonderful."

Carl Joseph nodded. "It is." His voice boomed. He pushed his glasses back into place. "It's so wonderful!"

"CJ . . . shhh." Daisy patted his hand. "We can hear you."

"Right." He covered his mouth with one hand and held up a single finger with the other. "Sorry."

Elle glanced at the circular drive out front. It was empty. She settled into a chair opposite Daisy and Carl Joseph. "Does your brother still ride bulls?"

"No . . . not anymore."

"Did he get tired of it?" Elle could imagine a person might grow weary of being thrown from a bull.

31

"No." Carl Joseph's eyes were suddenly sad. "He got hurt."

Daisy nodded. "Bad."

"Oh." Elle felt a slice of concern for Carl Joseph's brother. "Is he okay now?"

Carl Joseph squinted and seemed to mull over his answer. "After he got hurt, he rode bulls for another season. But then he didn't want to." He raised one shoulder and cocked his head. "Brother's still hurt; that's what I think."

"What's his name?" Elle spotted Carl Joseph's mother's car coming up the drive.

"Cody Gunner." Carl Joseph's pride was as transparent as his smile. "World-famous bull rider Cody Gunner. My brother."

Elle smiled. She was always struck by her students' imagination. Carl Joseph's brother was probably an accountant or a sales rep at some firm in Denver. Maybe he rode a bull once in his life, but that didn't make him a bull rider. But that didn't matter, of course. All that counted was the way Carl Joseph saw him.

"Your mom's here, CJ." Daisy pointed at the car. She stood and took Carl Joseph's hand. "It's your big day. Your brother's coming home tomorrow."

Carl Joseph's cheeks grew red and he giggled at Daisy. "Thank you, Daisy. For telling me that."

They walked off together, and at the door Daisy gave him a hug. They hadn't crossed lines beyond that, and Elle was glad. Their relationship needed to progress slowly. What they shared today was enough for now. As the last few students left, she and Daisy straightened chairs and tables and closed up for the day.

On the way home, Daisy was quieter than usual. Finally she took a big breath. "We should pray for Carl Joseph's brother. For the world-famous bull rider."

Elle was heading down the two-lane highway that led to their new house. "Because he might still be hurt?"

"Yeah, that." She furrowed her brow. "It's hard when you get hurt."

"Yes, it is." Elle looked at her empty hand, the finger where her ring had been four years earlier. "Very hard."

Daisy pointed at her. "You pray, Elle. Okay?"

"Okay." Elle kept her eyes on the road. "Dear God, please be with Carl Joseph's brother."

"Cody Gunner." Daisy opened one eye and shot a look at Elle.

"Right. Cody Gunner."

"World-famous bull rider." Daisy closed her eyes again and patted Elle's hand. "Say it all."

"Cody Gunner, world-famous bull rider." Elle allowed the hint of a smile. "Please help him get well so he isn't hurt anymore."

"In Jesus' name."

"Amen."

For the rest of the ride Elle thought about the

anniversary of a moment that never happened, and the picture of Daisy dancing in Carl Joseph's arms. The world would look at her and Daisy and think that Elle was the gifted one, the blessed one. Elle, who had it all together, the beautiful, intelligent daughter for whom life should've come easily and abundantly. Daisy—she was the one to be pitied. Short and stout with a bad heart and weak vision. A castaway in a world of perfectionism, where the prize went to high achievers and people with talent, star athletes and beauty queens. Daisy was doomed from birth to live a life of painful emptiness, mere existence.

Better to be Elle, that's what the world would say.

But the irony was this: Nothing could've been further from the truth.

Chapter Two

Cody Gunner sat next to professional bull riding's best-known cowboy and tried to find the passion for another go-round. They were in Nampa, Idaho, the last day before a six-week break. Cody wasn't signed up for the second half of the season. The way he felt now, he wasn't sure he was coming back.

"Folks, we've got a ton o' fun in this first bull." Sky Miller, four-time national champion, sat on Cody's right. He was the primary announcer for tonight's event. Cody would handle color. "No bull rider's lasted eight on Jack Daniels since February in Jacksonville."

Cody looked to the side, to the place where the barrel racers would've been warming up back in the days when the best bull riders rode the Professional Rodeo Cowboys Association circuit, back when he and Ali had toured together during that handful of amazing seasons.

Good thing he'd switched over to the PBR, the way most of the bull riders had. Here there were no blonde horseback riders tearing around the barrels, making him think even for a fraction of a moment that somehow—against all odds—she was here, in the same arena with him. The way she had been all those seasons ago.

"What do you say about Joe Glass, Cody? One of the tough guys, right?" The glance from Sky told him he'd missed his cue.

"One of the toughest." Cody grabbed a sheet and scanned it for the bull rider's information. "Joe's won three events this year and stayed on more than half the bulls he's drawn. That's one reason why he's sitting pretty at Number Nine in the overall standings."

Cody stayed focused for the next nine riders. When the network went to a longer break, he stretched. "Sorry 'bout that." He patted Sky on the shoulder. "Something to drink?"

"Coke. Thanks." Sky gave him a wary look. "You somewhere else tonight, Gunner?"

"Maybe." Cody took a few steps back.

The legend held his eyes for a beat. He knew better than to ask if the reason had something to do with Ali.

It was common knowledge in the rodeo world that Cody hadn't gotten over her. *There goes Cody Gunner,* they'd say. *Poor Cody. Still pining away over that wife of his.* Yeah, he'd heard it all, the whispers and well-intentioned remarks about moving on and letting go. That was okay. Cody climbed down seven stairs to the dirt-covered arena floor. Let them think he was crazy for holding on this long.

They hadn't loved Ali. Otherwise they'd understand.

It was eight years ago that they'd shared their last season on the circuit. Back when her cystic fibrosis had seemed like merely one more mountain they'd need to climb on the road to forever. Not like the eliminator it turned out to be. He steeled himself and stared at the ground as he walked back to the network food tent.

He and Ali had that one last season, and then they married. Cody gave her everything he had to give that year—his heart and soul, a lifetime of love, and one of the lungs from his own chest. "What happened?" people would ask when they heard about the lung. "You gave her a lung and it didn't take?"

Cody would only narrow his eyes and remember Ali, her honesty, the depth in her voice. "It worked." That's all he would say. *It worked.* Because it did. The doctors had told them the transplant would buy them only three years. And in the end that's exactly what it did. Three years. About a thousand tomorrows.

He would've given her his other lung, if he could've.

36

"Gunner!" The voice was familiar.

Cody looked up and into the eyes of Bo Wade, a cowboy Cody had competed against that last year—after Ali died, when Cody came out of retirement to do it all one more time, to win the championship for her, the one Ali never managed to win. Bo was in the top five back then, but he had hung it up a few years ago. Cody held out his hand and found a smile. "Bo Wade, watcha up to?"

"Workin' for the network." He grinned. "Hoping to be in your spot someday."

"Yeah." Cody grinned. "Same old story."

They talked for a minute or two about the season and the rise of the PBR. "Things are different now."

"No doubt." Cody checked his watch. He had ten minutes to report back. "Some of those bulls are wicked mean."

"And huge. Makes you wonder what they're puttin' in the feed."

Cody was about to wind up the conversation when it happened.

Bo's expression changed. He looked down at his dusty boots and then back up again. "Hey, man. I'm sorry about Ali. I never got to tell you."

Cody's breath caught in his throat, the way it always did at the mention of her. He'd tried a lot of different answers when people brought her into the conversation. He would sometimes shrug and say, "Things happen," or he'd look up at the bluest piece of sky and say, "She's still with us. I can feel her." Once in a while he'd say, "She's never really gone." All those things were true, but for the past year he'd kept his answer simpler.

"Thanks, Bo." Cody squinted. "I miss her like crazy."

"I bet." The corners of Bo's mouth lifted. There was no awkwardness between them. The two had ridden the circuit together for five years. That made them family on a lot of levels. "I remember back before the two of you got together." He shook his head. "Nothing could stop you like seeing Ali Daniels on a horse." He paused. "We had no idea she was sick."

"No one did." The conversation was too painful, the subject still too raw. Cody clenched his jaw. "Good seeing you." He shook his friend's hand again and nodded toward the arena. "Gotta get back."

"Okay." Bo slapped Cody's shoulder. "Take it easy, man. Maybe see you around the second half of the season. The network just made me permanent tech advisor."

Cody congratulated him, found a Coke and a bottle of water, and headed back to the booth. He kept his eyes straight ahead, but all he could see was Ali, her blonde ponytail flying behind her, racing around the barrels on Ace, her palomino, or standing in the tunnel after a ride, gasping for air while Cody brought her the inhaler. Ali in her compression vest back at the ranch her family owned. Ali beside him on a grassy bluff promising to love him until death had the final word.

He pursed his lips and blew out. He had to hold on to

the little details. The smell of her clothes after a ride, the mix of horse and perfume and lavender soap. The feel and exact color of her favorite faded jeans. The sensation of her breath on his face when they kissed.

He had to hold on to his memories, because otherwise they would fade and there would be no getting them back. But he had to live in a world without Ali. That was the balancing act working in rodeo. Here— among the smell of horses and bulls and arena dust— he could think of nothing else.

Cody reached the stairs and stopped. He still had three minutes. He slipped into a shadowy spot beneath the bleachers and leaned against the cool metal bars. He needed out. Otherwise the memories would drive him crazy. Besides, bull riding had taken enough of his time. A change in careers would be good for him. Maybe something closer to home.

Concern shot a burst of adrenaline through him. His mother's phone call this morning stayed with him, made him glad he was going home tomorrow. There was trouble with Carl Joseph. Big trouble. The kind they'd always feared for Cody's younger brother.

Yes, something closer to home would be better than this, than walking every day through a hallway of memories he couldn't escape. He could go home and be a rancher, raise cattle or competitive bulls. Or maybe find a job in sales, commodities—that sort of thing. He pictured Carl Joseph, the way his brother had clung to him last time he was home. Buddy was never happier than when Cody was home. So maybe he would go back and open a sports camp for kids with disabilities.

He heard the music blaring through the arena. Less than a minute before they went on again. He took the steps two at a time, dropped into the seat beside Sky Miller, and placed the Coke on the table between them. "Sorry, man. Got hung up."

Sky popped the top on the Coke and took a long drink. "Get in the game, okay?"

"I will."

He was sharp in the second set, but his heart wasn't in it. When he helped pack up the booth that night, he had the feeling that this was it, that he wouldn't be back for a long time. Maybe forever. Sky must've known, too.

When it was time to leave, Sky pulled him aside. "You're good, Gunner. You know your stuff."

"Thanks." Cody shifted, anxious to go.

"You could ride this gig for a lotta years." Sky paused. "Thing is, Gunner, you need to figure it out."

Cody didn't want to ask. "What?"

"Ali. Your past." Sky rubbed the back of his neck and exhaled hard. "You take her with you everywhere you go. You'll never be the best until you can walk in here"—he waved at the arena—"and see the stands, hear the bulls knocking around in the chutes, smell the sweat." He hesitated. "And not see her, too."

"That's the problem." Cody put his hand on his friend's shoulder. "I'm not *trying* to see her, man. She's just there, that's all. She's there."

Sky studied him, and for a minute it looked like he might launch into a speech about moving on and putting the past to rest. Instead he grabbed his bag. "Maybe over the break, Gunner. Maybe you can figure it out then."

"Maybe." Cody smiled, but he could feel the tears clouding his eyes. He looked down, and in that one simple movement, he gave it away.

"You're done, aren't you?"

"I'm not sure." Cody backed up, putting distance between them. The dam in his heart was breaking. He didn't want anyone around to see it happen. "Good working with you, Sky. I'll be around."

With that he turned and swung his bag over his shoulder. The hotel was across the street, and he had a flight home in the morning. He was waiting at the light when a carload of girls screeched to a stop.

"Hey, Cody Gunner—wanna ride?" The brunette behind the wheel wore red lipstick and had eyes that looked a little too bright.

"Yeah!" A girl in a cowboy hat and a tight T-shirt leaned in from the passenger seat. "We know every hot spot in Nampa."

The light turned green and the walk sign appeared. Cody tipped his hat at the girls. "Gotta get my sleep tonight, ladies." He started jogging across the cross-walk.

"Come on, Cody," the brunette called after him. He ignored them. Another thirty seconds and he was inside the doors of the hotel and headed for his room.

Every stop on the tour, every year he'd been a part of rodeo, he'd had offers from girls like that. Before Ali, he agreed to an offer here and there. But never now. The idea made him sick to his stomach, like throwing dirt in the face of everything Ali stood for.

Inside his room he washed his face, brushed his teeth, and crawled into bed. He pulled the framed photograph of Ali from the hotel nightstand and stared at it. The way her smile reached the depth of her eyes, how even now she seemed to be watching him, looking at him.

"Ali, girl"—he ran his thumb over the smooth glass—"I feel you everywhere tonight." His voice was a raspy whisper. "Like you're right here beside me."

But she wasn't. No matter how long he looked at her picture or thought about her, she was gone. They'd had that last year on the circuit and then three more years, and then she left him. Her body, anyway. Her spirit was still with him—always with him. Whether he was in a rodeo arena or not.

Some nights, like tonight, if he looked at her picture long enough, he could still hear her voice. They were riding double on Ace, taking the path out to the back of her parents' property where the clouds and trees and mountains all came together in a piece of paradise.

Cody . . . I want you to love again.

"What?" He had been outraged, of course, horrified at her request. "I'll never love anyone but you, Ali. Never."

But she insisted. *I mean it, Cody. I want you to love again. When I'm gone, you can't waste your life thinking about me.* She leaned up and kissed him—and for the sweetest moment he was there again. *Promise me, Cody. Promise me when I'm gone you'll find love again.*

She pushed him until finally, against everything in him, and only because it was what she wanted to hear, he promised. He blinked and the distant conversation faded. He wiped the tears off the glass frame. "Ali . . . I can't." He brought the framed photo to his face and pressed the glass against his cheek. "I can't do it."

Then he set the frame on the edge of the table so that her smile was facing him. He might forget the details but he wouldn't forget this—the sparkle in her eyes or the way she could see right through him when no one else ever could.

When she was alive he would've done anything for her. He forgave his father for her, and he gave up bull riding for her—to protect his lung, that piece of himself that belonged to her. The piece that bought them a few more years together.

But there was one thing he could never, ever do. No matter where the next season in life took him, he couldn't keep that one promise. The promise to love again. Because the idea was crazy. He hadn't known how to love at all before he met Ali. With her, love became real for the first time. She defined it.

He looked at her again. "You understand, Ali. Right?"

Wherever she was, whatever place in heaven shone a little brighter because of her presence, she would have to understand. Because the promise to love again was overshadowed by a bigger promise. The one he'd made to her that day on the bluff overlooking her parents' ranch. The promise to love her forever and always. He touched the frame once more. "Good night, Ali."

Death might've had the last word for Ali, but not for him. So he would love her and he would carry her with him every day, every painful step. Year after year after year.

As long as his remaining lung drew breath.

Chapter Three

Carl Joseph stood at the window next to the front door and waited.

He didn't mind waiting. Brother was coming home, and that was worth waiting for two minutes or two hours. Even two days.

"Cookies are ready!" Mom came to him and smiled. "Want a chocolate chip cookie, Carl Joseph?"

They smelled really good. Chocolaty and warm all through the house. Carl Joseph thought about saying yes. But he couldn't. "First cookies with Brother." He looked out the window. "I wait for Brother."

Mom said okay and went back to the kitchen.

One way to make the time go faster was to count. He counted the squares on the windows at the front of the

house. Then he counted the lines on the sidewalk outside—the part he could see. And he counted the tree
branches on the big tree out front. He was on the
thirty-seventh branch when Dad pulled up.

"He's here!" Carl Joseph shouted loud, but that was
okay. Daisy wasn't here to tell him to be quiet.
"Brother's home! Brother's here!" He jumped up and
punched his fist in the air. "Yeah for Brother!"

When he opened the door, he was out of breath. He
bent over and blew out, and then he stood up and there
he was! Brother! Brother stood up from the car and
grinned. The same kind of grin like when he was on
TV all those times and he lasted eight seconds on a
bull. That grin.

"Buddy!" He had his bag tossed back over his
shoulder because he was strong. Brother was very
strong. He ran to the porch and dropped his bag. "Give
me a hug!"

Carl Joseph wrapped his arms around Brother and
lifted him up. Then Brother did the lifting, because
Brother was stronger. Brother spun him around in a
circle and set him down. "I missed you, Buddy."

"Missed you more!" Carl Joseph stretched up and
looped his arm around Brother's neck. "Come on!
Mom has chocolate chip cookies. Just like every time
you come home!"

They went in and ate cookies and milk and all day,
the whole time, Brother stayed with him and talked to
him.

It was the best day Carl Joseph could remember for

the longest time. And the whole time he kept talking to God about his number-one wish. That one day Brother would stay at home. Because as good as hellos were, as good as it was to share warm chocolate chip cookies with Brother, there could be something better.

To never have to say good-bye.

BROTHER HAD BEEN home for a full day and life was happy times.

Carl Joseph planted his feet in the play yard and studied the sky. Clouds. All clouds. And clouds were not good for Daisy. They were on a short break, so maybe the rain would stay locked up there until they got back into the classroom.

"Fresh air is good." He linked his arm through Daisy's. "Tetherball?"

Daisy squinted up at the sky. "I guess so."

"Don't be afraid, Daisy. It won't rain today."

She looked at him and nodded. Very slowly. "Okay, CJ. Okay. I'm going to believe that."

They walked across the yard to the tetherball pole. Carl Joseph let go of her arm and walked backward a few feet in front of her. "Knock knock."

The first part of a smile was on her face. "Who's there?"

"Lena." Carl Joseph clapped his hands and laughed. Because if he laughed, maybe Daisy would forget about the clouds and maybe she would laugh, too.

"Lena who?" Daisy smiled bigger.

Carl Joseph stopped walking backward. He took a step toward Daisy. "Lena little closer!" Again he clapped, and he laughed harder than before.

"Lena little closer?" Daisy thought about that for a minute. Then her hands shot up in the air and her eyes lit up like sparkly diamonds. "Oh . . . I get it. Lean a little closer!" She put her hands on Carl Joseph's shoulders. "I like that one the best."

A funny feeling swirled around in Carl Joseph's stomach. His cheeks felt hot, the way they felt when he stood close to Daisy. He took her hand and skipped with her to the tetherball pole.

"I'm going to win today." Daisy hopped around beside him. "I'll beat you, CJ. Watch out!"

Carl Joseph laughed again. Daisy wasn't thinking of the clouds anymore. He could tell. He covered his face. "What do you see, Daisy?" His voice was muffled, but it was loud. When he covered his face he had to talk loud. That way Daisy could hear him.

"I see you're hiding from me!" Daisy took hold of his wrists. "Come on, CJ, take your hands down."

"Surprise!" He dropped his hands and held them out to his side. "You see me, Daisy? I'm the winner. That's what you see. The winner of all."

Daisy grabbed hold of the tetherball and gave it a hard shove. "Ready, set, go."

"Ahhh!" Carl Joseph squealed out loud. "I wasn't ready."

"Just kidding." She caught the ball by the rope and waited. "Ready now?"

"Wait." He held up one finger. His breath was fast, too fast. He put his head down and blew out—the way Brother had taught him. After seven breaths he looked up. "Okay . . . ready."

She slapped the ball and it came at him fast. Then he hit it so hard it soared up and over Daisy. Carl Joseph leaned his head back and laughed, but when he stopped laughing, the ball was already past him. "Ooops!"

Now it was Daisy's turn to laugh, but she didn't miss the ball. She smacked it loud, and it went round and round and round until it touched the pole.

"Winner!" She danced a pirouette. "Winner, CJ. I'm the winner!"

"Fine." He didn't want to play anyway. He pointed at the bench against the wall. "Let's sit there."

They each took one half of the bench, because it wasn't nice to make a girl feel crowded. When he had his breath back, he smiled at her. "Brother's home."

"I know. You told me." She swung her feet. "Is he better yet?"

"No." Carl Joseph looked at the ground. "He's riding Ace a lot."

"Ace the dog?"

Carl Joseph laughed so hard his glasses fell onto his lap. He helped them back up onto his nose. "That's funny, Daisy. You made a good joke."

She put her fingers over her lips and giggled. "Riding a dog, CJ. That's funny, right? Real funny."

"Yeah." Carl Joseph waited until he stopped

48

laughing. "Ace isn't a dog. He's Ali's horse. When Brother's sad he rides Ace."

"Oh." Daisy patted his hand. "I'm sorry about that."

Just as she said the word "sorry," the first raindrops hit Carl Joseph's forehead. He opened his eyes wide and looked at Daisy. "Uh oh."

At first she didn't know what was happening, but then she felt drops on her arm. "Rain! Raaaaain!" She spread her fingers over her face, stood up, and began turning in tight circles. "Rain!"

"It's okay." Carl Joseph looked at the sky. He felt scared and nervous all at once. He reached out and tried to catch her, tried to make her stop turning circles. But by the time she stopped, the rain was falling harder and harder. He pulled off his jacket and held it over her. "Come on, Daisy."

"CJ . . . I'm scared!"

He kept his jacket over her head and ran next to her toward the building. There was an overhang outside, and they reached the place beneath it at the same time as the other students. Everyone else walked past them into the classroom. A few girls patted Daisy on the back as they passed. "It's all right, Daisy. It's just rain, that's all."

When they were alone, Carl Joseph pulled her into his arms. "It's okay, Daisy. I'm here." He wiped the water off her back and patted her hair. Daisy was scared to death of rain. She had been ever since they met. Teacher said it was a good thing they lived in Colorado where the rain didn't come very often.

But when it did . . .

Daisy was crying. She put her face against his shoulder, and when she was done crying she looked at him. Fear was still in her eyes. "Water melted the Wicked Witch of the West, CJ. Do you know that?"

"I do." Carl Joseph nodded. "The witch in *The Wizard of Oz*. She died from water."

"Right." Daisy peered out at the stormy sky. "That's why I'm afraid."

He patted her cheek. "But you're not a witch, Daisy. You're not a witch at all."

"I know." She hugged him again. "But it's still water."

Carl Joseph thought about that. "True." The rain stopped then and he led her to the edge of the dry area. "Look out there, Daisy."

"I'm scared." She clung to him, and she wouldn't look up.

"Please, Daisy. Please look." He put his arm around her. "I have a secret for you."

That seemed to make her think. She relaxed her shoulders and sniffed. "What?"

"Good!" Carl Joseph clapped his hands together loud. "I knew I could make you look."

"But why?" Daisy shook her head. She looked ready to run away.

Carl Joseph didn't want her to run. "Look up there." He pointed at the sky.

She looked, but she stayed close to him. She was still afraid. "What?"

"There's sunshine up there, Daisy." He put his hand over his eyes and squinted. "Just beyond the clouds."

For a long moment she thought about that. "Really?"

"Really." He laughed but not because he had told a joke. Because he was happy. "Sunshine just beyond the clouds."

He was about to take her back into the classroom when Teacher came out. "Daisy . . . I was in the supply room. I didn't know it was raining." The two sisters hugged. "Are you okay?"

"Yes." Daisy looked at him, and her eyes were sparkly diamonds again. The fear was gone from her eyes. "CJ helped me."

"He gave you his coat." Teacher smiled at him. "That's very nice, Carl Joseph."

"No, not that." Daisy moved back beside him. She linked her arm through his the way she sometimes did. "He told me about the sunshine."

Teacher looked unsure about that. "Sunshine?"

"Yes." Daisy led Carl Joseph back to the place where they could see the sky. "Up there. Just beyond the clouds."

Teacher looked up at the sky and little bits of tears came into her eyes. She hugged herself and then she said something quiet mixed in with her breath. "Yeah . . . I never thought about it that way."

They went back into the classroom, but before they took their spots in the living room area, Carl Joseph watched Teacher. That's when he remembered something. Daisy had prayed for Cody. She had told him a few times already that he should, too. So maybe it was his turn to pray. He could ask God to help Teacher. He found his seat and covered his face.

God . . . help Teacher, please. Whatever she needs. That's all. Amen.

He opened his eyes and looked at Teacher again. She still looked sad. And those were for sure tears on her cheeks outside a minute ago. He understood when Daisy cried. She had a reason to be sad, because she was afraid of the rain. But Teacher needed a lot of prayers said for her. Because she was just as sad but there was no reason.

Teacher wasn't afraid of the rain even one tiny bit.

Chapter Four

C ody finally felt as if he could breathe again. His parents owned twenty acres in the foothills near Colorado Springs, and after two days at home Cody wondered why he'd ever left. He had a small house at the far western end of his parents' ranch. He didn't need his own place; not while he was living on the road. The PBR season ran from January to November with only a six-week break.

He could get a house later.

For now, his parents' place was enough. Ace was here, Ali's horse. He could ride and remember and spend time with Carl Joseph. And now he could even think clearly. He showered early that morning and walked over to his parents' house. The bad news about Carl Joseph was worse than Cody expected. He had epilepsy. Several times a week lately he'd fallen into major seizures—the type the doctors called grand mal. The seizures came along with another diagnosis. Carl Joseph's heart disease was worse. Not just his arteries, but the heart itself.

His prognosis for a long life was dim.

Cody wasn't willing to settle for that, any more than he'd been willing to settle for Ali's diagnosis. There had to be something they could do to help Carl Joseph strengthen his heart.

His buddy must've seen him coming, because he opened the back door and came running out. "Hi, Brother! It's a good morning!" He pointed at the sky. "See that? A bright sunny good morning."

"Yeah, Buddy." Cody smiled. What was it about the kid? Every time Cody was with him he felt happier, like he might just survive after all. "It's a great day."

"You know what?" Carl Joseph put his hands on his knees. His eyes lit up. "I think I wanna be a bull rider like you."

"I know, Buddy." Cody messed up his brother's hair. "You tell me that every time."

"Because I wanna be a world-famous bull rider like you, Brother."

"Bull riders get hurt." He put his arm around Carl Joseph's shoulders and they headed toward the back door.

"Yeah." Carl Joseph's smile faded. "That's true."

Cody pushed the door open and they moved inside to the breakfast table. Their mother was fixing scrambled eggs, cheese, and bell peppers. His favorite. When they were seated, Cody planted his elbows on the table. "You could work at the ranch here, Buddy. That's good work for you."

"No." Carl Joseph shook his head. It took a lot to fluster him, but this time talk about bull riding seemed to be more than a lighthearted way to carry on a conversation. "No, that's not okay. I wanna be a bull rider." He slammed his fist on the table. "Starting today."

"Whoa . . ." Cody looked from Carl Joseph to their mother. "What's this all about?"

His mother was stirring the eggs. She looked over her shoulder at Carl Joseph. "You wanna tell your brother what this is all about?"

"Okay." Carl Joseph sat up straighter in his chair. "Daisy likes bull riders. She told me so."

Cody blinked. "Daisy?" He looked at his mother. Inside, the beginnings of something unsettling stirred in his gut. "Who's Daisy?"

"She's my girl." Carl Joseph slapped himself on the chest. "My girl, Brother. She likes bull riders 'cause I told her you were a bull rider and she smiled really, really big. So you teach me, Brother, okay?"

"Tell you what"—he tried not to sound bothered— "let's start with Ace. You can take a ride around the arena with me. How 'bout that?"

" 'Cause that's a start, right?"

"Right." Cody stood. He tapped the table between them. "I'll be back, Buddy."

"Okay." Carl Joseph chuckled and clapped hard. Then he looked straight up. "I'm gonna be a bull rider. Thank You, God."

Cody turned his attention to his mother. She was stirring the eggs again, but she had to know he was coming her way. He reached her elbow and leaned around so she could see his face. "Who's Daisy?"

"He told you." She kept her eyes from his. "Daisy's his friend."

"I've been home for three days." He made an exaggerated move and looked out the window. "I haven't seen any girls hanging around the place. So who's Daisy?"

His mother released a loud sigh. "Look, Cody, don't overreact." She put the spatula down on the counter and faced him. "Your brother's getting older. He has friends now."

Cody's head was spinning. Carl Joseph had friends? "Is this that class thing you were telling me about?"

"Yes." She sighed and met his eyes. "I take him to a center in town. Everyone there has Down Syndrome."

"Including Daisy?" He felt himself relax. The idea of an able-bodied girl falling for Carl Joseph seemed wrong. He couldn't stand the idea that maybe his brother had fallen for a girl who would never have feelings for him. But if she had Down Syndrome like him . . .

"Yes." His mother picked up the spatula again and started stirring. "Daisy has Down Syndrome. She's

twenty-one, four years younger than Carl Joseph."
She turned off the stove and wiped her brow with the
back of her hand. "They like to swing dance and sing
Mickey Mouse songs, and they dream of going to Disneyland one day. Daisy helps Carl Joseph talk quieter,
and he helps her not be so afraid of the rain. It's a
simple, sweet friendship, Cody." She moved the pan
to the island countertop. "It's good for your brother."

"Okay." Cody felt much better. "So he's getting out
more, socializing. This class thing is . . . I don't know
. . . sort of a play group kind of thing." He looked over
his shoulder at his brother, then back again. "Right?"

His mother tilted her head sideways, considering his
definition. "Sort of. It's good for him, that's all I
know. I've seen differences."

Cody hesitated. "Good. Differences are good."

"If he can keep going." Her expression changed.
"With the epilepsy . . . the doctor isn't sure . . ."

"We can talk about it later." He reached for a stack
of plates in the cupboard just as he heard his dad's
voice behind him.

"Carl Joseph, you look good."

"Thanks, Dad. I'm seeing Daisy today."

"Yeah, I just found out about Daisy." Cody set the
plates next to the pan of eggs and gave his dad a tentative smile. "I guess I never thought about Carl
Joseph having, you know . . . a girl."

"It isn't like that." His mother pulled a stack of napkins out and set them on the counter. "Come and eat,
Carl Joseph."

Come and eat? Cody started to say something, but he stopped himself. The last time he was home, Carl Joseph was served at the table—same as always. He wasn't stable enough to fill his plate and carry it across the room without spilling or dropping it altogether. Cody tapped softly at his mom's arm. "He learned this?"

"Yes." His mom looked proud. "And table manners, too."

"Really?"

His dad joined them in the kitchen. "Really. Carl Joseph is capable of much more than we ever thought, Cody. It's amazing."

Carl Joseph was still on his way into the kitchen from the dining room, so he hadn't heard any of their conversation. Cody stared at his father and tried to think of a comeback. His comments bugged Cody. Maybe because Cody knew he was never happy about having a son with Down Syndrome. Back when Carl Joseph was two years old, their dad had left home and stayed away for nineteen years because he couldn't bear to be the father of a handicapped child.

So what was this? His dad's attempt at making Carl Joseph more like normal kids? Cody kept his thoughts to himself. He hung back and watched Carl Joseph choose a plate, scoop up a serving of eggs, and take a napkin and fork from the counter. He carried the plate back to the dining room table and sat down without even a little shakiness.

"Okay . . ." Cody filled his plate and took the place

across from his brother. "Buddy, you're doing great."

"Thanks." All his life, Carl Joseph had held his fork like a shovel, and after a few bites when his balance weakened, the food would fall back to the plate and he would shovel it into his mouth with his fingers. Then he would chomp hard, his mouth open, bits falling back to his plate as he chewed. Not today. He was concentrating, no doubt. But he lifted a forkful of eggs into his mouth, chewed with his mouth closed, and swallowed. Then he used the napkin to dab at the corners of his mouth.

"Cody's right." Their dad smiled at Carl Joseph. "You're doing very, very well. We're all proud of you."

"Daisy's proud." Carl Joseph put his fork down and folded his hands in his lap.

Cody watched his brother for a few more minutes. The classes must've been a very good thing for his brother. A few lessons on social graces, a little social interaction . . . Carl Joseph should've gone to the center years ago.

Carl Joseph focused on his breakfast, and Cody turned his attention to the reason he was home. He set his fork down and looked at his parents. "I need a change."

His mother hesitated midbite. "A change?"

"Yes." He pushed his plate back and rested his forearms on the table. "I'm not under contract for the rest of the season. They want me, but I haven't agreed yet."

His parents waited for him to continue.

"I love bull riding, don't get me wrong." Cody raked his fingers through his dark hair.

"Me, too." Carl Joseph looked up. "Brother's going to teach me to bull ride, right, Brother?"

"One day." Cody smiled at him. He turned back to his dad. "I want to do something different, something that matters. Maybe open a sports center, or raise bulls here at the ranch. So I can be around family more."

"You could do just about anything." His dad sat back in his seat and crossed his arms. "I didn't know you were considering a change."

His mother sat a little straighter. Her eyes were thoughtful. "I've been hoping for this."

Cody took a drink of his orange juice. "That I'd leave the circuit?"

"Yes." She dragged her fork through her eggs. "Because until you do, you'll never get over Ali. You carry her with you every time you hit the road."

For a long moment, Cody held his breath. His mother meant nothing by her comment, he knew that with every heartbeat. But how could he make them understand that he wasn't a victim of Ali's memory? He was the owner of it. He didn't want to move on or let her go. He just needed a place where her image wasn't around every corner.

"Don't be angry, Cody." She reached toward him and put her hand over his. "I loved Ali. We all did."

"But Ali makes you sad, Brother." Carl Joseph waved his fork in Cody's direction. At the same instant, he seemed to notice what he was doing. He brought his fork back down to his plate. "I think Ali makes you sad."

"What your mother's trying to say, son, is . . . well, it's been four years." His father's voice was tender.

Anger rose inside Cody. He focused on his eggs and ate them more quickly than he planned. When he was finished he stood and took his plate to the kitchen. "I'll be out back."

"Cody . . ." his mother called after him. "We're only saying that—"

He was out the door before she finished her sentence. He knew what they were saying, and it wasn't their fault. Four years was a long time. But not for him. He stormed out to the barn and a memory flashed bold and brilliant in his mind. The time when Ali had rushed out of her parents' house, the day she found out that he knew the truth about her illness.

She ran to the barn and climbed onto Ace just as he reached her.

"Ali, get down. We need to talk." He stood in front of her, his heart pounding.

"I didn't want you to know. Not yet." She pressed her fingers to her chest. "It was my place to tell you."

No matter what he said, she wouldn't climb down off the horse, so finally he climbed up behind her. With her at the reins, the horse raced across the open field to the trail and on out to the back fence. By then, Ali was so upset she could barely breathe. She fell into an asthma attack. He held her and coaxed her, and by some sort of miracle she found space in her damaged lungs to grab a breath.

Cody held on to the memory as he rounded the corner of the barn and saddled Ace. He brought the horse to a full run and set out on the trail that led to his house on the other side of the property. Atop Ace, he could almost feel Ali in front of him, almost sense her slight back against his chest, her hair in his face.

When his parents' house was out of sight, Cody stopped. His sides heaved and he had to concentrate to catch his breath. It had been that way ever since the transplant operation. He stared at the sky, at the white cumulus clouds dotting the blue. Of course he carried Ali with him every time he hit the road. Was he supposed to leave rodeo because of that?

Cody leaned over Ace and rested his forehead on the horse's mane. No one understood. It wasn't only the rodeo. He carried Ali with him everywhere he went. This break was supposed to give him a chance, an hour or two when he didn't see her face or hear her voice. When the sights and sounds and smells didn't make him think it was eight years ago and she was still by his side.

But now he was home, and things were no different.

She was still there when he fell asleep, there when he woke up. He saw her whenever he saw Ace, and when he looked into the wide open Colorado sky, and when he heard the crunch of dirt beneath his boots on the walk from his house to his parents'. She was everywhere, and until now that had been fine with him.

But his mother was right. Maybe that's why he couldn't shake the anger.

Four years was enough time, enough that it was no longer healthy to see her face and feel her breath against his skin every hour. Every few minutes. And so he was here because he was running from that truth and trying to find a way to embrace it—all at the same time.

"Ali . . ." He lifted his chin and stared into the blue.

There was no response. Only the whisper of wind in the distant pines.

How was he supposed to move on? The rodeo was over. He could feel it as soon as he stepped onto the plane in Nampa, Idaho. He couldn't take another cowboy coming up and offering condolences, couldn't stand another sad glance from the friends who knew how he was feeling, the way he was stuck back on some long-ago spring day when Ali was still alive, still sharing his bed and his life. When the lung he'd given her was still working.

He was finished with rodeo. He knew that for sure now.

So what was next? He'd read once in a book on grief that the only way to find new life was to get out of bed each morning and put one foot in front of the other. Breathe in, breathe out . . . and go after the next thing. In time, the pain would dull. One day, morning would come and the memories would no longer be part of every breath. Rather they would have stepped to the side, a favorite friend in a favorite place. Worth visiting every now and then.

Cody drew a long breath and ran his fingers through Ace's blond mane.

The horse whinnied and turned slightly, as if to say, "Well, where is she? Hasn't she been gone long enough?"

"Atta boy, Ace. It's okay."

He touched the horse's sides with his heels and they started moving. One foot in front of the other, huh? If that was true, then he had to find something to do with his time. He'd invested well. His prize earnings, his pay for three years' announcing on the circuit, and a consultation fee for two cowboy movies: All of it added up to a seven-figure bank account and land investments in three states. Money wouldn't be a problem, but what job would allow him to be as passionate as he'd been about the rodeo?

He removed his cowboy hat and ran his fingers through his hair. Only one person besides Ali had ever made him love so much it hurt. His brother, Carl Joseph. He thought about the conversation over breakfast, the idea that Buddy seemed smitten with a girl named Daisy.

Cody worked the muscles in his jaw. Of course the kid was smitten. He'd never been exposed to any sort of social environment until now. A group of friends was a good thing for Carl Joseph. But how was a daycare ever going to help him find long life and health here at home? His brother was forty or fifty pounds overweight, plagued by the same weak muscle tone that afflicted most people with Down

Syndrome. That and the epilepsy and heart disease.

A few years back, Cody had studied the idea of rehabilitation, finding exercises and routines for Carl Joseph that would help him overcome the limitations of Down Syndrome. At the time, he thought Carl Joseph would gain strength if he rode horses. And once in a while he'd helped his brother onto the back of a horse and led him around an arena. But that wouldn't help him find the strength and health he needed to live a long life.

Maybe the answer was a sports complex. He could look around the Springs and buy out a failing gym. Then he could turn it into a place where disabled people could come for physical training. Sort of a rehab program. The exercise would make Carl Joseph stronger, maybe buy him a decade of good health. Cody could run the place and the people who attended could be matched with trainers or placed in special classes. That way people like Carl Joseph could use their energy on something productive, something that would build their self-esteem. It would be a program that would complement the daycare thing Buddy was already involved in.

Cody eased Ace around and galloped the horse back to the barn. As he did, he was struck by a thought—something that proved the accuracy of the information he'd read a long time ago in the grief book. Do the next thing, the book's author had stated. And here—over the last few minutes—he'd done just that. He'd thought about his next move, his next career. His next passion. The book said that by doing such a thing, the memory of a lost loved one would naturally be pushed to the side. That must've been true, because when he was thinking about a center for kids like Carl Joseph a surprising thing had happened. Nothing else had filled his mind.

Not even his precious Ali.

Chapter Five

Elle sat with her mother at the kitchen table and tried to concentrate on their heated game of Scrabble. But Daisy's distractions were relentless. She was dancing in the kitchen, twirling and spinning and singing a song she was making up about field trips and the steps of a bus. It was Thursday, which meant tomorrow was another field trip day. Daisy would be dancing and giggling and celebrating until bedtime.

Field trips had that effect on her.

"Your turn." Her mother stood and headed toward the sink. "Elle, I'd swear your mind is somewhere else tonight. You don't usually let me get this close in Scrabble."

"I'll still beat you." Elle leaned down and scratched Snoopy's ears. The beagle was ten years old now, the hair around his eyes and nose more gray than brown. "I haven't had good letters all game."

"Shoulda swapped 'em!" Daisy twirled past Elle's chair. "I'd swap 'em."

"You're probably right."

Their mother poured three glasses of iced tea. She set one on the counter for Daisy and brought the other two to the table. "You ignored my observation."

"What?" Elle lifted her eyes and feigned innocence. "About beating me at Scrabble?"

She raised one eyebrow. "About your mind being somewhere else."

"Nah. Just thinking about tomorrow's field trip." Elle reached for her tea and took a sip. "Thanks for the drink."

"Tomorrow's field trip!" Daisy jumped in the air, both hands straight out in front of her. She began to hum. "I could've danced all night . . . I could've danced all night."

Their mother looked doubtful. "Where are you going?" She raised her voice so she could be heard over Daisy's gleeful singing.

"The park and out to lunch. Everyone's bringing money." Elle took four of her letter tiles and built the word "guilty" down along a double-word square. She grinned at her mother. "There. That should put me ahead."

Daisy stopped, out of breath, and dropped to the chair next to Elle. "Do you like bull riders, Elle?"

Elle looked at her sister and blinked. What was the fascination with bull riders lately? Ever since Carl Joseph mentioned his brother and how the guy had ridden bulls, Daisy brought it up nearly every day. "Not particularly."

Their mother leaned on her elbows and looked from

66

Elle to Daisy. "How'd you hear about bull riders?"

"From CJ." Daisy beamed. "His brother's a bull rider."

Elle gave her mother a side glance and the slightest shake of her head. With her eyes she conveyed her doubt. "He's probably an accountant or something. Just moved back to the Springs."

"He's a bull rider." Shock and indignation filled Daisy's face. "I said he's a bull rider and he's a bull rider."

"Okay." Elle patted her sister's hand. "He's a bull rider."

Daisy took a long drink of her iced tea. One ice cube plopped onto the table, and she quickly picked it up and dropped it back into her cup. "You didn't see that, okay, Elle? But he *is* a bull rider." She finished her tea with three big swallows and stood.

When she was out of earshot, Elle whispered toward her mother: "And I'm a ballerina."

Her mother smiled. "It doesn't really matter."

"Except Daisy's all caught up in the idea of bull riders now. Today at class Carl Joseph wore a cowboy hat and announced that he was taking up bull riding and one day he'd be a world champion like his brother." She made an exasperated face. "It's getting a little out of hand."

"I could've danced all night . . ." Daisy spun around the kitchen counter and into the living room. "I could've danced all night."

Her mother grinned. "Watch this." She used six of

her tiles with the word "sugars," placing the *s* at the end of "cage" and racking up points for both words. "That should seal it."

"Okay, okay." Elle added her mother's points to the score sheet. "I have to let you win once in a while. Otherwise you won't play."

"So"—her mother leaned back and ran her fingers along the damp sides of her iced tea glass—"is this bull rider brother guy single?"

"Mother . . ." Frustration poked pins at Elle's mood. "You promised."

Daisy skipped up to the table. "His wife was a horse rider. That's how he met her."

"Oh." Their mother sounded almost guilty. "So he's a married bull rider."

Elle was surprised, but not because she cared particularly. She hadn't heard about the guy's wife until now. "They're all married." Elle stared at her letters. "And that suits me fine. I'm not looking for a relationship, Mom." She lifted her eyes. "Remember?"

"I know. It's just . . ." Her mother checked the Scrabble board. "You need more than Thursday night Scrabble with us. You have your whole life ahead of you, Elle. I keep thinking God's going to bring the right man into your life, but weeks turn into months, months turn into years—and still nothing." Discouragement filled her tone. "It isn't right."

"You know what?" Elle met her mother's gaze straight on. "People think my students are handicapped. They look different, so they're disabled." Her voice fell and she looked at the board again. "But all of us are handicapped one way or another." She looked up. "The men I've met don't know how to love. Or they're married and looking for a cheap affair. That's more disabled than Daisy or Carl Joseph. Don't you think?"

Her mother sighed. "You're jaded, Elle. You had one bad experience."

"One?" She looked at her mother, astonished. "I got left at the altar on my wedding day! That's a little different."

"I'm just saying, you can't condemn all men because of what happened." Her mom sounded tentative, as if she knew she was pushing the subject a little too hard. "I'll drop it, but please, Elle . . . maybe talk to someone at church. Broken hearts are meant to be healed."

Elle had a standard answer when people asked her about love. She steeled herself against the pain and smiled at her mother. "I've said it before. If I'm supposed to fall in love, it'll have to find me. Grab me around the neck and sit me down face-to-face. Because I'm no longer looking." Daisy pushed a button on the CD player that sat on the kitchen counter. Waltz music filled the room, and she leaned her head back, overcome with joy. "I wish CJ was here." She swept around the table and held out her hand. "Come on, Elle. Dance with me."

The Dalton girls had always danced. Daisy's love for music and movement was probably the reason she didn't struggle with her weight the way so many people with Down Syndrome did. Elle took her sister's hand, stood, and began waltzing around the table. As they did, Daisy laughed the open-hearted, no-holds-barred laugh she was known for.

Her happiness was contagious, and Elle began to giggle. Never mind that her mother wouldn't give up on hoping she'd find a man. She'd already been down that road. This life—the one she lived at home with Daisy and her mom, the one she lived each day with her students—was fulfilling enough.

Snoopy stood and stretched and fell into line behind them. As they waltzed into the living room, he followed, and that made Daisy laugh harder. "Snoopy is a dancer! He's a dancer, Mom!"

"Yes, he is." Their mother stood and moved in time to the music. When she reached Elle and Daisy, she waltzed close to the beagle. "Snoopy's my partner this time."

Round and around the room they went, and Elle relished the feeling. When the song ended, they were all breathless from dancing and laughing. Daisy plopped down on the sofa and called Snoopy to her side. "Time for movie night."

"You're right." Elle went to the kitchen, found a bag of popcorn, and slipped it into the microwave. "Ten minutes to show time."

The movie that night was *Sweet Home Alabama*, starring Reese Witherspoon. Only a few minutes in, Reese's character daydreamed about a long-lost childhood love, and Elle felt the familiar ache in her chest. She could dismiss her mother's concern and laugh about the idea of needing more than she already had. But deep inside there was no denying the obvious. She had tried love once and failed. Badly.

Even if she were looking, she'd never find the sweet, guileless love that lived every day in the eyes of her students, a love built on honesty and transparency, a love strong enough to tear down the walls around her heart. Only that sort of love was worth letting go of her independence and trusting one more time. And that was the problem. Outside of Daisy's world, that sort of love wasn't just rare.

It was nonexistent.

THE FIELD TRIP to Antlers Park was in full swing, and Elle was proud of the way her students were handling their time in public. The bus ride had gone smoothly, all of the students demonstrating their ability to show their passes and stay seated until the appropriate stop. As always, Daisy led the way, with Carl Joseph right behind her.

Once in a while, Elle would watch the two of them and wonder what the future held. Daisy would be ready for independent living sometime in the next few months. Even now she could be successful, though Elle wanted to be sure Daisy understood her medical needs—monthly checkups because of her weak heart. She also needed a job. Already Elle was helping Daisy put together a resume.

The problem was Carl Joseph. He wouldn't be ready for at least another year. And with his epilepsy, his parents were thinking about pulling him from the program. When she tried to talk to Daisy about the situation, her sister only smiled and said, "I won't move out until CJ can move out."

Elle watched them now, Daisy and Carl Joseph, arms linked. They were at the front of the group, heading down a walkway toward Engine 168, the historic railroad car that had been placed in the park decades ago. It was a point of interest—something Elle wanted her students to understand.

She thought about her sister again. One of these days she'd have to sit down with Carl Joseph's parents and try to convince them. Epilepsy was fairly common for people with Down Syndrome. With the right medication and regular checkups, Carl Joseph could live an independent life even with his condition. Maybe they'd be more open to a group home setting where Carl Joseph and Daisy could live in the same complex. Not as some sort of romantic set-up, but as the best friends they'd come to be. For now, anyway.

They were twenty yards from the railroad car when Gus began to gallop around in circles. "We're going on a train . . . Hey, everyone, look!" He laughed loud and long and bobbed his head several times. "We're going on a train!"

Sid gave his classmate a disgusted look. He marched to the front of the railroad car and pointed at the ground. "Yeah, but no tracks." He shouted in Elle's direction. "See, Teacher. No tracks."

"No tracks is very dangerous." Carl Joseph stopped and looked around. "What's going to happen if no tracks for the train, Teacher?"

Elle held up her hands. "Everyone come here."

Slowly, with a variety of response times, the group formed a half circle around her. Sid was still mumbling something about the whole day being a disaster because no train could run without tracks. Elle waited until they were mostly quiet. "We are not going on a train today."

Gus pointed at the railroad car. "There it is, Teacher. That's the train."

"That's part of the park." She spoke loud enough for all of them to hear. Her tone was rich with compassion and confidence. "Today is a park day. The train is part of the park."

She had chosen Antlers Park intentionally, because she knew the sight of a full-size railroad car in the park would be enough to throw most of them. This was why they took field trips, so they could work through everyday obstacles on the quest for living an independent life. She motioned to the group. "Follow me."

When they reached the train, Elle positioned herself near a sign and directed them to come as close as they could. "This is a marker, a sign that explains why a train is here in the middle of the park. Who would like to read it?"

Daisy had her hand up first. About a third of the students could read, but Daisy was easily the most skilled. Their mother had worked hours each week making sure her youngest daughter could read—and she'd done it at a time when conventional wisdom held that a person with Down Syndrome might not be capable of such a feat.

It was one more area where Carl Joseph was far behind Daisy.

Daisy stepped to the front of the group and bent over the sign. Her eyes were worse than they'd been a year ago. She needed to squint in order to make out the words. But one line at a time she read the message on the sign out loud to the class. When she reached the part about the railroad car being a gift to the people of Colorado Springs, something to commemorate the railroad's part in the founding of the city, Gus waved his arms.

"I get it!" He pointed at the train. "It's a tourist trap. My mom told me about tourist traps."

Elle smiled. They finished up with the train and headed for the crosswalk. There, Elle reviewed the traffic signals. Sid lagged behind, and when they crossed, he was last to step into the road. By the time he did, the light had changed and a car honked at him. In times past, Sid would've shaken a fist at the driver or maybe dropped to the ground, weeping, reduced to the abilities of a five-year-old child.

Not this time. With Elle behind him, he stopped, looked at the driver and then waved at the man. Then he turned his attention to the other side of the street and, head high, finished his walk.

Progress! Elle stepped up onto the curb, stopped him, and smiled. "Sid! That was wonderful!"

"He didn't need to honk." Sid looked back at the driver, already speeding down the road.

"No, he didn't."

Elle and Sid joined the others at the Subway on the corner. Restaurants gave the students a chance to face other tasks that might've been daunting without the training they'd received at the ILC. They had to decide what type of bread and meat and fixings they'd have on their sandwich, and whether they wanted a meal package. And each of them needed to count out the right money to pay for the meal.

Twenty minutes later, when they had their sandwiches, the students found seats at five tables all on one side of the restaurant. Another improvement. A year ago, most of them would've wandered aimlessly around the dining area trying to figure out where to sit and who to sit with.

As they began eating, they fell into natural conversations. Another sign of independence. When one of them grew too loud, someone at their table would hold up two fingers—the sign that voices needed to be quieter. Elle sat at Daisy's table with Carl Joseph and Gus. It was one of those moments when she knew with every breath that this was the place God wanted her. Nevermind love and relationships, here—with these students, she was making a difference.

They were halfway through their meal when she saw a pickup truck park out front. A rugged dark-haired man in a white T-shirt and jeans climbed out and headed for the front door of the restaurant. Elle was struck by the guy's looks. In her world of working at the center and stopping at the grocery store and heading back home again, there were few guys who looked like this one. But the set of his jaw and his determined pace shouted that he was preoccupied.

She turned her attention back to her sandwich just as Carl Joseph dropped his sandwich and stood up.

"Brother!" He waved at the man. "Over here. Come sit with us!"

The guy's expression eased. Several students let out similar shouts. "Hi, Carl Joseph's brother!" "Come sit here!"

Daisy tugged on Carl Joseph's shirt. "Is that the bull rider?"

He puffed out his chest. "I'm a bull rider, too."

"Okay, everyone." Elle stood and looked at her students. "Let's remember our restaurant manners."

The guy gave a sheepish wave to the others and one at a time the excited students sat back down. Then he came to Carl Joseph's side and looked straight at him. "You remembered, right, Buddy?" His tone was kind, but his eyes looked troubled. Maybe even angry. "You and I have a date today?"

Carl Joseph did an exaggerated gasp. He covered his mouth and looked from Daisy to Elle and back to his brother. "I forgot, Brother. I'm sorry I forgot."

The guy gave a short laugh. In a way that made it clear he had no choice, he pulled up a chair and sat next to Carl Joseph. "Can you finish up?" A strained smile lifted his lips. "I have something to show you."

"But . . ." Carl Joseph pointed slowly at Daisy and Elle and Gus and then at the other tables. "These are my friends and . . . and this is Field Trip Day."

"Yeah." For the first time he looked at Elle. There was suddenly enough ice in his tone to change the temperature of the room. "Mom told me."

Elle held out her hand. "I don't believe we've met. I'm Elle Dalton. Director of the Center for Independent Living."

He took Elle's hand for the slightest moment. Long enough for her to see his wedding ring. "I'm Cody Gunner, Carl Joseph's brother."

"World-famous bull rider." Daisy's entire face lit up. She bounced in her seat. "Right here with us. World-famous bull rider."

Carl Joseph whispered to her, his frustration written into the lines on his forehead. "I'm a bull rider, too, Daisy. Remember?"

"Uh"—Cody gave an uncomfortable laugh—"sorry about this. I need to take my brother. We have plans."

"Okay." Elle looked at Carl Joseph. "The field trip is almost over. It's okay if you go with your brother."

"But Daisy and me wanna dance in the park." Carl Joseph's face fell. He implored his brother. "I didn't get to dance yet."

"Hold on, Buddy." Cody's pleasant facade seemed

to be cracking. He dropped his voice to a whisper and turned his attention to Elle. "Can I talk to you? In private?"

Elle felt her defenses rise. She stood and looked at her students. "I need to speak with Mr. Gunner outside. I'll be right back."

She led the way, and once they were out of earshot, he met her eyes. "What is all this?"

"Excuse me?" Elle could feel the anger flash in her eyes.

"This." He gestured toward the students inside. "Putting them on display so everyone can gawk at them." The guy kept his voice controlled, but just barely. "I thought my brother was taking social classes." He laughed, but there was no humor in it. "Now I find out it's some kind of independent living?"

Elle was too surprised to speak.

"Look—" Cody seemed to be trying to find control. "I'm sorry, it's just . . ." He paced a few steps away from her before whirling around and staring at her. "My brother's sick. He'll never live on his own. Someone should've told you."

Elle was still shocked by the guy's outburst. But now at least she understood it. "His epilepsy, you mean?"

"Epilepsy, heart disease . . . the fact that he can't read." Cody tossed his hands. "It's wrong to fill his head with ideas of independence." He turned his attention toward the students inside. "How can it be right for any of them?"

78

"Mr. Gunner." Elle worked to keep her tone even. "I care about each one of those students in that restaurant. I would never bring them into public to be laughed at." She narrowed her eyes. "This is part of their curriculum. If you'd like to know more about what your brother is learning, I'd advise you to make an appointment with me. I'm available every morning an hour before class."

"What's the point? My brother won't ever be well enough to leave home." He shook his head. "Don't you get it?"

"He can be independent even with his limitations." Elle worked to keep her anger in check. What right did Carl Joseph's brother have to disrupt the field trip?

"Nevermind." He took a step toward the door and held it open. His voice was still thick with frustration. "Thanks for your time."

Elle thought of a dozen things she could tell this guy, but why bother? Ignorant people like him came along every now and then. She didn't need to validate him by defending her work at the center. He was still holding open the door for her, so she went in.

Cody walked up to Carl Joseph and bagged the uneaten half of his sandwich. "Come on, Buddy. Let's get out of here."

"Wait!" Carl Joseph's voice was much louder than usual. "You didn't meet Daisy."

Cody smiled, but it was laced with impatience. "Fine." He looked at Daisy. His tone was kinder than before. "I'm Cody. You must be Daisy."

79

"Hi, Cody." Daisy gave him a bashful look. She batted her eyes. "You're cute."

"Hey, what about me?" Carl Joseph turned to Daisy, hurt flooding his eyes.

Daisy took his hand and pressed it to her heart. "You're the cutest of all, CJ." She whispered. "Even cuter than your brother."

At that moment, Cody seemed to notice the way his brother smelled. "Buddy? Are you wearing cologne?"

"Yes." Carl Joseph stood and beamed at Daisy. He pushed his glasses back up the bridge of his nose. "Mom bought me some. I wear it for Daisy."

Daisy leaned close to Elle. "He smells like a bull rider."

"Thank you." Carl Joseph puffed out his chest.

"This is crazy." Cody mumbled the words. He gave a curt nod to Daisy and Elle. "Nice to meet you." As he headed for the door, he stopped and looked back at Elle. "I'll stop in one day this week. Like you suggested."

Elle flashed her most professional smile. "You'll have to make an appointment, Mr. Gunner."

The two left, amidst a chorus of good-byes from the other students. As soon as they were outside, Cody put his arm around Carl Joseph's shoulders. Regardless of his intensity or his intrusion into the field trip, this much was clear: Cody Gunner was crazy about his younger brother. Cody opened the passenger-side door of the truck and gave Carl Joseph more help than he needed getting inside.

As the two drove off, Elle looked around the dining area at her students. Cody's visit had left a dark cloud of uncertainty over the group. But they knew this much: Carl Joseph's brother didn't approve of their field trip.

It was one of the things that made a person with Down Syndrome so special. Part of their makeup included an extraordinary sense of perception. Independent living courses were designed to help people with Down Syndrome recognize their feelings and talk about them.

Elle stood and cleared her throat. There was no time like the present for such a lesson. "Would someone like to tell me how you're feeling right now?"

At first no one responded. Finally Daisy raised her hand.

"Daisy?"

"I don't really think CJ's brother is cute." She shook her head. "Not anymore."

Sid tossed his hands in the air. "He didn't like us." He looked around. "Could anyone else see that? Carl Joseph's brother didn't like us."

Tears stung at Elle's eyes. As hard as it was to hear Sid voice his feelings, this, too, was progress. She moved between the tables so she was closer to Sid. "Why did you think that?"

"Because—" Sid pushed his sandwich back. His tone was more hurt than angry. "He didn't look at us."

"And something else." Gus raised his hand.

Elle pointed at him.

"He . . ." Gus looked at Daisy as if maybe this part might hurt her feelings. "I'm sorry, Daisy. I'm sorry to say something bad about Carl Joseph's brother."

"That's okay, Gus." She touched his shoulder. "You can say what you want."

"Okay . . ." Gus swallowed. "He said, 'This is crazy.' Maybe that means he thinks . . . he thinks we're crazy."

Elle's heart hurt. In that moment, if she could've, she would've whisked her students instantly back to the ILC, where they were safe and accepted, where living a life on their own seemed like one more fun activity. This reality was something entirely different. She went to Gus and lowered herself to his level. "Gus, no one thinks you're crazy."

Gus bit his lip and hung his head. "I think . . . maybe Carl Joseph's brother does."

"No." She stood and met the eyes of the students at every table. "Carl Joseph's brother is an angry person. Carl Joseph said he was hurt, so maybe he's in pain. His back or his knees, maybe." She wished he could see how his appearance had hurt her students. "We can pray for him."

"Yes." Tammy, the girl with the long braids, clapped her hands. "That's a positive idea. Right, Teacher? A positive idea."

"It is." Elle blinked back tears. If Cody Gunner were here she'd grab him by the collar and shake him. Then she'd tell him exactly how his careless words had hurt her students. But she couldn't think about that now.

Not with them looking for her to turn things around. "Tammy's right. If we pray for someone who's angry, then that's a very positive idea."

Gus looked around and then dropped from his chair to his knees. He folded his hands together and bowed his head. Elle was about to tell him he could pray from his seat, when around the room the others followed his example. Before Elle could find the words, every one of her students was kneeling in the dining area at Subway, head bowed.

"Dear God," Gus began, "be with Carl Joseph's angry brother. Anger is not a healthy choice. It's not a healthy life skill." He opened his eyes and smiled up at Elle. Then he closed them again. "So please be with Carl Joseph's brother, because maybe bull riders are angry people. Make him happy, Jesus. Amen."

Around the room, more than a dozen amens came from the group. Only then did Elle notice a table of teenage kids at the back of the room. The prayer had caught their attention. But instead of laughing at the handicapped people down on their knees, the teens were doing something entirely different.

They were smiling.

And at the end of the prayer, a few teens even stood and walked over, patting the shoulders of the students. Finally they nodded at Elle, and she mouthed the words, "Thank you," toward them. Then she sat down next to Daisy once more.

Two steps backward, three steps forward. That's the way it was with her students. The world was still getting used to the idea that people with Down Syndrome might be bagging their groceries or sweeping the floor at Wal-Mart. For every ignorant person like Cody Gunner, there was a group of people who understood, kids who had probably attended school with disabled students—because things were different today than they'd been a decade ago.

Elle was too choked up to take another bite of her sandwich. She sipped her water instead and watched as the cloud lifted and her students began interacting again. She could tell them later that it was probably best not to kneel in a public restaurant, that praying could be done in a chair as well as on their knees.

Or maybe not. Maybe if people had the chance to see an entire Subway dining room filled with people on their knees every once in a while, the whole world would be a little better off.

Chapter Six

Cody didn't say a word until they were a mile away from the Subway. He'd been wrong to storm in and demand that Carl Joseph leave right in the middle of his field trip. But why had no one explained the situation to him before? Here he'd thought Carl Joseph was involved in some kind of daycare program, a way to give him social interaction . . .

But a center for independent living?

Cody's knuckles were white from his grip on the steering wheel. The entire car reeked of Carl Joseph's cologne, the smell a pungent reminder of everything Cody hadn't understood until today. It had all come together that morning. He'd gotten a late start, and when he walked into his parents' house, he'd found his mother instead of Carl Joseph.

"Where's Buddy?" He grabbed an apple and peered into the living room. "I wanted to take him out today."

His mother was sitting at the dining room table writing a letter. "He had to be at the center early."

"The center?" He took a bite of the apple. "You mean the club, the social place?"

"Yes, Cody." His mother looked up. If he didn't know better, he would've thought she'd been crying. Her eyes looked weary, and there were circles beneath them. "He had a field trip today."

"What?" Fear took a stab at Cody. He walked closer to his mother. "Who's chaperoning?"

"The teacher's in charge. Her name's Elle Dalton. She has eighteen students like Carl Joseph. Friday is Field Trip Day."

"One teacher?" Panic welled up inside him. "You let Carl Joseph go on a field trip with just one able-bodied person? Are you kidding?" He paced to the other end of the dining room and then back again. "Where'd they go?"

"To Antlers Park and to Subway." She set her pen down. "Relax, Cody. Your brother's been going on field trips every Friday for three months." His mother explained that Carl Joseph had been to shopping malls and a skating rink and the zoo. "He'll be fine."

"No, he won't." Cody tried to picture Carl Joseph crossing a city street. "Buddy gets confused. He has epilepsy. You know that. He could wander off and get lost, have a seizure, and then what? He doesn't even know his own phone number."

"He does now."

The conversation had gone in circles, but in the end he made his decision. He and Carl Joseph needed a day to themselves. They'd talked about it when he first got home from the circuit. Cody had even mentioned that Friday might work. And today was Friday—field trip or not.

Cody took a left turn now and eased off the gas. Cody had read something in an issue of *USA Today* at a hotel in Montana earlier that year—how there was a push among educators to help adults with Down Syndrome and other disabilities find functioning independent lives outside their family homes.

Cody had shuddered at the idea. Innocent, tenderhearted Carl Joseph out in the real world, being laughed at and mocked and getting lost in the rat race? He wouldn't survive three days in that environment. And with his epilepsy, the idea was unthinkable. His mother even agreed that they were contemplating pulling him from the program. One of the quotations in the article said it all.

"We must be careful," a person who disagreed with the program was quoted as saying. "Sometimes in our rush to minimize disability, we unwittingly place a handicapped person in danger. The simple truth is that people with mental disabilities are not able to live on their own without great risk."

Cody agreed wholeheartedly. He had asked his mother why Carl Joseph was still taking part in field trips when he could have a seizure at any moment.

"Elle will take care of him," she'd said. "Elle knows what to do."

But now he'd seen Elle. She couldn't stay at Carl Joseph's side, and even if she did she wouldn't be strong enough to catch him if he fell. One seizure and he could crack his head open.

"Brother?" Carl Joseph turned to him.

"What, Buddy?" Cody glanced over.

Carl Joseph, the one who never got mad at anyone, had been quiet since they left the Subway. Now he looked hurt. "You weren't very nice to my friends."

"I'm sorry."

"So then"—he licked his lips—"why, Brother? Why weren't you nice?"

"I was afraid." Cody pulled up at a stoplight and looked at Carl Joseph. "I don't like you out on the streets, Buddy. You could walk into traffic or wander off. You could have one of your spells. Do you understand?"

Carl Joseph looked straight ahead. "Green, Brother. Green means go. Red means stop. White walk sign means walk."

Cody stared at his brother, and only after someone behind them honked did he finally press his foot to the accelerator. "Where did you learn that?"

"From Teacher."

They didn't talk again until they reached the parking lot of the old YMCA. Rumor around town was that the owner wanted to sell it. The city had passed on buying it, so now the place was open to anyone with the money to take it over. Cody parked his truck and turned to Carl Joseph. "Tell me about the center, Buddy."

Carl Joseph took a long breath. He twisted his fingers together, the way he did when he was nervous. "It's for independent living."

"You said that earlier." Cody was careful to make his tone kind. He reached out and took one of his brother's hands. None of this was Carl Joseph's fault. "Don't be nervous. I'm not mad."

"You seemed mad." He licked his lips again. "At Daisy and Gus and Teacher and Sid and Tammy and—"

"I'm not mad, Buddy. Just please . . . tell me about the center. Why . . . why do you need to go on field trips?"

"Because, see . . ." Carl Joseph looked out the window and then back at Cody. "Field trips get us closer to Goal Day."

"Goal Day?" Cody could feel his heart sinking inside him. There would be no goal day for a person as sick as Carl Joseph. "Tell me about it."

"Goal Day is when students move out and live on their own." Perspiration appeared on Carl Joseph's forehead. "All on their own. Independent living."

Cody felt sick to his stomach. So it was exactly what

he'd feared. This Elle Dalton was running a program that had somehow taught Carl Joseph to believe something impossible for his future. "Is that what you want?" The blood drained from Cody's face. "To live away from Mom and Dad, out here in the world all by yourself? Even with these spells you've been having?"

"Uh . . ." Carl Joseph began to rock. He looked at his feet and then held his hand up and examined it. "Yes. Buddy wants that."

For a moment Cody wasn't sure what to say. He'd already upset his brother. He had to undo this flawed way of thinking, the ridiculous and dangerous notions Carl Joseph had been taught at the center. But he had to do it in a way that didn't hurt his brother. Finally he squeezed Carl Joseph's hand. "Okay, Buddy. I understand." He hesitated. "We can talk about it later."

"Later." Carl Joseph nodded. He still looked uncertain, but he turned his eyes to Cody and smiled. "Goal Day can come later."

"Right." Cody's head was spinning. He wanted to get home as fast as possible and find his parents, confront them about how—since getting his recent diagnosis—they could possibly have allowed Carl Joseph to continue this way of thinking. He released his brother's hand, climbed out of the car, and went to Carl Joseph's side.

But before he got there, his brother climbed out and turned curious eyes in his direction. "Do you have your keys?"

"Yes." He held them up. What was this? Carl Joseph had never even comprehended the idea of keys before. When they went out on the town, Cody would open and close the door for him, helping him to the pavement and back into the car.

"Good." Carl Joseph pushed the lock button on his door and shut it. "You have to check first. Keys get locked in sometimes."

Cody was stunned. How much had his brother learned? Already more than Cody would've thought possible. They started to walk toward the building, and Cody focused on the reason they were here. "I'm thinking about buying this place."

"Really?" Carl Joseph was still trembling, still upset. But he was clearly trying to move past the earlier incident, same as Cody. "Why, Brother?"

"It's a gym." Cody kept his pace even with Carl Joseph's. "I thought maybe I could turn it into an exercise facility for people like you and . . . and your friends."

"You think we need exercise?" Carl Joseph stopped. His eyes lit up. "Teacher thinks that, too. She makes us dance and do sit-ups and stretches."

Cody felt his anger rise again. The woman was taking over every area of his brother's life. And what good was coming from her exercise program? Carl Joseph was no more fit than he'd been last time Cody was home. His heart was no stronger. "Well." He kept his voice upbeat. "I think maybe you could use a little more exercise than that. A regular exercise program."

"Okay."

"Yeah, and maybe you'll like this place better than the center." He made a funny face at Carl Joseph. "Might make you big and strong."

"Like a bull rider?"

"Right. Exactly."

"Oh, goodie." They went inside and Cody met the owner at the front desk. "I called about the facility here. I'm interested in purchasing it."

"Yes." The man shook his hand. "Thanks for coming." He hesitated. "But I'm afraid the other owner and I haven't decided whether or not we're going to sell."

Cody was about to ask how much longer before the owners might know more, when he heard someone laughing. He turned and saw Carl Joseph standing at a butterfly press machine, but instead of using it correctly, he was doing squats over the bench. A couple of scrawny guys in their thirties—long hair and pierced ears—had stopped to watch. One of them was pointing at Carl Joseph. "What's this—comic relief?"

"Yeah, since when do they let retards in?"

By the time Cody reached his side, Carl Joseph had brought his hands up and covered his face. Cody shoved the first guy he reached. "Leave him alone."

The guy had a beard and a mean face. He pushed Cody in return. "What's it to you?"

"That's my brother." Cody grabbed the guy's sweaty T-shirt. This time he pushed him hard enough that the guy fell to the floor.

At that point, the owner stepped up. "I'm going to

have to ask you to leave." He took hold of Cody's arm. "The club is for members only."

"Club?" Cody jerked his arm free. "Place is a dive." He snarled at the bearded man, still scrambling up from the floor. "Bunch of lowlifes." He glared at the owner. "No wonder you're going bankrupt."

The two men started to go after Cody, but the owner held them back. Cody led Carl Joseph out the door and back to the car. This time he didn't bother opening his brother's door. As soon as they were inside, Cody let his head fall against the steering wheel. What was happening? Nothing was going the way he planned it.

"Brother?" Carl Joseph touched his arm. "I think I like the center better."

Cody lifted his head. "I'll bet you do." He straightened and turned toward his brother. "I'm sorry about that. Those guys . . ." He swallowed his anger so Carl Joseph wouldn't think it was directed at him. "Those guys have a problem, Buddy. I'm sorry."

"Maybe they don't have life skills." Carl Joseph reached back and grabbed his seatbelt. He buckled it as if he'd done so a hundred times before. "Life skills help."

"Yes." Cody started the engine. Who would stand up for Buddy the next time some ignorant jerk laughed at him? Who would come along and take his hands down from his face and help him past the situation? He reached over and patted his brother's knee. "Let's get home, okay?"

"Okay."

As they drove, Cody asked more questions about the center. "How does a student get ready for Goal Day? Can you tell me?"

Carl Joseph seemed less upset than before, but he was still nervous. As if he could sense that Cody's questions were being asked not merely out of mild interest but because Cody disapproved. "You have to know the bus routes."

"How to get on a bus, you mean?"

"No." Carl Joseph brought his hands together and began twisting them again. "You have to know that Route Number Eight goes to the Citadel Mall and that Route Ten goes downtown."

Again the shock was so great, Cody could barely concentrate on the road. "You know the bus routes?"

"Not . . ." Carl Joseph looked up at the ceiling and for a long moment he moved his fingers against his hand like he was counting. "Not Bus Route Number Twenty-three or Twenty-five. Not Number Thirty-seven. Not Forty-one either."

"But you know the rest?"

"Not like Daisy knows them." He gave a weak smile. "Remember Daisy, Brother? She was at the Subway."

"Yes. She was nice." Cody clenched his fist. He'd been awful earlier. "I should've stayed and talked to her."

"Yes." Carl Joseph stopped twisting his hands. "She had a pretty shirt. You should've said she had a pretty shirt."

"Right." Cody stared at the road ahead. "Was the field trip fun? Before I came?"

"Yes. Gus wanted to ride a train."

"Through the park? I don't think there's a train that goes through Antlers Park."

"There isn't." Carl Joseph laughed. It wasn't as loud and carefree as usual, but at least it was a start, proof that he would recover from the events of the day—events that Cody knew he was completely responsible for.

Cody played along. "Okay, so why did Gus want to ride a train?"

"Because of the landmark at the middle of the park. Old Engine 168."

Carl Joseph was right. There was an old railroad car at the center of the park—something donated to the city ages ago. Cody looked at his brother, disbelieving. In all his life, he'd never had a conversation like this one with Carl Joseph. "Did someone explain that to Gus?"

"Yes." Carl Joseph rocked forward and laughed a little louder than before. "Sid told him, 'Look, no tracks.' And Teacher said, 'Read the sign.' "

This time Cody nearly hit the brakes. "You can read?"

"Not yet." Shame crept into his tone. "I'm learning my ABCs. Daisy's helping me."

"Daisy can read?"

"Daisy's a super-duper reader, Brother. She can read signs and bottles and recipes and *Adventures of Tom Sawyer*."

The idea was entirely new to Cody. A person with Down Syndrome could learn to read? That wasn't what the teachers had told their mother back when Carl Joseph was in grade school. But since then . . . Cody wasn't sure. Was he that out of touch?

It all came together. Carl Joseph wasn't involved in the center by his own choosing. Someone had to have found the place and convinced him that independent living was a good idea.

And that person could only have been his father.

The truth brought with it a host of familiar feelings—anger and resentment toward the man. Cody had hated his father most of his life. Ali had brought them together after a lifetime of being apart. Ali, who thought family was too important to hold grudges and harbor hatred. But that didn't mean Cody had forgotten.

Cody was seven and Carl Joseph two when their father climbed into a yellow taxicab and drove off—all because he wasn't willing to raise a son with Down Syndrome. Cody spent the next decade living with the growing understanding that something was different about his little brother. His father had been mean and unfeeling to reject a boy like Carl Joseph. Cody's entire bull-riding career was driven by the rage inside him, a rage that took root that day when his father's cab pulled away. Yes, Ali had brought healing between the two of them. His dad was back, and his parents were happy together. But maybe his father was still embarrassed by Carl Joseph. Why else would

Buddy be attending an independent-living center even with a diagnosis of epilepsy?

As Cody parked the car, he spotted his father's sedan. His dad was owner and manager of a restaurant—the same job he'd had since he moved home—and today he was home early. Cody was glad. He could hardly wait to talk to him. There were things he'd never said to the man once he returned, things that had seemed unimportant in light of everything with Ali. Back then Cody's days were too busy loving Ali, finding a way to soak a lifetime out of the three years they had together.

Cody climbed out of the car and waited for Carl Joseph to join him. He could already picture his father, sitting at the kitchen table with his mother, sharing a coffee break. What was he thinking, putting Carl Joseph's life at risk? And what had he been thinking all those years ago, when he climbed into that yellow cab and drove away? Carl Joseph never held any of it against their father. He was happy to see the man when he showed up again. But the things Cody had wanted to tell his father when it came to Carl Joseph stayed with him, stuffed in a corner of his heart.

And that was going to change in a few minutes.

Chapter Seven

Mary Gunner was aware that her world was about to be rocked.

She had called her husband minutes after Cody stormed out of the house. "There's trouble, Mike." She explained that Cody knew about the center, and that he was angry and scared about Carl Joseph being on his own. "Get home early."

Mike tried to downplay the brewing trouble. "Cody will get used to the idea, Mary. He has no say over Carl Joseph's future."

Mary did not like any sort of confrontation where Mike was concerned. They'd had more confrontation in their early years than most married couples had in a lifetime. Mike had played football in the NFL, and when an injury cut his career short, he found his ego best fed in the arms of other women.

When Mary learned the truth, she confronted him, ready to forgive him if he was sorry, if he promised to change. But Mike wasn't ready to make promises. Instead he told her that he couldn't be a father to Carl Joseph, and with almost no warning or conversation, he took two suitcases and met a cab in front of their house. He left that day with Carl Joseph crying in her arms, and he had never looked back until seven years ago.

By then Mary and Carl Joseph had built a life on their own. They had a comfortable routine, and Mary had only one source of heartache—the way Mike's absence hurt her oldest son. Cody lived most of his years angry, and for that Mary ached day and night.

If it weren't for Ali, healing might never have happened at all. But like an angel sent from heaven, Ali had a way of making people around her see love where before only hatred existed.

Eventually Mike returned home—full of apologies and regret. And every day since then he'd been the model husband, loving her and caring for her, and making up for all the years they'd lost.

In Ali's presence, Cody couldn't stay angry. His painful feelings toward his father faded until finally there wasn't a trace of hatred left. Mike gave blood before Ali's lung transplant, and as Ali grew sicker, Cody and his father grew closer. When she died, Cody wept in his father's arms. The past seemed as distant as if it had happened to someone else.

Until this morning.

So when Mike made light of the situation, when he complained that he was supposed to stay through the dinner shift at the restaurant, she did what she almost never did. She pushed. "Mike, this is serious. More than you know. Please . . ."

Mike must've heard something in her voice, because he hesitated for only a moment. "Okay." His tone expressed his change of heart. "I'll be there."

And now here they were, waiting, when they heard Cody's car pull into the drive. They were silent, side by side on the living room sofa, as the garage door lifted, and they heard Cody pull the car in.

"I don't want to talk about this in front of Carl Joseph." Mike paced to the window. "He doesn't need to listen. It'll confuse him."

Mary studied her husband, amazed. Sometimes it was hard to believe that this was the same man who had walked out on them. "You're right." She went to meet her sons at the kitchen door leading to the garage.

Cody looked from her to Mike and back again. He opened his mouth to speak, but she held up her hand. "Wait." She turned to Carl Joseph and smiled. "How was your field trip?"

"Good." He gave Cody a nervous look. "Pretty good."

"Carl Joseph, could you do me a favor?"

"Sure." Her younger son stood a little taller. He loved being trusted with assignments from her.

"Okay." This was something new, something that had come as a result of the center. Before, Mary would've assumed Carl Joseph was capable of only the simplest jobs. Not anymore. "Could you go out back and clear the weeds from the flower garden? And then could you spray the fertilizer on the stems? I meant to do that earlier today"—she looked at Cody—"but I didn't get to it."

"Sure." Carl Joseph nodded. He headed toward the back door. On the way, he waved at Mike. "Hi, Dad. How are you?"

"Good, son." Mike was still standing by the

window. "Did you see Daisy on your field trip?"

"Yes. We didn't get to dance in the park, though."

"Oh." Mike stuck his hands in his pockets. "I'm sorry about that. Maybe next time."

Cody shifted his position. Mary could feel his anger.

"Next time. Yes, maybe next time." Carl Joseph opened the slider and stepped onto the porch outside. "I'm gonna pull weeds for Mom and fertilize, okay?"

"Okay. Do a good job."

"I will." He smiled, and pride shone in his eyes. "I'll do my very best."

Mary wanted to follow him and pull him into her arms. The turmoil in their home wasn't his fault. And no matter how the doctor's recent diagnosis complicated things, Carl Joseph did want his independence. He'd been proving that ever since he started at the center. Mary returned to her spot beside Mike and braced herself for what was coming.

Cody waited until Carl Joseph was outside. Then he stepped into the living room and waved his hand at the sliding door. "You're trying to get rid of him. Is that it?"

"Lower your voice." Mike's tone was stern.

Mary could feel her husband's body tense up beside her. As in all those years when Cody was growing up, it would be her role to keep her son's anger at bay. "No one's trying to get rid of Carl Joseph. That's not what this is about."

"Yes, it is!" Cody paced toward the patio slider and back again. "Independent living?" He laughed, but the sound was colored with fury. "That's like packing an eight-year-old's bags and sending him on his way." The muscles in his jaw flexed. "Carl Joseph is as gentle and innocent as a little kid. He has epilepsy. I mean, come on. You can't really think you're going to send him into the world and everything'll be okay."

"The center has a plan for each student, a list of goals that have to be met before the student is introduced to independent living." Mike was calmer now. He moved to the sofa and Mary followed. When they were seated, Mike put his arm over the back of the sofa and leaned into the cushions. "You haven't been around, Cody. You don't know how much this means to him."

"Oh, sure." Cody bent at the waist, his words directed at Mike like bullets. "It's not how much it means to Carl Joseph. It's how much it means to *you,* right, Dad? Big Mike Gunner, former NFL hotshot." He pointed at Mike. "You walked out on him because he wasn't like other kids. Remember?" Tears worked their way into Cody's voice.

"You're right." Mike leaned forward, his elbows on his knees. "I was young and ignorant, and I didn't know how to handle things."

Mary couldn't sit by and let Cody say these things. Not when Mike had so completely changed. "Things are different now. Your father loves Carl Joseph very much." She held her hand out toward Cody. "Can't you see? Both of us only want what's best for your brother. Whatever that is."

Cody let his hands fall to his side. "I'll tell you what that is." He looked back toward the sliding glass door, out to the place where Carl Joseph was smiling and making his way around the garden, tossing weeds into a bucket. When he spoke again, Cody's words were squeezed through clenched teeth. "What's best is keeping him home where he can be happy and loved, where no one will laugh at him and call him a retard the way they did when we were out today. Where he'll be safe if he has a seizure, and he can get emergency medical help if he needs it." Cody's eyes were wet, and his emotion spilled into every word. "Carl Joseph is the most precious kid I know, but regardless of his age he's just a kid. Keep him home and protect him. Love him the way he deserves to be loved." Cody dragged the back of his hand across his cheek. "That's what's best for him." He hung his head and made both his hands into fists. Then he glared at Mike. "What do you have to say to that?"

Mike waited. He was calmer than Mary had ever seen him. "Are you finished?"

"Yes." Cody spat the word.

"Okay." Mike took a long breath. "First of all, everything we're doing for Carl Joseph these days is because we love him. We love him very much." Mike stood and went to the far window. He sat against the sill and faced Cody. "Have you watched your brother lately?"

Cody's voice rose. He pointed to the place where Carl Joseph was still working. "I watched him cover his face and start rocking when the guys at the gym called him a retard. So, yes. I guess I've been watching him."

"Getting made fun of is part of life." Mike was unfazed. "I'm talking about his day-to-day activities, the way he lives now. Six months ago, your brother would struggle out of bed, drag himself to breakfast, and barely be able to feed himself when your mother set a plate of eggs in front of him. After breakfast he would curl up on the couch and watch cartoons for a few hours. He'd eat again and maybe walk outside to visit Ace. Then he'd play video games until lunch." Mike grabbed a quick breath. "After lunch he'd fall asleep watching Nickelodeon until I got home at five." Mike paused. "It wasn't much of a life, Cody. You have to admit."

"But he was safe and he was loved." Cody's response was immediate. He took a step closer to his father, his words filled with passion. "The doctor said he won't live very long, anyway. Another ten years, maybe. At least let him live it here, where he's loved. Where he has everything he needs."

Mike didn't blink. "He doesn't want that."

"No, of course not." Cody shook his head. "Not now that you've filled his head with impossible ideas."

"Cody." Mary leaned forward and waited for him to look at her. "What your father's saying is, Carl Joseph's not the same person he was back then."

"He's not." Mike looked out the back glass door and a smile tugged at the corners of his lips. "Even with the dangers of epilepsy, your brother gets up early now. He comes to the kitchen wanting to make his *own* eggs. He eats with table manners and then he helps with dishes. He talks about his friends at the center, the issues they're struggling with, and when he walks around this place he stands three inches taller than before." Mike turned his attention back to Cody. "You know why? Because he's proud of himself. He has a plan and a purpose. He's excited about life." He paused. "And you mean to tell me you'd deny your brother all of that?" He let out a single, frustrated laugh. "You're supposed to love him most of all."

"I do!" Cody shouted the words. Then he gritted his teeth and forced himself to lower his voice. "I love him the most because I love him the way he is. I don't need him to perform some sort of circus act in order to feel good about him."

"That's not fair, Cody." Mary went to him, but he pulled away. "You were with Carl Joseph today. Didn't you see how different he is? How he gets into a car by himself and buckles his own seatbelt? He has more to talk about, and he's excited about reading and getting around by himself. Didn't you see that?"

"And that's worth risking his life?" Cody stared at the ceiling for a moment and then back at her. "Okay, fine. Take him to the center and let him learn how to buckle his seatbelt. But don't fill his head with ideas about independence. Can you imagine it, Mom? Can you picture *Goal Day*?" Cody made the last two words sound ominous. He pointed to the entryway.

"Carl Joseph packs his bag and walks out that door and what? He gets an apartment? He'll burn down his place or get hit by a car the first week, Mom! He'll have a seizure and choke on his dinner. It's insane."

"We understand the risks. More now, since our meeting with the doctor." Mike's expression fell. "Independent living might not be possible for Carl Joseph." His eyes lifted to Cody's. "But we have to try. It's what Carl Joseph wants."

Cody's anger eased some. "So maybe I can help him feel more independent. We can run errands together and he can keep taking classes—so long as he doesn't make a plan to move out."

"We've thought about that. We're even thinking about taking him out of the center." The struggle they'd been living through was evident in Mike's voice. "But that's not what Carl Joseph wants."

"Of course he wants the center." Cody's tone softened. "He thinks it'll make you happy. If you asked him to drive the car out onto the interstate, he'd do that, too. Whatever it takes to get your approval. But here's the problem. Carl Joseph doesn't know how dangerous this is. He's trusting you." He looked from Mike to Mary. "And you. And that Elle Dalton teacher of his. He's a kid. He doesn't know the difference. He's believing the adults around him, with no idea what independent living really means."

For the first time, Mike didn't have a response. He hung his head, and when he looked up, his focus returned to Carl Joseph working outside.

Before he could think of something to say, Cody crossed his arms. "I'm sorry for my temper. It's been a long day." He headed for the front door, but then he stopped. "Please . . . think about the doctor's diagnosis. Don't let Carl Joseph dream about something that can never happen. I love that kid." His voice broke. "I love him too much to see him hurt."

When he was gone, Mike pulled Mary into a hug. "What're we supposed to do?"

She searched his eyes. "Maybe it's time to pull him out."

Mike was quiet for a minute. "Elle's been doing research on people with Down Syndrome and epilepsy living on their own, right?"

"That's what she said."

"So we can't pull him out yet. Not while there's still a chance he could reach his goal."

Mary wasn't sure, but she didn't want to talk about it anymore. She leaned up and kissed his cheek. "Okay, Mike." She eased back. "I'm going for a walk."

He looked over his shoulder. "I'll be outside with Carl Joseph."

Mary nodded, but only because she couldn't speak. If she did, the torrent of tears building inside her would release for sure and she wouldn't have any strength left to make it to the front door.

On the way out, her eyes fell on a picture of Carl Joseph at age twelve, back when she knew without a doubt what was best for her son. His past, his present, and everything about his future. Back when independent living for a child like Carl Joseph would've been absolutely ridiculous.

The way maybe it still was today.

Chapter Eight

When Mary stepped outside, she looked around for Cody, but her oldest son was gone. Probably jogged back to his house on the other side of the property. She sighed and began walking toward the long, winding driveway. When she needed to think, this was where she went. She would set off down the drive and then right and up the hill to the end of the road. The area was wide open with only a few clusters of pine trees and mesquite bushes and enough sky to clear her head.

But today she kept her eyes down, and for the first few minutes she replayed everything Cody had just said. It was easy to mistake Cody for an angry man with no willingness to bend, opinionated, always thinking he was right. But that wasn't the true Cody.

Cody wasn't trying to be right or strong-headed. He loved Carl Joseph. For most of his childhood and adolescence he cared more about his little brother than he did about anyone else. He was Carl Joseph's friend and mentor, and together those two boys had filled her heart with joy.

When Cody first started riding bulls, he'd come home every few weeks and Carl Joseph would be waiting for him at the door, a big, wide grin on his face. He'd fling open his arms and run toward Cody. "Brother! You came back, Brother!"

Mary felt tears in her eyes and sniffed. She could hear him still, the joy in his voice, the anticipation whenever Cody came home. Almost always, Cody would bring video from the rodeo events, and he and Carl Joseph would sit in front of the TV watching Cody's rides over and over and over again. "You're a good bull rider, Brother. Very, very good!"

Even now, Carl Joseph wanted nothing more than to be a bull rider like Cody. Yes, because Daisy was impressed by the idea. But also because it would make him a little bit more like the brother he idolized. Four years ago, when Ali died, Carl Joseph brought Cody more comfort than all the rest of his friends and family combined. Carl Joseph was the one who pulled Cody aside at Ali's funeral and pointed toward heaven. "You know what I think, Brother?" he said as he put his arm around Cody's shoulders. "I think up there in heaven Ali has the fastest, most beautiful horse of all."

Mary had been standing close enough to hear the conversation. "Yeah, Buddy. Maybe you're right." Cody looked up, his eyes filled with pain.

"I am right, Brother. God would definitely give Ali a horse in heaven."

It was the first time that terrible day that Mary saw Cody smile. Because Carl Joseph had known exactly what Cody needed to hear in the wake of such a devastating loss.

Of course Cody didn't want anything to happen to Carl Joseph—none of them did. But was that reason enough to hold him back, to keep him home in front of a television when there was a chance he could manage his epilepsy and heart disease on his own? Mike was right about the changes in Carl Joseph.

Mary hugged herself and slowed her pace. This was never how she'd pictured things going with Carl Joseph, not since the day she first held him.

Mary reached the end of the driveway and turned right. As she did, as she faced the long hill before her, the years disappeared and she was there again, in the hospital, celebrating one of the happiest days in her life—the birth of her second son.

The day they laid Carl Joseph in her arms, Mary knew something was different about him. His cry was different from Cody's, and his neck looked shorter and thicker. The thought of Down Syndrome crossed her mind—because she remembered once during her pregnancy, when she'd stopped to admire a newborn in the grocery store with her mother. Conversation between Mary and the woman lasted the better part of thirty minutes, and at the end, the woman stroked her baby's forehead. "She has Down Syndrome. The doctors think she'll need to be institutionalized." Tears glistened in the woman's eyes. "But I won't let that happen. Not to my little girl."

The scene had terrified Mary and plagued her for the next week. But then she let the possibility go. She wouldn't have a child with Down Syndrome. It wasn't something that ran in her family, and besides, she was taking great care of herself. Her child would be even healthier and stronger than Cody, because she knew more about being a mother the second time around.

But that day in her hospital bed, looking down at Carl Joseph, the fears returned. What if there was something wrong with him, something that would affect him all his life? She shuddered at the thought. Her baby was perfect. Beautiful and whole and healthy, no matter what doubts plagued her.

Not until the end of his first week did doctors do a blood test to confirm her fears. Carl Joseph had Down Syndrome; there was no doubt. One in a thousand babies were born with the chromosomal defect, and in this case, he was that one. He had an extra chromosome 21.

The doctor went on to say that had Mary submitted to an amniocentesis, they might've found out about the birth defect sooner. "Then"—the doctor pursed his lips—"you might've had options."

"Options?" Anger flooded Mary's veins. "You mean abortion? I could've aborted my baby if I'd known—is that what you're saying?"

"Just a minute." The doctor held up his hand. "I'm only saying I advise all my patients to have an amnio. You declined." He looked at Carl Joseph. "Now your options are far more limited."

"Look"—Mary pointed to the door—"you can leave now. I never . . . never would've aborted Carl Joseph just because he isn't like other children. And I never want to see you in this room again."

The doctor left, and Mary sat in her bed trembling. The baby in her arms looked up at her, all innocence and tenderness and love, and Mary realized something. This child needed her more than Cody ever had. "You're a miracle, little Carl Joseph. A miracle from God. Everything's going to be okay."

She cooed and kissed Carl Joseph's cheeks until an hour later when a new doctor entered the room, a man with kind eyes and a gentle manner.

"I'm Dr. West," he told her. "I understand you've heard the news about your little boy."

"Yes." She didn't realize it until that moment, but she had tears on her cheeks.

"Your son will always be different, but that doesn't mean he won't bring a great deal of love into your life."

"Arc you . . . are you recommending an institution?" The thought horrified her. She couldn't imagine taking her baby home, feeding him and holding him and rocking him all so when he was three or four years old she could drive him to some brick building and say good-bye.

She didn't wait for Dr. West's response. "I can't put him in an institution, Doctor. I can't do it."

Dr. West put his hand on her shoulder. "I wasn't going to recommend that. That's an old way of thinking, the idea of institutionalizing children with Down Syndrome. Now most doctors will tell you to take your baby home and love him. You feed him and read to him and cuddle him."

"Until . . ." She wasn't sure she understood.

"Indefinitely." Dr. West smiled. "Having a child with Down Syndrome is like having a child that will never grow up. Your baby, Mrs. Gunner, will level off in cognitive thinking and social interaction at about the age of a second-grader. He won't learn to read or write or live on his own. But these days, we're finding that children with Down Syndrome who are allowed to live at home live longer than those who are placed in institutions." He opened the folder in his hands and studied the information inside. "Carl Joseph has a healthy heart for now. He could live into his forties, if things go well for him."

The doctor talked to her for a few more minutes. Then he smiled and patted Carl Joseph's head. "You and your baby need some time alone."

"Yes." She held Carl Joseph closer. "Thank you."

After Dr. West left, Mary wept over her tiny baby. He would never talk clearly or walk normally, and he wouldn't look like other children. He wouldn't have a first day of kindergarten, and he'd never play high school football. He wouldn't graduate and he wouldn't have a career goal. He'd never fall in love.

But he would be hers forever.

And as her tears fell that day, she felt herself bonding to Carl Joseph as she'd never connected to anyone or anything in her life. Mike spent much of his time away from home, and Cody was independent from the moment he could walk. But Carl Joseph . . . Carl Joseph might have Down Syndrome, but he would be hers and always hers. Forever and ever.

Now as she walked away from the house, images from that day filled Mary's heart and overflowed into her soul. She kicked at a few loose pebbles as she made her way up the hill. After Mike left all those years ago, her feelings for Carl Joseph only grew stronger. She protected him from strange glances and mean comments, and she made sure he never wanted for anything. If he needed his shoes tied, she tied them. If he wanted breakfast, she made it. She waited on him and looked after him and treasured the times when they cuddled together in front of the television. When he left for his special school on the short bus, she thought about him constantly until he returned home safely.

School taught Carl Joseph very little, as it turned out. He learned to color and stack blocks and how to share a puzzle during carpet time. But after a few years it became clear to Mary that special education— at least at their small-town school—was little more than glorified babysitting. She pulled Carl Joseph out after fifth grade.

When Mike's child support wasn't enough to pay the bills, Mary took a night job. And throughout those years she comforted herself with the truth that was a balm to her hurting heart: Carl Joseph would always be hers. That was the balm. Never once during Carl Joseph's childhood or teenage years had she ever considered that he might want to move out on his own one day.

She slowed her pace. Independent living was Mike's idea, of course. Cody was right about that part. But not for the reasons Cody guessed. Mike was not embarrassed by Carl Joseph, nor did he want their youngest son to achieve great things to make the two of them feel better about having a handicapped son.

After Mike returned to their lives, it took only a few weeks before he came to her on the front porch one day. His eyes were red, his cheeks tearstained. "Mary, I'm sorry."

She looked long and deep into his eyes. "About what?"

"About all I've missed." He coughed, struggling with his words. "I'm so sorry. I never . . . never should've left."

"Ah, baby." She put her arms around his waist. "You've already told me that a dozen times. It's okay. We're together now; everything's different."

"But . . ." He fought back another bit of sorrow. "I haven't told you how sorry I am about Carl Joseph. I ran from him, the affairs, the other women. I was always running away from Carl Joseph. When . . . when I should've run *to* him. I should've embraced him." He pressed his fist to his chest. "That kid has worked his way in here so fast it makes my head spin. He's wonderful, Mary. I love everything about him."

Mary blinked and remembered how it felt to hear those words, how it made her want to shout to the heavens that finally Mike understood how wonderful it was to have Carl Joseph as a son. Mike had missed so much, all the years when Carl Joseph's wonderment at the world around him was enough to make Mary see all of life through new eyes.

She reached the top of the hill and looked out over the fields. Ever since that day, Mike had grown more and more attached to Carl Joseph. But Mike was also busy, making a name for himself in the restaurant business. When Cody was home, Carl Joseph never left his side. And Mike was usually at the restaurant. It would've been easy for Cody to miss how close Carl Joseph and Mike had become.

But that didn't change the facts.

The idea of independent living came up quite innocently. One day after work, Mike went to the doctor for a checkup. When he came home that evening, his eyes were shining. He handed her a brochure. "Read this." His voice held a sense of awe. "I had no idea."

Mary looked at the flyer. Written across the top it said, *Independent Living Center—give your disabled child every chance for a bright future.*

She drew a deep breath and closed her eyes. Never in a million years would she forget how she felt in that moment. Her heart skipped a beat, and she almost handed the pamphlet back to Mike, almost told him to rip it in half and never mention the words "independent living" again.

She'd heard of such a thing more than once in the years leading up to that moment. She'd heard about it, and every time she'd felt sick to her stomach. Carl Joseph, independent? The boy would be lost in the world without her, without the safety and security of the home she'd made for him.

But with Mike standing there, she had no choice. She read about the full-time program offered at the center, and the testimonials from family members of people with Down Syndrome. How they were grateful to the center for giving their son or daughter a chance at the sort of life everyone deserved.

Mary wanted to scream at those parents. At first, she'd felt the same way Cody felt, that a child with Down Syndrome couldn't possibly understand what he did or didn't deserve. The entire idea felt like something created by able-bodied people and from the viewpoint of able-bodied people. A program that tried to force people with Down Syndrome into a mold that seemed normal and acceptable to people without disabilities.

But it was the photo on the inside page that caught her attention. There, smiling bigger than life, was a young man with Down Syndrome. Beneath his picture it said, "I'm a man now, not a little kid. This is my life. All my dreams are coming true—Gus, Age 22."

Mary stared at that photograph, and everything she'd believed about her life with Carl Joseph began to crumble before her eyes. Was this the life Carl Joseph deserved, the one she'd unwittingly denied him?

Mary stared at the brochure for a long time. Then

she handed it back to Mike and in a voice pinched with emotion, she said, "Let's talk to Carl Joseph."

Mike had done the talking when they brought the topic up to Carl Joseph later that night. Mike explained that maybe it was time for Carl Joseph to attend adult school, time to learn how to handle money and take the bus places. Maybe even time to get a job.

Carl Joseph took a minute or so to absorb what was being said. But as it all started to click, he sat up and looked from Mike to Mary. "You mean . . . I get to be a man like Daddy?"

What was left of Mary's doubts fell away in that instant. She crossed the room and knelt in front of Carl Joseph. Then she put her arms around him and hugged him. Independent living was the most terrifying thing she could imagine. But if it made Carl Joseph feel like a man, how could she possibly deny him the chance?

They enrolled him at the center the next morning.

Mary smiled at the memory. Gus was one of Carl Joseph's friends now, someone who was also working very hard toward his Goal Day.

She reached the bottom of the hill and turned left into their driveway. There, standing on the front porch, was Carl Joseph, his hand shading his eyes. "Mom?" he shouted.

She was too far away to yell back, but she waved at him, big so he could see. With that he hopped down from the porch and ran to her. Mary stopped and admired him. He did not run with the grace of an able-bodied person, but he ran with gusto and determination, huffing and puffing as he came. When he reached her, he stopped and fell into place beside her. "Hi, Mom." He gave her a big, openmouthed smile.

"Hi, Carl Joseph." Mary swallowed her sadness. Never mind Cody's anger. What they were doing was right—as long as they could feel safe about Carl Joseph's epilepsy treatment. The classes were helping Carl Joseph feel good about himself and good about life. "Did you finish weeding?"

"Yes." He spread his arms out wide. "I did the whole thing. All of it."

"Good." She nodded. "You're a hard worker, Carl Joseph."

"I am." He stuck out his chest. "Teacher says I can have a real job by Christmastime."

"Really?" A chill ran down her arms. "By Christmastime?"

"Yes." He held up one hand and made an exaggerated show of counting, his brow knit in concentration. "Seven months, Mom. It'll happen in seven months." He laughed out loud, the excited laugh of a child. "Then I'll be almost ready for Goal Day."

She hid her fears. "That'll be exciting."

He moved closer and took hold of her hand. "It's okay if I hold your hand still, right, Mom? Even if I'm a man?"

"Yes." She felt her heart melt. "Of course. It'll always be okay."

"Good." They walked for a few seconds in silence.

118

Then Carl Joseph turned to her. "I'm not sure about Cody."

Mary smiled. "Me, either."

"'Cause you wanna know why?" Carl Joseph's smile faded. Concern filled the lines in his forehead.

"Why?"

"'Cause he was mad at Teacher today." He shifted his jaw to one side and looked away. "He was mad at my friends, too."

"Mad at them?" As difficult as the idea of Carl Joseph's independent living was for Cody, Mary couldn't picture him being rude to his brother's friends.

"He came into Subway and said I had to go. He said it was crazy."

"What was crazy?"

"Something Daisy said." Carl Joseph wrinkled his brow a little more. "He said it was crazy."

"Oh." Mary wasn't sure she understood, but that wasn't the point. Carl Joseph had always been perceptive about people's feelings, and this was no different. If Cody was upset, Carl Joseph was bound to pick up on it and feel confused. "Well, honey, I don't think he thought you or Daisy were crazy."

"Maybe the field trip."

"Maybe."

"'Cause know what I think?" They were almost to the house. Carl Joseph peered at the porch as if he was looking for Cody.

"What?"

"I think Cody's heart needs fixing again." Carl Joseph stopped and turned to her. His eyes were very serious. "The way it did before he met Ali, the horse rider."

"Yes, maybe that's it." Mary felt a familiar sadness. Ali had been so good for Cody. She had taught him to love when it didn't seem—outside his feelings for his brother—that he'd ever learn. And now, the best thing for him would be to meet another girl, to find those feelings once more. But it would be easier for Carl Joseph to earn his independence than for Cody to fall in love again. She took Carl Joseph's other hand. "How can we help fix Cody's heart?"

"We can pray." Carl Joseph gave a series of small nods. "We can close our eyes and pray to Jesus."

Though once in a while Mary would pray in the quiet of her heart, prayer wasn't mentioned around the Gunner household with any consistency. She smiled at her youngest son. "Okay, honey. You go ahead and pray."

"Close your eyes." Carl Joseph waited until she'd closed them. "Okay. Dear God, here I am. Carl Joseph Gunner. This time I have a prayer for Brother. His name is Cody. Please help him . . ." He hesitated, as if he were trying to remember what help Cody needed. When he spoke again, his words were rushed and so thick it was hard to understand him. "Oh, yes! Please help him have a fixed heart. So he isn't mad at me and my friends, and so he doesn't say it's crazy. Amen."

He squeezed Mary's hands and she opened her eyes.

"That was wonderful, Carl Joseph." Mary pulled him close and hugged him. "How did you learn to pray like that?"

They began walking toward the house again. Carl Joseph shrugged. "It's a life skill. Teacher says we can't be independent if we don't know how to talk to God."

"Of course." Mary could barely draw a breath. Carl Joseph went into the house, but she stayed outside on the porch. Prayer, a life skill? She sat on the glider a few feet from the door and stared at the distant mountains. Her fears about Carl Joseph's independent living had always seemed to be about him. She was afraid he wouldn't survive without her. But maybe she wasn't really worried about how Carl Joseph would do without her.

She was worried about how she would do without Carl Joseph.

Which was exactly how Cody was feeling. Now it would be up to her oldest son to see that, too. Because not until Cody understood his own fears would he stop fighting the idea of Carl Joseph's independence and do the one thing Carl Joseph wanted his brother to do.

Let him go.

Chapter Nine

All weekend, Cody ran from his anger. He didn't want to talk to his parents, didn't want to go online and look at studies about independent living or hear testimonials from other people with Down Syndrome. He wanted his brother to stay the way he used to be. Safe and loved and accounted for, without any threat of a life that could bring him harm.

So he spent the weekend with Carl Joseph.

Saturday morning he helped his brother onto Ace and led him around the arena.

"This is a start, right, Brother? Every bull rider starts on a horse, right?"

"Right." He patted Carl Joseph's leg as they walked. "Not everyone who gets on a horse can get on a bull, though. You know that, right?"

Carl Joseph didn't hesitate. "But I will." He grinned. "Daisy likes bull riders."

Cody tried another approach. "But you need a bull first."

That stopped Carl Joseph cold. He frowned, and as he did, he pulled back on the reins. Ace stopped sharply, irritated.

"Buddy, let up. You shouldn't pull back so hard."

"Right." Carl Joseph relaxed his hold. "Sorry." He gave Cody a concerned look. "Where are we gonna get a bull?"

"We might not get one." Cody had to be honest. "But that's okay. Know why?"

"Why?" Disappointment rang in Carl Joseph's voice. "Daisy likes bull riders."

"Yeah, but Daisy likes cowboys, too, right? Wasn't that what you told me?"

"Yes."

"Okay, so see!" He took a step to the side and waved

his hand at the picture Carl Joseph made atop the horse. "You're already a cowboy. So she'll already like you."

"Oh." Carl Joseph pondered that for a moment. "I never thought about how she already likes me."

"Yeah, Buddy."

"But, Brother"—he knit his brow together, his lips slightly open—"are you still mad at me?" He had asked the question ten times on Saturday alone.

Cody sighed and gripped Carl Joseph's knee. "No, Buddy. I'm not mad, remember? I was never mad."

"But you said it was crazy."

"I was wrong. I'm sorry." He tightened his hold on the lead rope and tried to think of another way to make his brother understand. "I was having a bad day. That's all."

"Oh." Carl Joseph sounded relieved. He faced straight ahead. "Bad days happen."

"Yes, Buddy. Bad days happen."

"Like when Ali died. Ali the horse rider."

"Yes." Cody swallowed back the pain. He patted Ace. "Yes, Buddy—like that."

After riding horses that day, they watched old footage of Cody's bull-riding days, and then they settled in for back-to-back movies, one of their favorite ways of spending a day together. By Sunday afternoon, Carl Joseph was no longer asking whether Cody was mad or not. It was a victory, and Cody promised himself he would never again act in such a way as to make Carl Joseph doubt him.

But that didn't mean he was going to sit by and let

his brother be pulled along toward some sort of crazy idea of living on his own. He would keep warning his parents of the dangers, begging them to remove Carl Joseph from the center. And he would make the appointment with the teacher—so he could explain his fears in person. When Monday came, he showered and dressed and appeared at the breakfast table, relaxed and smiling.

He hadn't said more than a few words to his parents all weekend, so his mother gave him a wary glance. "You look nice."

"Thanks." He dished himself a bowl of oatmeal and took the seat next to Carl Joseph. The smell of his brother's cologne was so strong he could taste it, but he didn't say anything. Instead he smiled. "Buddy and I are going to school together today."

Carl Joseph looked at Cody for a long moment and then dropped his eyes to his oatmeal. "Right," he muttered. "Me and Brother are going to school together."

"Really?" Their mother gave Cody a disapproving look. But when Carl Joseph turned his attention to her, she smiled. "I . . . I didn't know that."

"Well, we are." Cody kept his tone upbeat. "He's going to show me what they do at the center."

"That's not crazy." Carl Joseph cast an innocent look at their mother. "Right, Mom?"

"Right. Not at all."

She waited until they were finished eating. Then she stood and turned to Cody. "I'd like to talk to you for a minute, please."

"I have to brush my teeth." Carl Joseph cleared his bowl, rinsed it in the sink, and loaded it into the dishwasher. He didn't clank his dish or drop anything or let the water run too long. He waved at them and headed down the hall. "Teeth need brushing."

When he was gone, Cody turned to his mother. "I know what you're going to say. But it's my right to go. His teacher asked me to come in before class and talk with her. I want to hear her thoughts on epilepsy." He walked a few steps toward the dining room, and then back again. "I want her to know that we're all worried."

She looked distraught. "Maybe she'll tell you her plan. She has a way she thinks it could work. Carl Joseph living in a group home, taking medicine for his seizures."

"No." Cody said the word a little too loud. He had to keep a grip on his temper. "You can't let that happen." He went to her and gently took her hand. "You and Dad need to get him out of that center. It's only going to hurt him when he can't reach Goal Day. And clearly he can't." He paused, quieter than before. "That's what the doctor said, right?"

His mother had never come right out and said so. But now she looked down and after a few seconds she nodded. "Yes. The doctor doesn't think it's possible."

Cody felt the weight of Carl Joseph's disappointment. He gestured down the hall where Carl Joseph had gone. "Think how hard it's going to be for him, Mom. When he finds out he can't live on his own."

Cody took a breath. "Even if Carl Joseph could manage his epilepsy on his own, he couldn't live by himself. He couldn't live in a group home without people helping him every hour of the day." He looked down the hallway toward Carl Joseph's room again. "I want to see what this Elle Dalton is teaching them. Let me see a person with Down Syndrome who can manage all those things, and maybe I'll feel differently."

His mother held his gaze for a long time. "Okay. Go, then. But your brother's already nervous. He knows you're not going just because you're interested." She let loose a sad sigh. "He senses everything you feel, Cody. Don't forget that."

"I won't." Cody allowed his tone to soften. "I don't want to fight. It's Dad who wants Carl Joseph out of the house, not you."

"No." She shook her head. "You're wrong." Her voice rang with sincerity. "I see what the center has done for Carl Joseph, how it's made him happier." She paused. "I want it, too, Cody. Don't make this a battle with your father. We're both in this."

Cody could hear Carl Joseph coming. He didn't want anything to trouble his brother that morning. "Okay." He leaned in and kissed her cheek. "I'll try to remember that."

"Good."

They spent the next half hour getting ready. Carl Joseph needed to bring a bag of flour and a bottle of vanilla to class, because Monday was Cooking Day. "We're making shortcake, Brother," he said as he rummaged through the kitchen. "Everyone loves shortcake. People at Disneyland love shortcake."

"Disneyland?" Cody stood back and let his brother do the work. If he wanted to be independent, he needed to be able to locate ingredients in the kitchen.

"Yes." Carl Joseph heaved a bag of flour onto the counter. He looked intently at the label. "F-l-o-u-r. Flour." He turned to Cody. "Teacher said she had strawberry shortcake at Disneyland once."

Carl Joseph set the ingredients in a paper bag, grabbed his backpack, and grinned at Cody. "Time for school."

The drive to the center took fifteen minutes. The whole time Cody wrestled with his purpose for going. He didn't care if Carl Joseph knew how to make shortcake. How would that keep him from getting lost or running out of food? How would it help him know how to handle a seizure by himself? What was Elle Dalton teaching her students that would keep them from getting run down by a car on their way out the door of a grocery store?

As they walked up to the center, Carl Joseph twisted his hands together. He stopped just as he reached the door. "Brother, you're not mad?"

"No, Buddy." Cody hugged his brother's shoulders. "I'm not."

Carl Joseph didn't look sure. But he nodded anyway. "Good."

"Let's go in, okay?" Cody was suddenly anxious to let the teacher know he was there.

"Okay, right. Let's go in." Carl Joseph opened the door and led the way.

Inside the room was full-blown chaos. Loud music filled the place, and even louder voices and laughter. There were more than a dozen young adults with Down Syndrome—the same students who had been on the Subway field trip. A few were sitting on an old sofa, talking animatedly to each other, and three others were huddled over a stuffed turtle, laughing their heads off.

In another corner of the room were Daisy and three students, all of them swaying and twirling and clapping to various rhythms in the loud music. An able-bodied older woman was talking with two students at the far end of the room, but no one seemed to be in charge.

Carl Joseph gave him a nervous look. "Free time comes first."

Cody could barely hear him. "I see that." He was about to find a seat where he wouldn't be noticed, when Daisy spotted him.

Her eyes grew wide and her mouth came all the way open. "Carl Joseph brought his brother to class!" She skipped toward Cody, took his hand, and began pumping it. "I'm Daisy. Remember me?"

"Yes." Cody was very comfortable around Carl Joseph. When he looked at his brother, he never saw a handicapped person, but only the kid who adored him. But he didn't know Daisy. He tried to hide his discomfort. "I remember you, Daisy."

She came closer and made a dramatic show of smelling him. Then she nodded her head at Carl Joseph. "You're right, CJ. He smells like a bull rider, same as you."

The other students gradually stopped whatever they'd been doing and gathered around Cody and Carl Joseph. One stepped up, his expression blank. "I'm Gus."

"Hi, Gus." Cody shook his hand.

"So you like us now? But not the other day?" Gus looked at the other students around him. "Carl Joseph's brother doesn't like us, that's what we said at Subway."

"I liked you then, too." He laughed, but it sounded weak. "I was in a hurry the other day. I'm sorry about that."

"We prayed for you." A girl with long brown braids waved her hand. "You might not have life skills so we prayed."

Cody felt his cheeks grow hot. The entire class had prayed for him because he didn't have the life skills to be cordial? That had to be Elle Dalton's doing. He was about to ask where she was, when he spotted her near a doorway at the back of the room. Her eyes met his, but she directed her words to the students. "Okay, everyone. Let's give our visitor some space." She turned off the music and moved to a section of the room with two rows of chairs and an oversized black-board. "We're getting a new bus route today. Everyone find your seats."

She held Cody's eyes a little longer and then turned to her students, making small talk with them. As Cody watched her, something inside him stirred. She was the enemy, no doubt. She was willing to risk Carl Joseph's life to see her idea of independence played out. But there was no denying that she cared for her students. She took time with each of them, speaking to them at an adult level instead of talking down to them the way people did who weren't used to being around someone with Down Syndrome. And from his place by the door, Cody couldn't help but notice something else.

Elle Dalton was beautiful. Breathtaking, even.

Not in the way some girls were, with flashy clothes and makeup and jewelry. She had a quiet beauty about her, and something that could only have come from inside. Cody clenched his teeth and turned away. None of that mattered. He wasn't here to admire her.

Cody turned his attention to his brother. Carl Joseph was sitting next to Daisy, talking with his hands. His cheeks were red and his smile took up his entire face. Cody realized what was happening. Carl Joseph didn't come to the center to learn about independence. He came because of Daisy. This was his first crush, and that was innocent enough. He watched his brother for another minute, watched him play with Daisy's hair and her hands. It might be innocent, but where could it possibly lead?

He shifted, and without meaning to, his eyes returned to Elle, to the graceful way she moved in and out of the rows of students, speaking to each of them. Finally she took her spot at the front of the area. "Everyone turn to a partner and go over the details of Bus Route Eleven, the one we used last week on our field trip."

"Subway eat fresh!" The girl in braids stood up and grinned with the proclamation. She clapped her hands the way Carl Joseph sometimes did. Fast and loud, with her hands raised up close to her face. "Subway field trip. Eat fresh."

"Thank you, Tammy." Elle wasn't flustered by the student's outburst. "Please sit back down and turn to your partner."

Cody watched Carl Joseph turn to Daisy and take her hands. In that moment Cody saw something in his brother's eyes he'd never seen before. The sort of adoration and puppy love that indicated he was right about Carl Joseph. His brother was completely taken by the girl.

Great, he thought. Carl Joseph would never give up the idea of living on his own if it meant letting go of Daisy.

As soon as the students were busy, Elle said something to the older woman—who was obviously an aide or an assistant. Then Elle walked over to him. The kindness he'd seen in her eyes a few minutes ago was gone. She never broke eye contact as she approached, and when she reached him, she nodded to the door. "I'd like to speak with *you* outside, Mr. Gunner."

He followed her. What was this about? She had no

reason to be angry with him. Not yet, anyway.

When the door shut behind them, Elle put her hands on her hips. "I didn't appreciate the way you disrupted our field trip last week."

"Yeah, well." He forced himself to stay focused. He wasn't angry, but his frustration was rising. "If all it takes is an unexpected visit from me to disrupt things, maybe you shouldn't be taking field trips."

Elle searched his eyes. "What exactly is your problem? The entire class felt bad after you left."

Cody fought his emotions. Guilt and shame and anger and confusion. He looked down and rubbed the back of his neck. He clenched his jaw. "I heard. I'm sorry." Cody met her eyes, and he felt his breath catch in his throat. Even angry, her hazel eyes were gorgeous. He had to work to remember his point. A grin tugged at his lips. He didn't want to fight with Elle Dalton. He only wanted Buddy home where he belonged. "You asked the whole class to pray for me, right? You told them I didn't have the right sort of life skills."

Elle's anger dimmed, but only a little. "Based on my limited experience, you don't."

Cody wasn't sure what to say. And his attraction to Buddy's teacher was irritating. He pursed his lips and inhaled sharply through his nose. He pointed at the classroom. "What you're teaching those young people isn't right for all of them."

"I disagree." Her eyes flashed, indignant.

"Okay." He held up his hands and took a step back.

"I'd like permission to watch class today, but I have to be honest. My goal is to have Carl Joseph removed from your program as soon as possible."

The anger in Elle's face became sadness. "You're serious?"

"Yes. This morning Carl Joseph said something about making shortcake."

"Monday's Cooking Day." Elle held her ground. Her gaze didn't waver.

"And how, Ms. Dalton"—he leaned against the stucco wall and slipped his hands into his jeans pockets—"will making shortcake help Carl Joseph when he's lost on a bus route somewhere? When he's bagging groceries at the market and someone calls him a name or pushes him or confuses him? Is he supposed to whip up a batch of shortcake then? Or maybe drop down on his knees and start praying? Is that your answer?"

Elle looked at him for a long time. The emotions in her eyes changed from outrage to hurt, and finally to quiet resignation. "I can see I have a lot of work ahead."

"No work, Ms. Dalton. I'll sit in the back and keep to myself. Don't change your routine for me."

"I won't work to impress you." She lifted her chin, pride smoothing out the concern in her face. "I'll work to convince you. Because you're wrong. And before you and I are through, you'll see that for yourself. I promise."

"Is that right?" Cody wanted to laugh at her spunk.

If things had been different, if life had been different, he might've been drawn to Elle Dalton. But even if he had room in his heart to love another woman, it wouldn't be the arrogant young teacher standing before him.

She took a step toward the door. "I know what you're thinking, Mr. Gunner."

"You don't know the first thing about me." He gave her a lazy grin. Why did he have to find her so attractive? She was the single reason their home was in turmoil. He reminded himself to focus on that, and not the way her hazel eyes caught the morning sunlight.

She lingered at the door for a moment. "I'm not the only one intent on proving something here, right?"

"Exactly." His tone grew more serious. "Independence is more than being able to eat at a Subway, Ms. Dalton."

She gave him a final look and then returned to her students. His heart was pounding as he followed her into the room and took a seat near the door. The longer he watched Elle, her gentle way and patient voice, the more he felt convinced that he'd pegged her wrong. She wasn't the enemy. She was a confused do-gooder. Someone whose intentions were right, but whose ideas were way off.

So maybe he wouldn't ask his parents to pull Carl Joseph from the class after watching for just a day. Maybe he'd come every day this week and prove to Elle Dalton that he wasn't an irrational, irate, overly protective older brother. He would earn her trust, and then they could sit down and talk about the reality of what she was trying to pull off. Especially with a sick student like Carl Joseph. She was an idealistic teacher. She hadn't spent her life with a Down Syndrome sibling. Cody settled back in his chair and tried not to notice the way Elle walked or the way her face lit up when one of her students made her laugh. Yes, he would come every day that week. He would come for the simple reason that he needed to invest time at the center in order to gain Elle Dalton's trust. Not for any other reason.

Even if at times that morning it took all his strength to focus on anyone or anything in the classroom but her.

Chapter Ten

Elle could barely concentrate on the coursework that day. Having Cody Gunner watching her from his seat near the door was a distraction that rivaled any she'd ever had. Not because of his dark good looks. He was married, after all. No, he was a distraction because of the threat he represented. If Cody convinced his family to pull Carl Joseph from the center, Daisy would be devastated. So would every one of her students.

Carl Joseph's departure would raise countless questions, fears, and anxieties for them. No doubt they would figure out the reason he left. The truth that his family no longer supported his plans to be independent would be glaringly obvious. And that could quite possibly start a chain reaction of events that would undermine everything the center stood for. Everything she was passionate about.

Elle maintained her composure until break time. It was nice outside again, not a cloud in the sky. She dismissed them to the outdoors, and then, without a glance at Cody Gunner, she retreated to the break room.

And there she fell back on the one life skill she couldn't live without. She poured herself a cup of coffee, held the warm mug close against her chest, and closed her eyes. *God . . . what's happening? Who is this Cody Gunner and why did he have to come home in the first place?* She kept her eyes closed and thought about that. The timing was all wrong. If Cody had come home six months from now, he could've seen for himself how independent Carl Joseph had become. They would have a plan to manage his heart disease and his epilepsy.

Instead Cody could see only the early stages of progress.

Lord, I'm up against a wall here. Help me show Carl Joseph's brother that it's possible, that even sick people with Down Syndrome can *lead independent lives. Please, Father.*

She opened her eyes and her breath caught in her throat. "Mr. Gunner!"

"Sorry." He was leaning in the doorway, watching her. "I was a little harsh earlier. You have a way with your students." He studied her. "I'm impressed, Elle Dalton."

She flashed proud eyes at him. "Is that why you're standing there? To tell me that?"

Regret colored his expression. "I don't want to be enemies."

She waited, suspicious. "You're opposed to what I'm doing here, Mr. Gunner. That much is obvious."

"I am. For my brother." He straightened. "But I'm willing to hear you out, willing to see what the program's all about." He sighed, and the conflict in his heart was obvious. "I love my brother, that's all. I want what's best for him. What's safest."

"I understand." Her tone softened. Still, she wasn't sure where he was headed with this. "What are you saying, exactly? That you'll stay around the rest of the day without making a judgment?"

"I'll stay all week." He took a step back. "If that's okay. But at the end of the week, let's talk about whether this"—he looked back at the class space—"all of this is really good for Carl Joseph."

She narrowed her eyes. What had Carl Joseph said? That his brother was hurt, that he'd been injured in bull riding, right? Whether the bull riding was true or not, maybe the guy had been injured somehow. Maybe that's why Cody didn't want to see anything happen to Carl Joseph. Because he understood that one injury could change everything. "You've spent all your life protecting your brother, haven't you?"

"Yes." He held her gaze for a long moment.

Elle took a sip of her coffee, but she never took her

eyes off him. Behind his brash approach and bitter words, Cody Gunner cared. "There were times"—he caught her eye again—"when Carl Joseph was the only person who kept me going, when everyone else felt like a stranger." A steely look came over him, and his eyes penetrated to her soul. Not with anger, the way they had before class started, but with a passion that caught her off guard. Each word was measured, full of intensity. "I can't let anything happen to him. Do you understand that, Ms. Dalton?"

"Yes." She considered him. "I hope at the end of the week you'll see that I feel the same way. I would never put your brother in danger. Not for anything."

"Okay." Cody gave her a polite nod. "I'll be in the classroom, then." He hesitated. "No hard feelings about my attitude earlier?"

"None." She didn't smile, but she did feel more relaxed. The rest of the day went smoothly. Cody stayed glued to the action as she went over the bus route again, and then directed the students to move into the kitchen.

"We're making shortcake today." She found an apron in a drawer and tied it around her waist. "Who remembers why we make shortcake?"

Daisy shot her hand in the air. She grinned at Carl Joseph and then at Elle. "Because people at Disneyland like shortcake."

"Disneyland is good for shortcake." Carl Joseph held his hands toward the other students, looking for their approval.

A chorus of nods and affirmations came from the crowd.

Elle smiled. "Okay, yes. There's a little restaurant in Disneyland that makes the best strawberry shortcake." She thought she caught Cody grinning at the back of the room. "But that's not *why* we make shortcake. Anyone remember why?"

Sid made an exaggerated sigh. "I know." He raised his hand. "Pick me, Teacher."

"Sid, why do we make shortcake?"

"So we can entertain."

"Right. Very good." Elle held up a laminated over-sized card with a photo of shortcake. "Shortcake is a dessert, and it can be used in many ways when you entertain."

This time she saw Cody shift his position. She could read his mind, even midstream in front of her class. What was the point of teaching people with Down Syndrome how to entertain? That's what he was thinking. She tried not to let the negativity she felt from him ruin her mood. She'd been looking forward to this cooking assignment since last week when they'd learned how to prepare broccoli.

"Shortcake is very attractive." Tammy swung her braids and smiled. "Very attractive."

"I think I could entertain twelve people if I had shortcake." Gus looked around at the others.

Carl Joseph reached back and patted Gus on the knee. "I would come to your party if you had short-cake, Gus."

"Okay, then." Elle regained control. She moved to the long countertop area that separated her from the students. "First let's take a look at our ingredients."

"I brought flour and vanilla, Teacher." Carl Joseph stood up. He slid his glasses back up his nose and then grinned at Daisy. "Flour and vanilla."

Before a landslide of comments followed, Elle motioned to Carl Joseph. "Could you get nine mixing bowls from the supply cupboard? Then place them in a row along this counter, okay?"

Carl Joseph looked as if he'd won the lottery. He jumped up and hurried to an oversized cupboard. He was the newest of her students, and even he knew where everything was kept. Elle continued explaining the ingredients, but she kept watch on Carl Joseph. Clearly his brother would be scrutinizing this assignment, seeing whether Carl Joseph could follow multiple orders without needing help.

Sure enough, he took the mixing bowls out one at a time and set them in two stacks. Then he counted them again, just to be sure, and distributed them along the counter. The counter area had been built so that a team of two people could stand facing each other and work on a recipe together. Elle had nine copies of the shortcake recipe. "Okay, find a partner and station yourselves near one of the mixing bowls."

Daisy danced her way over to Carl Joseph. She stood opposite him and laughed a few times. "Is this spot taken?"

"No, madam." He hunched over, giving her his

shyest giggle. "Not unless Mickey Mouse shows up."

Daisy laughed at that as if it were the wittiest thing she'd ever heard. "Mickey Mouse! CJ, you're funny."

Over the next hour, with Elle and her aide over-seeing the project, each team of two students followed the shortcake recipe and created a bowl full of batter. At one point, Cody stood and circled the work area from a distance.

As he walked near Carl Joseph and Daisy, Elle expected her sister to get excited again and say some-thing about Cody smelling like a bull rider. But this time the laughter that had marked their work time faded as Cody came closer. Carl Joseph gave Daisy a secretive look, and she nodded in a way that wasn't quite subtle.

"Good job, Buddy." Cody peered over his brother's shoulder at the bowl. "I bet your shortcake is best of all."

"Yeah . . . thanks." Carl Joseph didn't look up. He kept his eyes moving between the batter and Daisy. Then he looked at Cody. "I don't need help, Brother. Thanks, but I don't need help."

"Okay." Cody angled his head and glanced across the room at Elle. "I'll try to stay out of the way."

"Yeah, 'cause then it'll be a surprise." Carl Joseph waved at his brother. "Go back to the chair and thanks anyway."

Cody raised his brow and chuckled, clearly not sure how to take the gentle rebuffing from Carl Joseph. One at a time, Elle directed the teams of students to spoon their batter into greased pans and place their shortcake in one of the center's two ovens. The hardest task, the one that would matter most when they were living on their own, was to work against their short-term memory problems and remember the shortcake after it was in the oven.

Elle and the aide oversaw the project, but neither of them would rescue the students. Sure enough, the first two teams forgot about their shortcake. Elle waited until the cake was burned but not on fire before reminding the teams. "Gus's team and Tammy's team, do you smell something burning?"

All four students lurched into panic mode. They ran into each other, and then across the room into the kitchen, all of them talking at once. Elle stood with her arms crossed. "You'll need potholders."

"Potholders." Gus raced to the right drawer and found one for each of them.

"What next?" Elle could feel Cody watching, disapproving. If she hadn't reminded them about the short-cakes, they eventually would've caught fire. But this was part of learning. If Cody didn't understand that, then maybe by the end of the week he would. "What next, people?"

"Turn off the ovens." Tammy had an oven mitt on her hand. She stared at the oven and did a nervous little dance in place. "We should turn off the ovens."

"Yes, do that." Elle kept any frustration from her voice.

Gus and Tammy each reached for the controls on

their separate ovens and turned them off. Elle felt a ripple of satisfaction. At least here, even in a time of panic, they remembered how to turn off the ovens. She moved in closer. "What next?"

"Take out the shortcake!" Gus looked at his baking partner and swallowed hard. "I'll do it, okay?"

The other young man nodded. "I'll get the hot pad."

Gus pulled a blackened shortcake from the oven, while a few feet away Tammy did the same thing with hers. They set the burned desserts on the hotpads, stepped back, and stared at them dismally. Gus looked at Elle. "No entertaining tonight."

"No." Elle smiled. "But we learned something."

All four students stared at her, mouths open, as if they weren't sure what they'd learned by burning their shortcake. Then Gus gasped and his hand shot straight in the air. "We learned not to forget." He pointed back at the oven. "We could use a timer."

Elle felt her heart soar. "Exactly." She hadn't mentioned that to any of them, because the timer was something all of them should've known by now. The other students gathered around to gawk at the blackened shortcake.

"Gus, you can have some of mine," Daisy said.

"Yeah, mine, too." Carl Joseph tapped his fingers on the counter near the burned dessert. " 'Cause yeah, a timer would be better." He turned to Daisy. "They use timers at Disneyland."

It was a victory. Without her prompting, Gus had remembered that a timer would've saved the shortcake from burning. Carl Joseph and Daisy were one of the teams to use the ovens next, and Carl Joseph raised his hand. "We'd like a timer, Teacher. If that's okay."

She laughed. "Yes. Go right ahead."

With textbook precision, Carl Joseph and Daisy worked to get their dessert into the oven. Carl Joseph turned on the oven while Daisy set the timer. Then, using a potholder, Carl Joseph placed their pan of shortcake batter onto the hot rack and Daisy shut the oven door.

Elle wanted to hug them both, but she couldn't over-react. This was the sort of thing that would have to come easily for them before they could celebrate Goal Day. Thirty minutes later, when the timer went off, all four students promptly and calmly found their oven mitts and potholders, turned off their ovens, and removed their shortcakes. Both were a light golden color on top, cooked perfectly.

"Carl Joseph." Elle walked up and whispered to him. "I think maybe when it cools, your brother would like a piece."

"Yeah." Carl Joseph's eyes sparkled. "Brother should get a piece."

An hour later, when Carl Joseph brought a piece of shortcake to his brother, Cody thanked him and com-plimented him. And as he took his first bite, he raised his fork in Elle's direction. She gave him a sly smile and then turned back to her students. Maybe they would find common ground yet.

The day wore on, and by the time her students left,

Elle was exhausted. It was twice as hard, teaching and trying to make things work well for Cody Gunner all at the same time.

"You look tired, Teacher." Daisy came up, her backpack slung onto her shoulder. She twisted her head upside down and stared at Elle. Then she straightened and laughed at her own silliness. "Are you tired?"

"School's over, Daisy." She gave her a knowing look. "You call me Elle now, remember?"

"I know." She laughed again. "Elle . . . Elle . . . Elle." She set her backpack on the floor, unzipped it, and peered inside. "The shortcake's in there."

"Yes." All the students took home a large piece of shortcake.

"We can entertain tonight. You and Mom and me." She jumped into the air and came down in a perfect ballet first position. "And we can dance for fun."

"First we need to go to the market." Elle had none of her usual energy. It had been draining being watched by Cody all day. He was giving her a week to prove that the students were learning skills that would one day make them capable of living on their own. One week. She sighed and grabbed her bag. "You ready to go to the store?"

"Yes." She stuck out her tongue and curled it up over her lip, something she did when she was concentrating intently. She looked through her backpack, rummaging around and finally pulling out a calculator. She grinned and held the calculator straight up over her head. "I'll keep the budget."

Daisy had been at the center longer than most of the students. That she was thinking about staying on a budget at the mere mention of grocery shopping was further proof that she was almost ready. Depending on how the next few months went, she could have her Goal Day before the holidays.

A sense of bittersweet joy came over Elle. Letting go of a sibling with Down Syndrome would never be easy. There would always be risks, but then life for able-bodied people held risks, too. She was proof.

"Okay, Daisy." They linked arms and headed out toward the parking lot. Elle turned off the lights and locked up on the way. "You keep the budget. Let's make sure we don't spend more than a hundred dollars today, all right?"

Daisy did a few short laughs. "Wow, Elle. A whole hundred dollars."

For the rest of the ride to the market and even after they parked and were heading inside, Daisy kept a running dialogue about what they might be able to buy with a hundred dollars. When she'd hit just about every combination of groceries, Elle thought of a way to change the subject. "Daisy."

"And peanut butter and mayonnaise and string cheese and—"

"Daisy." Elle's frustration rose a notch.

Her sister fell silent. She pulled out a cart and opened her eyes wide at Elle. "I was making a budget."

"I know, but I have a question."

Daisy pushed the cart into the store and they walked toward the produce section. She looked a little put out, but she turned her attention to Elle anyway. "What question?"

Elle wanted to know more about whatever exchange had happened between her sister and Carl Joseph while they were making the shortcake batter. It was the first time Daisy hadn't acted thrilled about Cody Gunner. "About Carl Joseph's brother."

As soon as Elle said the words, Daisy's expression closed. She lifted her chin, pride having its way with her. "I don't like CJ's brother. Not anymore."

"I thought he smelled good and he was a world-famous bull rider."

Daisy allowed the hint of a smile. "He does smell good." Her smile fell off. "But I don't like him any-more."

"Why?"

"CJ's brother doesn't want him at the center." She looked straight ahead and stopped at a display of bananas. "He doesn't want him there because he doesn't like us."

Elle took a bunch of bananas and weighed them. "Three pounds, Daisy. Let's start with that."

Daisy took her calculator from her pocket and squinted at the sign above the bananas. "Forty cents a pound." Her mouth hung open while she punched in the numbers, but after a short time, she laughed aloud. "One twenty. One dollar and twenty cents. That's how much so far."

"Excellent." Elle gave her sister a look that expressed how proud she was. "You're doing so well, Daisy."

A shadow fell over her expression. "But Cody Gunner doesn't like us."

"He will." Elle allowed Daisy to take the lead as they moved to a display of apples. "One day he will."

And as they finished shopping, as she allowed her sister time to gain the experience of finding eggs and peanut butter and mayonnaise and string cheese along with a cart full of other items all for under a hundred dollars, she could only pray quietly that what she'd told Daisy was right.

That someday—by some sort of miracle—Cody Gunner would like not just the students at the ILC. But he would also like her work well enough to believe in Carl Joseph's place there.

Chapter Eleven

Carl Joseph was at his parents' computer trying to write a letter. But he was having trouble. Something maybe was wrong with Brother. He had heard the yelling and shouting that day when he was pulling weeds. And now it was Wednesday and Brother was still coming every day to the center.

Daisy said he was coming because he didn't like them. "Your brother doesn't want you at the center," she had told him earlier that day.

And maybe Daisy was right. But maybe not. Because Brother had a smile and a happy voice when he was at the center. He sat in his chair and he watched and he thought a lot. And sometimes Brother would get up and find him next to Daisy and see what they were doing. Three times he said, "Good job, Buddy."

Also he thought Teacher was pretty. Carl Joseph knew because Brother's eyes were the same at Elle as they were at Ali the first time. When Brother and Ali were at the rodeo together. Because Carl Joseph would come with his mother and sometimes with his dad, and he could see Brother's eyes then. His eyes for Ali. And that was the same as his eyes for Teacher.

But even all that didn't mean he was happy.

Carl Joseph looked out the window and bit his lip. Plus the letter was hard 'cause he was a little scared 'cause of the bus routes. And that kept filling his head. He knew Number Eight and Number Three. But Number Eleven was scary because there were two changes. And two changes had to happen. Otherwise no Goal Day. Yes, bus routes were scary.

He turned his eyes to the computer screen. There was nothing on it so far. He adjusted his glasses and looked at the keyboard. He could at least type her name. He found the *D* and tapped it. Then he tapped out the rest of her name. *A-I-S-Y.*

He lifted his eyes and made a happy laugh. Daisy. That's what it spelled: Daisy. He wanted to write Daisy a letter because of Disneyland. Teacher said that when you entertain you have to invite someone. And he wanted to entertain Daisy at Disneyland. So maybe he had to write her a letter and invite her first.

He heard a noise and he saw Brother's truck pull into the driveway. That made him feel nervous, because he wasn't sure about Brother anymore. He didn't want to make him mad. 'Cause maybe Brother was mad that he and Daisy were friends and maybe he wanted Carl Joseph to leave the center.

He watched Brother park his truck and head up the walk. "Uh-oh." He grabbed the mouse. But not Mickey Mouse, 'cause that was different. Then he moved the arrow fast, faster. Fast as he could until he found the X marks the spot. Then he clicked and the letter was gone. 'Cause he could write a letter to Daisy later.

But he didn't want Brother to be mad. Not ever.

Because Daisy was his number two best friend, but Brother . . . Brother was his best friend of all. So he could hide letters to Daisy. Because he didn't want Brother to see what he was doing and be mad. He stood and slammed the chair back against the desk. His heart pounded like a drum. He moved quickly away from the computer and over to the door. That way Brother wouldn't see what he was doing. Then he ran and held open his arms. "Brother!"

"Hey, Buddy." He came up and they hugged. "Whatcha been doing?"

"Nothing." Carl Joseph answered fast. "Not writing a letter to Daisy. Not me."

Brother stopped and crossed his arms. He looked around at the computer and then back again. "Are you lying to me, Buddy?"

"Yes." Again his answer was fast. Because Mom said you don't love someone you lie to. And you don't lie to someone you love. He nodded, very serious. "Yes, Brother. I'm lying."

"How come?" Brother put his arm on his shoulder and looked at him. Straight at him.

Carl Joseph felt his heart slow down a little. Brother still loved him. 'Cause he put his hand on Carl Joseph's shoulder and that meant, "I love you, Buddy." Carl Joseph put his hands on his knees and breathed out like when he raced Gus at break time. When he looked up he licked his lips first. "You don't like Daisy."

"What?" Brother looked hurt. So maybe he did like Daisy. "Buddy, that's not true. I like her a lot. She has cute blonde hair."

" 'Cause she has cute blonde hair and she likes Minnie Mouse." Carl Joseph looked down at the floor. His heart was pounding again. "And Brother likes Minnie Mouse."

"That's right." He sounded tired. He led Carl Joseph back into the office and pulled out the computer chair. "Sit here."

Carl Joseph did as he was told. He sat down and looked at the blank screen.

"You were writing a letter to Daisy, right?"

"Yes." He didn't look around. He didn't want to see if Brother was mad or not. "A letter to Daisy."

"Okay, Buddy. Then go ahead." He reached down and hugged Carl Joseph from the back. "Go ahead and write to Daisy. I like when you write letters."

" 'Cause"—Carl Joseph turned around and looked at Brother's eyes—"I was inviting her to Disneyland with me." He looked at the screen again. "Teacher says when you entertain, you need to invite someone."

Brother sounded a little more tired. "Fine. Go on and write your invitation. I'm not mad at you, Buddy." He came around and sat on the edge of the desk. Then he looked straight at Carl Joseph. "I love you, Buddy. Okay? Remember that?"

Carl Joseph thought for a moment. "Yes, I remember."

"Good. I'm not mad and I like your friends."

" 'Cause after Daisy I can write a letter to you." He smiled at Brother. "And maybe you think Teacher is pretty."

Brother opened his mouth but no words came out. Carl Joseph closed his eyes because this might be where Brother got mad. But instead, laughter came from him. Lots of laughter. Carl Joseph opened his eyes. "Brother?"

"How do you know I think your teacher's pretty?" He leaned in and messed Carl Joseph's hair.

" 'Cause your eyes looked at her like . . ." Carl Joseph stopped. Every time he talked about Ali the horse rider, Brother got sad. Brother was laughing now, so he didn't want to make him sad. He pushed his glasses back up his nose. " 'Cause your eyes said she was pretty."

"Well." Brother stood and took a step away. "You're

right about your teacher. She is pretty. But that doesn't mean we agree about everything. Okay?"

"Okay, Brother. Except Disneyland. We can agree about Disneyland."

Brother was still smiling, and his face said he thought Carl Joseph was silly. "We can definitely agree about that."

"You and me and Daisy."

"Yes, Buddy." Brother waved at him. "You and me and Daisy."

When Brother left, Carl Joseph remembered everything he wanted to say to Daisy. Because he wasn't afraid anymore about Brother. Brother liked Daisy and that meant no more heart like a drum. But before he started back on the letter, he closed his eyes and folded his hands and talked to God out loud.

"One day, God, please let Brother and me and Daisy and Teacher go to Disneyland together. 'Cause the Magic Kingdom has shortcake and Mickey Mouse and Minnie. And thanks that Brother isn't mad. So maybe we can all go there. Amen."

When he opened his eyes, he felt ready for the letter. 'Cause Teacher said it felt good to use life skills. And praying to God was one of the best life skills of all. You could say what you want to God anytime, anywhere. Teacher said that. And talking to God meant God was with you. And sometimes being a grownup was scary. Except with God it was never scary at all.

Even when you had to know all the bus routes in the whole wide world.

Chapter Twelve

Elle couldn't wait to get Snoopy out on a leash. All afternoon she'd been looking forward to taking her dog to the park up the street. It wasn't a big park like Antlers. Just a patch of grass in the middle of twenty rows of modest homes. A place where mothers could take their preschoolers and find a swing set and a slide and a set of monkey bars. The park was one of Elle's favorite places after a long day.

The sunshine from earlier had disappeared behind a layer of clouds, and she was about to find something warmer to wear when her mother approached her.

"You look tired."

Elle chided herself for not hiding her feelings better. "I'm fine. Just a long day."

"That's nearly a whole week of long days." She frowned. "What's happening at the center?" Her mother touched her arm, her eyes curious. "You've been more tired, quieter."

Daisy overheard the question. She stepped up and clucked her tongue to the roof of her mouth. "CJ's brother. He happened this week."

Their mother wrinkled her nose. "The world-famous bull rider?"

Elle rolled her eyes. "Please, Mother. Don't feed the fantasy." She headed for the coat closet and found an old sweater. "I'm taking Snoopy for a walk."

Her mother stayed on her heels. "So he's not a bull rider?"

"I don't know what he is." Elle looked past her mom. Daisy hadn't followed them. "The guy shows up Monday morning unannounced, and now he's a regular fixture at the center."

"Oh." Her mom stepped out of her way as she slipped on the sweater and moved back toward the kitchen. "Is he curious?"

"No." She stopped and looked at her mom. After being calm and gentle with her students all day, she didn't have the patience for this. Even so, her mother didn't know what was happening with Cody Gunner, and Elle couldn't blame her for being curious. She exhaled and tried to explain the situation better. "He wants Carl Joseph removed from the center. That's his bottom line." She leaned against the nearest wall. Everything about Carl Joseph's brother made her feel worn-out.

"Why on earth?" Her mother's expression told the story. She couldn't fathom someone opposed to independence for people with Down Syndrome. "Are you sure?"

"Yes. He thinks that Carl Joseph is safer and happier at home, that because of his epilepsy and heart disease, we're filling his head with impossible ideas. That sort of thing."

"Oh." She wrinkled her brow. "Of course it's up to Carl Joseph's parents."

"Since his diagnosis, they're unsure, too. Cody's

opinion could be enough to sway them."

"I see." Her mother looked into the next room, where Daisy was sitting in a weathered old recliner. She was reading *Heidi* for the third time. "Regardless of his health, I can't imagine standing in the way of someone with Down Syndrome. Not when there are so many options for them now."

"I know. Me, either." Elle leaned in and kissed her mother's cheek. "Let's talk about it later. I need to get out."

"Okay." Her mom patted her arm. "I'm sorry, Elle. You don't deserve that."

"I just wish he didn't make me doubt myself." She gave her mother a tired smile. "It feels like I'm spending my time defending myself, instead of getting my students closer to their goal."

"It'll pass."

"I know." She pulled Snoopy's leash from a drawer in the kitchen and headed for the door. Their small house was one of hundreds in this part of Colorado Springs. It was the best they could do with the money from the sale of the old house, and it was cozy. More than they needed. She smiled at her mother. "I'll be back in an hour."

The moment she stepped outside, she felt her mind begin to clear. She walked more slowly than usual and studied the new leaves on the branches of the trees that lined the street. Colorado Springs didn't have many deciduous trees, but this neighborhood's developers had seen to it that there were at least a few mixed in between the common evergreens.

She took in a long breath and walked a little taller. Cody Gunner had been driving her crazy this past week, between his wary glances and his subtle smiles. He wasn't critical or mean, exactly. But his scrutiny exhausted her. Once in a while, for a brief moment at a time over the past several days, she would catch herself watching him, admiring his strong jaw and intense eyes, or the way his broad back tapered down to his waist.

Each time she would turn away, angry with herself. He was married. That she would find him attractive was appalling.

No, she definitely couldn't be attracted to Carl Joseph's brother. But now that she was outside, now that the cool evening breeze played against her face and the smell of jasmine filled her senses, she had to be honest. Her attraction to him was part of the problem.

Not only did she want him to finish the week convinced that her work at the ILC was necessary and important, and that it was the right place for Carl Joseph, but she wanted him to go back to whatever he used to do with his days. Go back home to his wife and leave the educating to her. She spotted another dog owner across the street. They nodded to each other and Snoopy looked up and whined

"I know . . . you want to play." She stopped and patted the old beagle's head. "Too bad, Snoopy. We have ground to cover."

At the end of the street, Elle turned right. The park was just three blocks up on the left. It was impossible to think about Cody Gunner and not let her mind wander back to where the damage had been done. If things hadn't fallen apart, she would be into her fourth year of marriage, maybe talking about having children or buying a first home.

She narrowed her eyes and tried to fight the memories. But then, in a rush, they came at her with a gale force and she could do nothing to hold them off. It wasn't as if she thought about the past every day. For the most part she could live without thinking about it. But once in a while it helped to go back. The memories reminded her of why she was the way she was, why she had no intention of trusting love again unless God, Himself, brought the right person into her life.

Anyway, Elle wasn't waiting around. It was better to keep existing, keep following her passion for helping her students, keep playing Scrabble with her mother. That way no one could ever hurt her the way she'd been hurt that terrible spring.

She looked ahead as she walked, but she no longer saw the cars passing by or the budding trees or even the park. She was seeing all the way back to the beginning.

His name was Trace Canton, and he was the principal at Pinewood Elementary where Elle received her first teaching job. She was just out of college at Colorado University and she'd taken an apartment not far from campus. She applied to four schools—all in separate tricts—and Pinewood was the first to offer her a job.

The ironic thing was she didn't meet Trace until after he was hired. He was on vacation during the hiring process, so the assistant principal and the district superintendent had made the decision without him.

That fall she was hanging posters in her classroom when she felt someone watching her. She turned and jumped. "Oh, sorry." There was a man standing in the doorway, and not just any man. He wore designer slacks and a button-down silk shirt. He wasn't built like the guys she'd dated in college. He had the slender frame of a model—like someone who had stepped out of the pages of *GQ* magazine. Elle set the poster down on the desk and cleared her throat. "I didn't know you were there."

"Don't mind me." Trace smiled at her, and that simple smile cut straight to her heart. "I wanted to get a look at your classroom, that's all."

Elle figured the guy was the father of one of her students. "Did someone in the office tell you about Back-to-School Night this Friday?" She glanced at his hand, his ring finger. It was bare.

He chuckled and took a few steps into her classroom. "I'll be there."

She was flustered by his confidence. He acted as if he owned the place, and suddenly she wondered. Should she be nervous? Was he some psycho who had stumbled into her classroom off the street? She took a step back. "Excuse me, I didn't get your name."

"Trace." He stopped a few feet from her and

grinned. "Most everyone around here knows me a
Mr. Canton."

Elle was mortified. She could've slithered under the
carpet and wormed her way to the parking lot. How
could she have missed that this was the principal? She
felt her cheeks grow hot. "I didn't . . . I had no idea
that . . . I guess I haven't . . ." She sat on the edge of
her desk and made an exasperated sound. "I'm sorry."
She shrugged and gave him a crooked grin. "I didn't
know you were back."

"Don't worry about it." He pressed his shoulder into
the wall and studied her. "Everyone in the office tells
me you're beyond dedicated." He surveyed the room.
"I wanted to see for myself."

It took that long for Elle to catch her breath.
"Well"—she waved her hand at the walls, at the work
she'd already done—"what do you think?"

"I think the staff is right." He cocked his head and
held her eyes. "Welcome to Pinewood, Ms. Dalton.
I'm sure you'll fit in very nicely." He nodded at her
and turned to leave. He stopped at the door and looked
at her again. "Oh, and I'll make a point of stopping in
on Back-to-School Night." He grinned, and then he
was gone.

That visit was the first of many.

It was an unspoken rule that there would be no frat-
ernizing between staff members. Two of the teachers
were married to each other, but that was the exception,
not the rule. Still, Elle felt a connection between herself and the principal every time they were together. A

month into the school year, she found the courage to mention him to one of the old-timers, a teacher who had been there since before Trace Canton arrived at Pinewood.

"What's his story? He doesn't have a wedding ring." They were in the teachers' lounge, so Elle kept her voice low.

"No one knows." The older woman gave Elle a curious look. "He's a looker; everyone can see that. But in the five years he's been here, no one has learned a thing about his private life."

"Strange." She kept her comments casual. She didn't want to appear too interested.

"Want the rumor?" The teacher looked around. When she was sure there was no one else around she lowered her voice. "People say he's gay. That would explain a lot."

"Gay?" Elle felt her stomach drop. That wasn't possible, was it? Not based on the way he looked at her. Even so, it gave her a reason to keep her distance. If he wasn't interested in her, then she wouldn't make a fool of herself by talking to him more than was absolutely necessary.

Over the next few months, Elle stayed away from Trace Canton. Better to learn more about him from afar than to put herself at risk for humiliation.

Just before Christmas break, Trace found her alone in her classroom. "Is it true you're reading the Nativity to your children?"

Elle taught a second-grade class. She was working

at her desk but she set her pen down to give him her full attention. "Yes, sir."

"Please"—he smiled at her—"don't call me sir. It makes me feel old."

"Okay." She swallowed and glanced at her desk, at a stack of papers her students were to color the next day. Each one had a picture of Mary and Joseph and the manger, with an enormous star overhead. She looked back at Trace. "Yes, I'm reading them the Nativity story. I researched it with the district. We're allowed to talk about religious holidays, right?"

"Definitely." He walked up to the desk and sat on the edge of one of the student tables. "I'm not upset, Ms. Dalton. I admire your determination." He crossed his arms. Whatever cologne he was wearing, it made her knees feel weak. "I'm a Christian. The day we lose the meaning of Christmas in our public schools will be a sad one, indeed."

She could barely find the wherewithal to speak. "Yes. Indeed."

Before he left her classroom that day, he took his time examining her wall of papers and posters. She returned to her work, preparing the blackboard for the next day's lessons. When she turned around, she caught him looking at her, his eyes glancing at the length of her. In the same heartbeat, he refocused and held her gaze a little longer than necessary. "You impress me, Ms. Dalton." He headed for the door, but stopped and spoke the next words straight to her soul. "More than you know."

When he left that afternoon, she was convinced of two things. First, there was something special developing between her and the principal—however complicated that might be. And second, the man was not gay. He was a Christian, after all.

The rest of the school year was made up of a series of casual meetings and conversations between them, none of which Elle sought. Once he came close to asking her out for coffee, but he stopped himself. At the end of the school year he called her into his office.

"Ms. Dalton, there are some things you need to know." He was sitting at his desk, and he looked broken. The confidence he carried as he strolled the halls of Pinewood was completely missing.

Her heart skipped a beat, and then slid into a strange rhythm. Was this where he would bare his deepest secrets? Was the old teacher in the lunchroom that day right about him, despite everything she'd come to believe? She sat forward and folded her hands. "Okay."

"First"—he adjusted his tie and glanced at the door. He looked so nervous she felt sorry for him. "First, my role as principal of this school is one I take very seriously. My plan has always been to work here for ten years and then move into the district office. It's my dream, and I wouldn't harm that dream for anything in the world. Education has been my life since I entered college. It's left me no time to pursue anything personal."

Elle had no idea where he was headed with this. "I

see," she said, simply because it seemed right for her to answer somehow.

He rested his forearms on his desk and slumped his shoulders forward. His eyes met hers and he looked tormented. "Second, I've developed feelings for you, Ms. Dalton. Feelings that go"—he looked down for a moment and then back at her—"far beyond my admiration for you as a teacher."

Relief spilled into her veins, and her heart found its normal beat again. Trace Canton was not gay. She didn't break eye contact with him. "Really?"

"Yes." He laughed, and it relieved much of the tension between them. "Whew." He shook his head. "That's one of the hardest things I've ever said."

"I . . ." She felt shy now that his intentions were clear. "I sort of wondered. I mean, I guess I hoped you might feel something for me."

His eyes danced as he realized what she was saying. But just as quickly, he grew serious again. "The trouble is, it would be completely inappropriate for me to ask you out, for us to see each other given our current working relationship."

"I agree." The palms of her hands were damp. "It's one thing for teachers to date. But you're my boss."

"Exactly." He slid a document across his desk. "Look at this. It's a request to have you transferred to Barrett Elementary three miles west of here. It's the same district, but it would allow us . . ." He paused, and she could hear a tremble in his voice. "It would allow me to do what I've wanted to do since the day I met you."

Elle could hardly believe her good fortune.

All along, she'd been telling her mother about Trace, how he was a cheerful man, great with the kids, but how his private life was a mystery. Now, though, the mystery was solved. Trace had been so caught up in education and working his way into the role of principal that he hadn't had time to date. No wonder he was single.

Elle accepted the transfer the next day, and when school let out for summer, she and Trace went to dinner. That night, for the first time, he called her by her given name as he opened her car door for her. "You look beautiful, Elle." Before she climbed in, their eyes held. "I've wanted to call you that since September."

The connection between them happened quickly and with an intensity that left her dizzy. Of course, they'd already spent nine months pretending they didn't have feelings for each other. Now that they were able to express themselves, the romance between them took on a life of its own.

All summer and into the next school year, they were inseparable. They hiked Pike's Peak and three other trails into the mountains surrounding the Springs. They went snow skiing in Vail over a four-day weekend, and golfing at the Broadmoor.

The subject of purity was one they both agreed on. God wouldn't bless their relationship unless they put off temptation. On the trip to Vail, they stayed in separate rooms and never considered breaching the boundaries.

"He's a perfect gentleman," Elle told her mother that Christmas. "I never dreamed I'd meet a man like him."

Her mother listened, but it took a moment before she said anything. "He sounds a little too good to be true."

"Not really." Elle didn't want anyone saying anything to mar the way she was feeling. "He's a man of God, Mother. What more could I ask for?"

One afternoon, her mother explained her concern. "How old is he?"

"Thirty-one." Elle grinned. "Eight years older than me, but that doesn't bother us. He says I'm more mature than him most of the time."

Her mother nodded, thoughtful. "Thirty-one and never been in love. Sort of unusual, don't you think?"

"No." Elle bristled. "He's been getting his education and training. That's not unusual, Mother. It's dedication."

Her mother dropped the subject and pulled Elle into a tender hug. "I'm glad you're happy, honey. You deserve this."

Elle's happiness grew tenfold that New Year's Eve when Trace took her to dinner at the Broadmoor, and after dinner—out on a patio overlooking the beautifully lit golf course, he lowered himself to one knee and pulled a velvet box from his pants pocket. His eyes were damp as he searched hers. "Marry me, Elle."

"Trace . . . yes." She brought her fingers to her lips and then took the box. Inside was a diamond solitaire surrounded by a ring of smaller diamonds. She gasped, and before she could take a breath they were in each other's arms, hugging and kissing and laughing.

Their engagement was more of the same, one amazing day after another. The plans came together quickly, and the wedding was set for May. Elle and her mother went to Denver and found a stunning dress, tight along the bodice with a spray of glittery white that made up the skirt and train.

Three hundred people were invited—the staffs at both elementary schools and family on both sides. Together they picked out the DJ and the ballroom—at the Broadmoor, of course. They laughed as they strolled through Nordstroms, registering for new dishes and crystal and fine china.

Elle didn't notice anything amiss until a month before the wedding. They had plans for dinner and a walk, time to talk about the wedding plans and go over the details of the reception. But Trace called half an hour before he was supposed to pick her up. "Um, Elle . . . I can't make it tonight. Something's come up."

She was puzzled by his behavior, but she figured it had something to do with the wedding. Maybe he was meeting with someone about the honeymoon. Or maybe he was cooking up some other surprise. She let the incident pass without commenting. But when it happened again later that week, she felt the first tremblings of fear.

"Trace . . . is everything okay? With us, I mean."

"Of course." His answer came fast, his tone a little too forced. "Don't worry, Elle. This is about me."

She tried not to think too long about his answer, but his strange behavior continued into the next week and the week after that. Finally, one day after school she showed up at Pinewood and strode into the reception area. She nodded at the woman still seated at the front desk. Then she walked past and into Trace's office.

"Hey." He was on the phone, but at the sight of her he slammed the receiver down and stood. "You can't walk in here unannounced."

"I just did." She couldn't make out the emotions in his eyes, but they were nothing she'd ever seen before. "We need to talk, Trace." She shut the door behind her. "I'm sorry I didn't call first. But I couldn't wait. What's happening with you?"

He lowered himself to his desk and shielded his eyes with his fingers. He exhaled, almost as if he was still recovering from the sight of her. When he lowered his hands, his expression had changed to one she was more familiar with. "Honey, I told you. This isn't about you."

"Okay, so what's it about?" Panic coursed through her. She wanted to scream at him. "We're getting married in ten days, Trace. And you can't keep a dinner date. Doesn't that strike you as strange?"

"I know." He uttered a weak laugh. "I can imagine how it looks." He reached across the desk.

For a moment she didn't respond. She was too angry. "I can't live this way. With you keeping things from me. Secrets." She looked around the room as if the answer might be tangible. "Whatever it is, I can't take it."

"I'm sorry." He stretched his hand out a little farther. His expression was still pinched, his voice nervous. "Elle, come on, honey. I love you. I told you this isn't about you."

She didn't want to, but she took his hand anyway. Whatever damage had been done, feeling his fingers against hers was necessary if they were going to find their way back to where they'd been before. She blinked back tears. "I'm about to commit my entire life to you, Trace. Whatever you've been dealing with, you need to talk to me about it."

"No, Elle." Something cold flashed in his eyes, and just as quickly it was gone. "No, Elle. It was my problem, and I took care of it. Just some leftover business from my old life." He smiled at her, the smile that had won her heart. "The lonely life I lived before I met you."

She wasn't satisfied with his answer, but she didn't know what to do to change his mind.

Finally, he stood and came around to her side of the desk. "I'm sorry for reacting when you walked in." He eased her to her feet and drew her into his arms. "I've been dealing with a lot, Elle. One of the new teachers isn't adjusting very well, and I've been needed more because of that." He touched his lips to hers. "Nothing's changed. Trust me."

Despite Trace's reassurance, Elle's suspicions

remained, but there was nothing that justified her breaking things off. She loved Trace, and if he was feeling stressed about the pending wedding, that only made him human, right? Over the next week, he slipped back into his usual self, making time for her and spending evenings at her apartment going over the details of the wedding.

The Saturday of the ceremony dawned with thick clouds. Looking back, Elle should've seen it as an omen. Especially since the forecast had called for nothing but sunshine. Her mother and Daisy were in town, staying at her apartment, and her other two sisters were at a nearby hotel. The five of them gathered early that morning and fussed over each other's hair and makeup. Finally, at ten-thirty, they were ready to go. The wedding was slated for eleven, and the drive to the church took just ten minutes.

A friend at school knew someone who owned a limo service, and arrangements had been made to have one free of charge for Elle and Trace's big day. The limo whisked them off to the church and they arrived fifteen minutes early. Lots of guests were already there, but the pastor found them in the bridal room. "Have you heard from the groom?"

Fear colored black streaks across Elle's perfect morning. "He's coming by himself. The groomsmen are meeting him here."

"Very well." The pastor looked at his watch. "Is he usually punctual?"

Elle caught her mother's nervous glance. She

eared her throat and adjusted her veil. What could he say? Trace was one of the most punctual people she knew. She smiled at the man. "Usually. But if we have to wait for him, we'll wait."

"Absolutely." He smiled. "See you in a few minutes."

Elle's insides tied in knots. She couldn't look at her mother, couldn't imagine the unfathomable thoughts whispering in her mind. Instead she turned to Daisy. "Are you excited about today?"

"I love to dance." Daisy smiled. She came to Elle and looked her dress up and down. "You look like an angel, Elle. A pretty angel."

"Thanks, Daisy. That's sweet." She kissed her sister's cheek. "You look like an angel, too."

The bridesmaids' dresses were red. Daisy looked down at herself and adjusted her skirt. Then she cast a questioning look at Elle. "Maybe I look like Minnie Mouse."

Elle laughed, and for a moment she didn't feel suffocated with doubts. "Yes, Daisy. You look like Minnie."

The minutes slipped away slowly, painfully. When the time reached five till eleven, Elle stationed herself near the window. Her sisters had gone out into the foyer to mingle with the guests. Only her mother remained in the room with her. "Go, Mom. Please? Find out if he's here."

Her mother didn't say anything. Her pale face said it all. At eleven o'clock sharp, she returned and

171

shook her head. "Does he have a cell phone?"

"Yes." She was shaking by then, shivering from head to toe. She could hear her veil crinkling from the way her shoulders shook. She dug through her purse and only then realized that she'd had her phone set to the vibrate mode. When she opened it, she saw that she had four missed calls.

Frantically she scrolled through them. Each one was from Trace. Her head was spinning and she could barely concentrate. She sat on the edge of a desk chair and put her head down. Anything to get the blood to flow to her brain so she wouldn't pass out.

"Elle . . . what is it?" Her mother knelt by her side, her hand on her shoulder. "Talk to me, sweetheart."

"It's Trace." She lifted her head. "He's called four times."

"Okay, then." Her mother nodded to the phone. "Call him back. He's probably just running late."

Elle couldn't stop the spinning in her head. Running late? She clung to the idea. Yes, that had to be it. He had gotten stuck in traffic or his car had broken down, or a pipe had burst beneath his sink. Or maybe he'd stopped to help someone in trouble. There had to be a reason.

She tried to swallow but her throat was too dry. She lifted the cell phone, but she was shaking too badly to dial his number. "Here." She handed it to her mother. "Call him for me. Please."

Her mother looked as frightened as she was. She took the phone and scrolled through the missed calls.

Then she hit the send button. After a few seconds she handed it back. "It's ringing."

On the third ring, Trace answered. From the beginning she could tell he was crying. Weeping, even. "Elle . . . I'm sorry, honey. I'm so sorry." Every word was another sob.

Her heart pounded so hard she was certain it would burst through her chest or stop altogether. She gripped the phone and paced to the window. "Talk to me, Trace. What happened? Were you in an accident?"

"No." He had never sounded so distraught. "I can't do it, Elle. I can't marry you." He moaned. "God, why do I feel this way? Why is this happening?"

She was seeing black spots now. Was he praying? And why now, why his doubts at the very hour they were supposed to be saying their vows? "Trace . . ." She steadied herself against the window sill and closed her eyes. "I . . . I don't understand."

"I've fought it all my life, Elle." He stopped crying long enough to explain himself. Even so, his words were punctuated with quiet sobs. "I'm in love with someone else. Another teacher. I tried . . . I tried to let him go, but I couldn't."

Elle's breathing grew shallow and she gasped for air, grabbed at any way to understand what he'd just said. "*Him*? You're . . . you're in love with a man?"

Across the room, her mother dropped to another chair. "Dear God, no . . . no."

Trace was going on, saying something about it being wrong. "All my life I've had to choose. God and His

173

goodness, or the desires of my flesh." He let out a cry that cut through her. "I can't promise you forever when . . . when I'll be looking for every chance to be with him. Oh, Elle . . . I'm so sorry."

It wasn't happening. The only way Elle was able to fill her lungs, to keep from passing out or having a heart attack, was by convincing herself that what she was hearing was all a lie. It was impossible. Trace Canton, her one true love, wasn't leaving her stranded at the altar for a man. No way.

She let the shock work its way through her body, through her heart and soul. He was still going on about getting counseling and knowing it was wrong and wanting God's will, when she interrupted him. "I have to go, Trace." Her voice was cold, unfeeling. "Good-bye."

Her phone felt like a burning piece of coal. She closed it and dropped it at the same time. Then she turned to her mother, but the words wouldn't come. Not that she needed words. Everything that could've been spoken had already been said. Her mother, too, looked ready to pass out. Always in their growing-up years, Elle had been the strong daughter, the one who rubbed her mother's back when the task of raising four daughters without the help of a husband seemed daunting to her.

Elle was the daughter who took responsibility for Daisy, helping her with kitchen tasks and reading to her when their mother was busy with the other girls, and she was the one who, of course, had gone into teaching—just one more way she could help people. But here, with three hundred wedding guests sitting in the sanctuary down the hall, Elle couldn't take another step.

Her mother must've known. Because she stood and drew a long breath. "I'll talk to them. I'll say there's been a change of plans."

The shock was still exploding through her, but Elle had never loved her mother more than in that single moment. An hour later, when the wedding guests were long gone and she and her mother and sisters had wept together until they had no more tears to cry, they went back to Elle's apartment.

She stayed the summer with her mother and Daisy, unwilling to talk about Trace or the disastrous wedding day. In July, she received a letter from him. He had quit his job as principal of Pinewood and had relocated to Los Angeles. He was still seeking God's will, still aware that acting on his passions was sinful. He asked her to pray for him.

A year later, on what would've been their first anniversary, she pulled the letter out and realized that God had been healing her heart even when getting up every day had been a struggle. Because on that day, with tears streaming down her face, she did the thing she couldn't do until that moment.

She prayed for Trace Canton.

And then she folded up the letter and tucked it into a box with the invitations and napkins, and the guestbook that had never been used.

People who knew her well said things intended to make her feel better. "Better to find out now, Elle. Better than living your life with him and having him leave you three years from now." Or, "You're not the first one to be left at the altar. It's not a reflection on you, Elle. It was his problem, and it's his loss."

The truth about why he left never came fully to the surface, although the whispering in the lunchroom at Barrett Elementary must've been only a fraction of what it was at Pinewood. People talked, and she assumed they knew. But no one ever said a word to her.

No one but her mother and her sisters. "It's a lie," her mother told her one evening, a week after the broken wedding. "Trace is believing a lie. The truth is we all struggle with sin and we all have a choice whether to live life for God or against Him." She ran her fingers over Elle's hair. "Don't let this change how you feel about yourself or about love, Elle. Please, sweetheart."

But there was nothing her mother could say or do to undo the damage. If the devil was lying to Trace, he was doing the same thing to her. Because from the moment Trace explained himself on the phone that day, from the moment she stepped out of her wedding gown, sobbing so hard she could barely breathe, she became convinced of one thing.

Love was a lie.

And she could live the rest of her life without having anything to do with it.

That was her determination. Yes, she could love her mother and her sisters. And over the next two years she threw herself into getting a master's degree in special education so she could help Daisy find a better life.

But she would never open her heart to a man again.

SHE AND SNOOPY finished two full laps around the park, and Snoopy started whining again. He didn't like to walk more than two laps, not this close to suppertime. She stopped at a bench and he took the spot on the ground next to her, his warm body pressed against her ankles.

Once in a while, when she felt particularly close to God, she would allow herself to imagine that if love burst through the doors of her heart some far-off day, she wouldn't stop it. She wouldn't pursue it, but she wouldn't resist it, either. Not if God had a plan for her to find love again. Even that was a stretch. She thought about the past few days, and the visitor who had plagued her classroom and her thoughts. Yes, God might bring love into her life again. But not in the form of a married man. The one thing she could never, ever do was allow herself to have feelings for Cody Gunner. Because the first time her heart was broken, she was lucky to escape with her life. Elle had no doubt that the next time wouldn't merely set her back a few years.

It would kill her.

Chapter Thirteen

Cody had planned to make his mind up about his brother's involvement at the ILC before the Friday field trip. But the closer it got to Friday, the more he knew he wanted to attend the trip with Elle and her class. He loved her compassion, loved the way she worked with her students.

Or maybe he just loved watching her.

Whatever it was, he didn't want to stop spending time with her. The days with Carl Joseph at the center had given him the distraction he'd been looking for. Even if he hadn't been looking for a girl with hazel eyes.

After watching her work with the young adults at the center every day that week, he couldn't deny the obvious. She was helping them. Even if a person with Down Syndrome lived at home in a safe, loving environment all his life, it wouldn't hurt for him to know how to cook or eat correctly, how to shop on a budget or take the bus.

Elle Dalton was dedicated to her students in a way that surprised him. He had studied her all week, trying to see past her beauty. Whatever drove her, it wasn't a temporary incentive. She was committed to changing the lives of handicapped people, and she went about it as if that alone were the purpose of her life.

At the end of class Thursday he found her in the break room again. Most of the students were gone, but aisy and Carl Joseph and Gus were outside taking urns at the tetherball pole. "Mr. Gunner"—she was making copies of something, probably the bus route—"thanks for not scaring me this time."

"You're welcome." He smiled, but he was careful to keep the moment professional. "Look, Ms. Dalton—about your field trip tomorrow. I was wondering if I could join you. If it wouldn't be too much trouble."

Elle stopped and put her hands on her hips. She studied him for a moment before she answered. "You've already made up your mind about me"—she waved to the room beyond—"about the work I'm doing here at the center." She wasn't angry, merely pointing out what she clearly thought was a fact. "Why come with us?"

"Because—" He wanted to look away, but he couldn't. She had that effect on him. "The truth is, I'm impressed by your work here. You're giving your students skills they wouldn't have otherwise."

She raised an eyebrow. "Really? I changed your mind that easily?" There was teasing in her tone.

He smiled. "You haven't changed my mind about putting people like Carl Joseph out in the world to fend for themselves. But"—his voice grew more serious – "your work, your passion for these people, is a great thing. A very great thing."

"Thank you." She glanced down at her feet. Her cheeks grew red and she turned back to the copy machine and pressed a few buttons. When she spoke, it was hard to hear her. "You can come with us, Mr.

179

Gunner." She faced him once more. This time her expression was no-nonsense. "But I take these field trips very seriously, and so do the students."

"I know that." He hated how she thought of him, critical and ogre-like. Maybe that's why he needed to spend more time with her. Not so she could change his mind about the purpose of the center, but so he could change *her* mind about him. "The Subway thing . . . it won't happen again."

She narrowed her eyes. "Do you know where we're going tomorrow?"

"To a dance class downtown?"

"A dance class and then to an old church. One of the oldest in Colorado Springs. It has a midday Friday service."

Cody clenched the muscles in his jaw. He and God had been on a roller-coaster since Ali died. She had faith enough to move mountains, but it hadn't helped her in the end. After her death, there were times when he wanted nothing to do with Ali's faith, and other times when it made perfect sense, when he was thankful beyond words to Ali's God for giving them as much time as they had.

Even so, over the last few years he'd fallen away from even thinking about faith. It hadn't been a part of his life before Ali, and truthfully it hadn't helped much to believe there was a higher power, a Great Being who watched over the moves of His people and helped when He was called upon. Cody crossed his arms. "Carl Joseph has never been to church.

ur family, we've never been churchgoers."

"I know that." She no longer seemed flustered. "I talked to each of the students. Every one of them wants to go."

"Because prayer is a life skill." It wasn't a question. He had seen Elle remind them about prayer time and again during the week.

Elle drew a long breath. "Yes, Mr. Gunner. Because prayer is a life skill." She studied him. "Are you opposed to God in some way? Do you want to keep Carl Joseph from attending the church service?"

"No." He shrugged. "I guess I haven't seen a lot of proof of God, that's all. If you want to take your students to church, I won't stand in the way."

"And you won't mumble under your breath or give angry looks to the pastor, rolling your eyes, that sort of thing?" The hint of teasing was back in her voice.

He was beginning to understand Elle Dalton, at least the public Elle. She hid behind a layer of professionalism and mild sarcasm. He understood that. But the time he spent with her left him no closer to knowing the real her. Not in the least. He considered her question. "I'll sit in the back. You'll never know I'm there." He angled his head. "I might even learn something."

"All right then." She went to a filing drawer and pulled out a single sheet of paper. "We're meeting here an hour earlier than usual." She handed him the paper. "Here are the details."

He thanked her and was headed toward the door

when he stopped and faced her again. "What's you̶ interest, Ms. Dalton? That's the part I can't figur̶ out."

"My interest?"

"Yes." He wasn't being combative, not this time. He was simply curious. Maybe if he understood her motives, he could consider the reasons for putting someone like Carl Joseph out into the world by himself. He searched her eyes. "Why isn't it enough for people with Down Syndrome to live at home with their parents, safe and loved and cared for?"

"Because"—passion filled her tone—"people with Down Syndrome have dreams and hopes, Mr. Gunner. Did you know that? They look at magazines and television, and they picture themselves dressed in a suit, headed off to work. They see married couples, holding hands and kissing, and they dream of knowing love like that."

Cody could feel himself frown, despite his determination to stay neutral. "They want to be married?"

"Yes." She leaned against the counter. "Before I took this job, I interviewed a married couple with Down Syndrome. They had assistance from a twice-weekly caregiver, but they managed just fine on their own. Even with a variety of health issues." She stared at him, her voice intense. "Do you know how long those two people waited for permission to marry?" She didn't wait for him to answer. "Twenty years, Mr. Gunner. Because people like you and me kept denying them the right to be together."

"It's like letting grade-school kids get married."

"No, it isn't." She crossed her arms. "Down Syndrome makes a person less capable cognitively. But not emotionally. They still mature at an age-appropriate rate."

"You mean, Carl Joseph has the feelings and desires of any other twenty-four-year-old guy?" Cody let loose a single laugh, and it expressed how ludicrous he thought the idea. He had never considered such a thing. Carl Joseph was a child; he would always be a child.

"That's exactly right." In that instant, Cody could think of only one person. His precious Ali. Wasn't that her philosophy? People had to choose life every day if they were going to really live. He blinked back her image and took another step toward the door. "We'll be here in the morning, Ms. Dalton. Thank you."

He left the break room and headed across the center's main area. He stepped outside and saw that Gus was gone. Only Carl Joseph and Daisy remained in the yard, and neither of them heard him walk out. He stood near the door and studied them.

They were singing as loud as they could, though it took a minute for Cody to understand them. When he did, he was struck by the simplicity of the moment. Daisy was dancing in a sort of box step, and Carl Joseph was trying to follow her lead. Together they were singing, "M-I-C . . . K-E-Y . . . M-O-U-S-E!"

Something stirred in Cody's heart. Even now Carl Joseph was in danger. He could have a seizure at any time, though Carl Joseph hadn't had one since Cody had been home. He was on a new medication, but the risk remained. That's what the doctor had told his parents yesterday at Carl Joseph's appointment. The doctor was adamant.

Carl Joseph's condition was unstable. Independent living couldn't even be considered unless his health improved.

Cody felt a rush of sadness as he watched his brother. Carl Joseph put his hands around Daisy's waist and the two of them waltzed to something Daisy was humming. Whatever the future held, he hoped Carl Joseph could keep his friendship with Daisy.

For both their sakes.

"I LOVE DANCING with you, Daisy. 'Cause you're the best dancer in Disneyland!" Carl Joseph smiled so big it became a laugh.

Rain was in the forecast, and Carl Joseph kept looking up, checking the clouds. Cody felt a surge of protectiveness for his younger brother. Lately Carl Joseph had been almost obsessed with clouds, peering at them and staring at them, frowning at them, as if a tornado were in the forecast when all that floated overhead was a layer of cumulus clouds.

It was this exact sort of thing that would make him a danger to himself if he were on his own in the world. He could be walking across a street and get distracted by the sky. That quickly he could step off a curb into the path of a bus.

Carl Joseph and Daisy had moved on to some other play-acting. They were doing some other kind of dance step—and but for Carl Joseph's awkward clumsiness, it almost seemed they were following a regular pattern.

That had to be Daisy's doing. Clearly she was as taken with Carl Joseph as he was with her. No doubt she encouraged his new interest in faith, since she'd been attending the center longer than he had.

A gust of wind blew across the courtyard, and the first raindrops began to fall. In the distance, a low rumble of thunder echoed across the valley. Suddenly Daisy began to cry, loudly and in short bursts. She covered her face and turned in a tight circle, frantic. At the same time, Carl Joseph sprang into action. He pulled off his jacket, put it around her shoulders, and whispered something into her ear. Then he led her with fast, jerky steps to a covering of trees and a small cement bench.

Cody watched, mesmerized. As they reached the dry area, Daisy began brushing the raindrops off her arms and legs and face, her movements quick and compulsive. If Cody didn't know better, he'd think the raindrops were burning her skin. He moved closer, but before he could make his presence known, he saw Carl Joseph put his arm around her shoulders and gently, tenderly, rock her.

Cody was close enough now to hear what they were saying, though they were too distracted to notice him. Carl Joseph was still rocking her. "It's okay, Daisy. The rain won't hurt you. Not the rain."

She looked up, her expression paralyzed with fear. "I could melt."

"No, Daisy. That was the Wicked Witch of the West. You're not a witch and . . . and you're not a wicked witch. You're Minnie Mouse."

A slight smile appeared in her eyes. "And you're Mickey."

"Right." He laughed hard, the laugh that would tell anyone within listening range that he was not like other people. The laugh that made Cody love him more than anything in life. "Right, Daisy, I'm Mickey. Mickey Mouse." He pointed at her, his eyes big. "And I'm writing you a letter. So I can entertain you at Disneyland."

For a moment Daisy's eyes lit up, too. But the rain was falling harder and she looked out at it. As she did, terror filled her face. "But the rain . . ." She began to cry. She pressed her forehead into Carl Joseph's shoulder. "Keep me dry, CJ. Okay? Keep me dry."

Cody was stunned by the scene. His throat felt thick as he watched it play out. This was why Carl Joseph had become obsessed with clouds. Because he was driven to protect Daisy from her obvious fear of the rain. His heart swelled inside him. The friendship between the two of them was painfully genuine.

He gave a little cough so he wouldn't startle them. "Buddy . . . it's time to go home."

Carl Joseph gave him a frustrated look, the sort of look he had never given Cody in all his life. "Not yet." He tightened his hold on Daisy's shoulders. "Not with n." He pointed at the wet pavement. "Not now."

"Okay." Cody wasn't sure what to do next. Behind him he heard a sound and he turned. Elle was locking up, and as she came out she realized what was happening. "Carl Joseph, are you helping Daisy again?" She smiled at the two and headed toward them. Along the way she glanced at Cody, and her eyes told him how Carl Joseph's display of friendship touched her as well.

When she reached Daisy, she touched the young woman's shoulder. "Are you okay?"

"CJ keeps me dry." She looked up but made no effort to move.

"Carl Joseph has to go home with his brother." Elle tilted her head. "I'll make sure you don't get wet, okay?"

Carl Joseph lifted his eyes to Elle and then turned to Cody again. He stood, his hand still on Daisy's back. For a moment he looked unable to express himself. That happened often with Carl Joseph, and when it did he sometimes hid his face and resorted to a slight rocking motion.

Not now.

With his options limited, Carl Joseph looked around and spotted the covered area near the center door. He pulled his jacket up around Daisy's shoulders again and over her head. "Come on, Daisy. Run with me."

Her blank expression made it clear she didn't know where Carl Joseph was taking her or why they were supposed to run. But she trusted him. Because she ducked her head and with quick steps, the two of them ran across the rainy yard to the covered area.

There Carl Joseph eased his jacket down aroun Daisy's shoulders. Cody could barely make out wha he was saying.

"Brother wants to go."

Daisy smiled at Carl Joseph, but then glared at Cody. "I want you to stay."

"Me, too." He stood squarely in front of her and patted her shoulders. "You stay dry with Teacher."

"Okay." Daisy ran her tongue over her lower lip. "Come tomorrow, CJ."

"I will." He pulled her into a hug then, and for a moment the two held on as if they might never let go.

Cody watched, awed. He barely noticed Elle coming up beside him. "See?" Her tone was gentle. "Carl Joseph doesn't want you making his decisions. Can't you feel it?"

"Yes." Cody kept his eyes on his brother. "I feel it." But in that moment, he felt Elle's nearness more. The softness in her voice and the subtle smell of her shampoo. He tried to focus. "Does Daisy have a ride?"

"I'll take her."

"Oh." He had sensed that Elle was fonder of Daisy than some of the other students. That was fine; maybe Daisy had no other way to the center. He tipped an invisible hat. "See you tomorrow."

In the car on the way home, Cody looked at his brother. "Daisy's afraid of the rain?"

"Yes." Carl Joseph was grumpy. His short answer was loaded with attitude.

"Why's she afraid?" Cody turned his attention back

to the road. He tried to keep his tone upbeat, casual.

Carl Joseph uttered a loud breath and turned impatient eyes toward Cody. "She isn't the Wicked Witch of the West. She's Minnie Mouse. And Minnie Mouse doesn't melt in the rain."

"Oh." Cody blinked. He made one more try. "So she's afraid she'll melt, Buddy? Is that it?"

"Yes." Carl Joseph lifted his hands and let them drop in his lap. "I keep her dry, okay?"

"Okay." They rode the rest of the way in silence. Not until they pulled into the driveway did Cody sense that Carl Joseph had cooled down some. "Are you okay now, Buddy?"

"Yes, I'm okay." He reached out and patted Cody's knee. "Sorry, Brother. Sorry for being mad. We still wanted to dance, okay?"

"You and Daisy?"

"Yes." He smiled, even though the look of it was still a little subdued. "Me and Minnie Mouse."

That night Carl Joseph couldn't stop talking about the field trip. They were going to get a dance lesson from a real dance instructor. "So maybe I can learn the Lindy Hop," he told their parents after dinner. He hopped around the table, laughing as he went. "Hop . . . hop . . . hop!"

Neither of his parents had spoken to Cody about the center since he started attending with Carl Joseph earlier that week. Now, though, his mother caught his eyes, and the concern in her face told Cody she'd been worrying about the situation since their last conversation. "You're going on the field trip?"

"Brother wants to dance!" Carl Joseph's mood was considerably better than it had been in the car on the way home. He grinned as he danced past Cody. "Right, Brother?"

"Dancing and church." He raised a forkful of mashed potatoes in a mock sort of cheer. "Should be interesting."

Carl Joseph stopped in his tracks. His smile faded. "But you're happy to go, right, Brother? Not mad like the Subway field trip?"

Elle's request ran through his mind. Remorse hit him like a truck, and he immediately changed his tone. "Yes, Buddy. I'm very happy." He held his hand out, the sarcasm from earlier gone. Carl Joseph took hold of his fingers. "The field trip will be lots of fun."

Doubt lingered, but only for a moment. Then Carl Joseph smiled again, the big open-mouthed smile he was known for. He pushed his glasses back up his nose. "Goodie! Field trip day is fun!"

The rest of that night and the next morning as they pulled up in front of the center, fear shot darts at Cody. What if Carl Joseph had a seizure today? He could fall and get hurt and . . . the worst scenarios played out in his imagination in as much time as it took him to draw a single breath. He couldn't lose Carl Joseph, his buddy. His friend. Not after losing Ali. He wouldn't survive it.

He could only hope that of all days, Carl Joseph's medication wouldn't give out today.

Chapter Fourteen

Cody kept his thoughts to himself as the group waited inside the center. Once they were all together, Elle took her place at the front. "Everyone remembers the bus route?"

Several voices began talking at once. Elle held up her hand. Her patience seemed to know no limits. "One at a time."

Daisy raised her hand. "Me, Teacher."

"Let's ask someone else. We all know that Daisy knows the bus routes." She gave Daisy a quick smile. "Gus, why don't you tell us the bus route today."

"Uh . . ." Gus pulled a piece of crumpled paper from his pocket and opened it. He turned it one way and then another and for a few seconds he did nothing but stammer.

Cody raised his brow, waiting.

Finally Gus looked at Elle. "Walk to Adler Street. Take the west bus past four stops to Cheyenne Street. Get off." He looked up at the ceiling and tapped one finger on his temple. He checked his paper again and suddenly his eyes got big. "I know. Take the orange bus south to Pine Street. Get off and take the south bus to Main Street." His mouth hung open, eyes unblinking. "Right, Teacher?"

"Yes." Elle beamed. "Exactly right."

With that, the group gathered their things and left the center, walking toward Adler. Cody lagged behind, watching. Every now and then a car would slow down as it passed. Cody wanted to shout at the driver to keep moving and not to stare. It was hard enough for this group to get anywhere without people gawking at them.

Like every other day, Carl Joseph walked next to Daisy. They were the same height, but Carl Joseph stood taller in her presence. When he seemed to think no one was looking, Carl Joseph linked his baby finger through hers. It was something Cody tried not to notice. Because Carl Joseph loved this life, these friends. So what would happen when his parents did what they needed to do? When they broke the news to him that independent living wasn't possible for him?

As they reached the first bus, Carl Joseph walked more slowly. This time Daisy put her arm around him. "It's okay, CJ. This bus is right."

Carl Joseph stopped at the bottom of the steps. He pulled the directions sheet from his pocket, looked at it, and scratched his head. Then he pulled his bus pass from the other pocket and looked at it. "This bus is for Cheyenne Street?"

"Yes, CJ." Daisy tugged gently at his arm. "This bus."

Cody shuddered to think how Carl Joseph would handle this moment without the support of Daisy and Elle and his classmates. His brother tucked the papers back in his pocket and looked up at the bus. He was stiff with worry, and he began wringing his hands. "This bus?"

"Come on, CJ." Daisy released his arm and moved onto the first step. There were still four other students waiting to board.

One of them peered around the others. "Move it, people. Teacher wants to move it."

Elle was hanging back, watching the drama unfold. She kept from saying anything, and after a minute, his legs trembling, Carl Joseph followed Daisy onto the bus.

Cody came up behind Elle. She smelled wonderful, and for a crazy minute he wished it was just the two of them on the trip. "Is he always like this?"

"Yes." Elle didn't look troubled. "Most of the students are nervous about the bus until they get used to it. That's the purpose of the field trips."

Cody swallowed. His heart was beating faster than usual. "How can you know they won't act this way when they're by themselves for the first time?"

Elle reached the top step. She looked back at Cody. "We don't just drop them off at an apartment and wish them luck, Mr. Gunner. Every stage is carefully monitored."

"Oh." He held her gaze a beat longer than necessary. Then he swallowed. "I didn't know."

They reached the dance studio on Main Street and filed into the lobby. The instructor was an older woman, and she and Elle seemed to know each other. The students moved into the dance room, and for the next two hours they learned a variety of swing dance moves, including the Lindy Hop. Cody couldn't help but smile as he watched the smiles on the faces around him. Clearly they loved to dance.

As they left, Cody caught up to Elle and walked beside her. "You taught them about dance, right?"

"Yes." Her eyes sparkled. Then her gaze dropped to his left hand and her guard seemed to go up again. "People with Down Syndrome need more exercise than other people. Dance is an exercise they enjoy, so it's something they'll do without being told."

"They could benefit from something tougher— weight training or cycling." He put his hands in his pockets, his pace easy and in line with hers. She had a dizzying effect on him, something he couldn't shake. "I was thinking of starting something before I came home."

"Really?" Her enthusiasm took him by surprise. "The owner of the center wants to expand. He wants a fitness center, an addition to the existing building." She looked at him, her eyes thoughtful. "He won a grant from the state, so the money's already in place." She angled her head. "I'm supposed to find someone who could run it, develop a fitness program for the students. That way we could open it up to other disabled people, as well. People who don't have the opportunity to learn independence." She gave him a curious look. "Are you returning to work, wherever you were before you came home?"

"No." He waited for the usual comments about rodeo and how difficult life must be on the road. But they didn't come. He smiled to himself. She was maybe one of the first women he'd ever known who wasn't part of the rodeo world. He looked straight ahead. "I'm sort of at a crossroads. Looking for the next thing."

"Oh." Her look became the more familiar subtly sarcastic one. "That's why we were blessed to have your scrutiny this past week. Because you have nothing better to do."

"Look, Elle . . ." He wanted to keep the air between them light. Her nearness was intoxicating, but his feelings went beyond that. He liked her, liked the way she didn't back down from him and the way she cared for her students. He liked her passion most of all. But still he had to make himself clear. "I'm here for one reason." He nodded at Carl Joseph walking next to Daisy a few people ahead of them. "I love that kid."

She hesitated and then moved over some, creating more space between them. "I understand that, Mr. Gunner." She gathered the students in a circle there on the sidewalk. "Who besides Daisy can tell me the next bus route?"

The students pulled out their direction sheets. One of the students gave the right answer and they were off again, this time toward the church service. As they climbed off the bus across from the old downtown church, Elle threw what must've been a curve at them. "Who would like to eat lunch?"

Several hands shot up.

"I'm very hungry, Teacher." Gus looked at the others. "We're starving."

"Yes." Tammy twirled one of her braids. "I could eat a cow."

"Cow isn't always good for you." Sid pointed at her. "Cow should be cooked."

Elle stifled a smile. "Very well." She took in the faces around her. "How many of you brought money?"

All week, Elle had talked to them about field trips, and how if they were going out on the town they should be prepared. Preparation was a life skill, she told them. They should have their directions, and a cell phone, and ten dollars in case they needed to eat while they were out.

Now all but two students raised their hands. Some of them actually raised their money.

Elle told them to put their money back in their pockets. "Tommy's Burgers is one block south." Elle pointed in the right direction. "We have an hour before the church service. Let's go eat."

"See," Tammy announced loudly. "We are having cow." She stuck her tongue out at Sid as she walked past. "Cooked cow, Sid. Burgers are cooked cow."

The first trouble of the day came at the restaurant.

One minute everything seemed to be going smoothly, and the next Tammy was standing and screaming, pointing at Gus. "Help him! Someone help him!"

Gus's face was deep red, and he was grabbing at his throat. Drool hung at the corners of his mouth and he was stomping his feet in panic.

"Help him!" Tammy's scream incited the rest of the

roup, and in an instant, all the students were on their feet shouting the same thing. "Help him! Someone help him!"

Cody was sitting by himself. As soon as he realized what was happening, he cut his way through the crowd, reached Gus, and positioned himself behind the young man. "Stand up straight, Gus."

The guy did as he was asked. By now Elle was at their side. "Dear God." She covered her mouth, her voice filled with fear. "Help us, Lord."

Cody stayed behind him and slid his arms beneath Gus's. He made a fist with one hand and cupped it with the other, then he pressed the fist against Gus's stomach, in the hollow where his ribs met just below his chest. He pressed hard, jerking his hand in an upward motion. Then he did it again.

Some of the girls were screaming now, moving in tight circles. On the third thrust, a large piece of barely chewed hamburger flew from Gus's mouth out onto the floor. He gasped for air. His eyes wide, he dropped to his knees and grabbed his throat with both hands.

Cody put his hand on the young man's shoulder. "Gus, you're okay. Breathe out."

But panic still had the best of him. He shook his head, fast and frenzied.

"Gus." Cody used a stronger tone this time. "Breathe out. You're okay, now just breathe out."

Elle worked her way through the students, telling them that Gus was fine and asking them to sit back down. Two of the girls were still crying.

"Breathe out, Gus." Cody leaned in closer. "You'r okay."

Finally Gus did as he was told. He pursed his lips and blew out. He still had his hands around his throat, his eyes still bugged out of his face. But after a minute he struggled to his feet. He stared at Cody and then at Elle and back again. "I laughed."

Tammy was shaking, but she approached Cody and explained what had happened. "Gus was telling a funny story." She looked at the other two students who had been sitting at her table. "And he was eating and telling a funny story."

"And"—one of the others grabbed his throat and stuck his tongue out—"no more words."

Cody didn't realize until then that he was shaking. Gus had waited longer than necessary to stand up, probably because choking was an unfamiliar concept to him. Carl Joseph had choked once when he was around ten or eleven. Cody still remembered their mother giving him the Heimlich maneuver and saving his life.

Gus finally relaxed the hold he had on his throat. He lowered his hands and, moving like a ninety-year-old man, he returned to his table. When he reached his chair, he turned and pointed at Cody. "He likes us now."

"Yes, he likes us." Tammy bent over in dramatic fashion, catching her own breath. When she straightened, she lifted both her hands toward the ceiling. "Thank You, God. Carl Joseph's brother likes us."

Cody felt the sting of tears in his eyes. It had taken this, but at least now the students trusted him.

Elle made her way to his side and touched his elbow. "Mr. Gunner . . ."

"Call me Cody." He braced himself against the nearest chair and tried to catch his breath.

"Cody . . . thank you." Her eyes still held fear, but it was mixed with an undeniable admiration. Maybe even an attraction. Her tone was drenched in relief. "Nothing like that . . . That's never happened before."

Cody looked at Carl Joseph. His brother had his hands over his face, and he was rocking. Daisy was talking to him through the spaces between his fingers. Cody sighed and turned to Elle again. "People with Down Syndrome sometimes have trouble swallowing."

"I know. It's one of the reasons we make sure the students are paired up when they move out on their own."

Cody looked deep into her eyes. "Even then . . ." He wasn't being defiant, just honest. "This sort of thing could always happen." He walked over and crouched next to Carl Joseph. "Buddy, it's okay. Gus is fine."

Carl Joseph opened his fingers wider and peered at him. "Gus?"

"Yes, he's okay." Cody wasn't sure if his brother was reacting this way because he remembered what had happened when he was younger. Either way, the event had traumatized him.

It took a half hour before the group relaxed enough

to set out for the church. They walked together, and again Cody hung back. Ali had always wanted him to go to church with her, but they'd never gone. Their time was too short, and being around other people always represented a possibility of infection for her.

The day was overcast again, but Cody looked up and saw a slice of blue. *Ali, you'd be proud of me. I'm going to church.* A sad smile lifted his lips. It was happening. Her memory no longer consumed him. Thoughts of her were never far away, but they weren't a part of every breath anymore. That would explain the feeling in his heart, the emptiness. He looked up ahead at Elle. She walked between Gus and Tammy, the three of them laughing.

And maybe it explained why he couldn't stop thinking about a certain young teacher.

When they reached the church, Elle brought her finger to her lips and shushed the students. Cody was last in line, and she repeated the motion for his benefit. Then she added, "I mean it."

Cody saluted her and filed in. A change had happened today, maybe because of the incident with Gus. There was a bond between him and Elle now, something he couldn't quite define. He took a pew just behind the students, and watched how they filed in and found their seats. Two of the guys wore baseball caps. As they reached their seats, they removed their caps and placed them on the floor. Awe and wonder filled their faces. Gus dropped to his knees and bowed his head immediately, and several of the others did the same. A few rely looked around, spellbound by the old church.

An organist played two hymns, and then the pastor got things started. He welcomed Elle's students and explained that God has a plan for every one of his children. Cody swallowed back a rush of emotion. *Down Syndrome, God?* Is that the plan You have for Carl Joseph and his friends?

There was no answer, nothing audible. But he remembered something his mother had said over the years when she spent time with Carl Joseph.

"Here on earth, we think Carl Joseph is handicapped. Won't it be funny if we get to heaven one day and find out it was the other way around."

Cody watched Carl Joseph, his head bowed in prayer. Their mother had a point.

He crossed his arms and lost focus on what was being said up front. Instead he thought about Ali, how she had believed so firmly that she would go to heaven, that she would meet up with the sister she lost as a child, and the two of them would ride horses forever across endless fields of green.

Cody wasn't so sure.

He caught very little of the rest of the sermon, but when it was over, collection baskets were passed. Cody sat a little straighter and felt his blood begin to heat. Certainly the church wouldn't be so bold as to take money from handicapped people. He slid into a pew adjacent to the group so he could see better.

Sure enough, the basket made its way back to Elle's students, and one at a time they pulled out wads of

one-dollar bills and coins and tossed them in. Wh●
the basket reached Carl Joseph, Cody watched hi●
take out a stack of money, count five twenty-dolla●
bills, and place them in the basket.

Cody was on his feet before the basket could make
it to the next person. A hundred dollars? Where would
his brother have gotten that sort of money, and how
could he throw it into a collection basket? He quietly
approached the pew where his brother was sitting next
to Daisy. When the basket reached the end of the row,
Cody dug in and discreetly took out the five twenties.
Then he whispered toward his brother. "Buddy, we
need to go."

"What?" Carl Joseph pushed his glasses up. He
looked stunned by Cody's request. He glanced at the
students around him. Several of them noticed Cody
and were clearly waiting to see what Carl Joseph
would do. He looked back at Cody, and his face red-
dened. He leaned over Daisy's legs and whispered
loud, "Not now! This is church."

"Come on." Cody couldn't wait another minute.
They needed to catch a cab back to the center and get
home. He gave his brother a stern look. "Now."

Carl Joseph respected him too much to argue.
Despite his angry expression, he stood and moved
past Daisy out into the aisle.

It was at that moment that Elle noticed what was
happening. She excused herself and came to them, her
eyes full of alarm. She, too, kept to a low whisper.
"What's going on?"

We're leaving." Cody could feel the apology in his ~~cs.~~ "My brother just dropped a hundred dollars in ~~he~~ plate." A sad, whispered laugh escaped. "This isn't ~~or~~ us. I'm sorry."

He led the way and despite the horrified looks from the other students, Carl Joseph followed. When they were outside on the front steps of the church, Cody turned to Carl Joseph. He held up the five twenties. "What's this, Buddy?"

Carl Joseph's anger became sorrow. His shoulders fell a little. "My gift, Brother. My gift for Jesus."

"Jesus doesn't need a hundred dollars, Buddy." Cody waved the bills at his brother. "You don't know the first thing about money."

"I know the first thing." Carl Joseph held up his hand and stared at his fingers. He was so nervous, his entire arm shook. He appeared to be counting and after several seconds he held up his pointer finger. "I know one thing. Gifts are for Jesus."

Cody's heart broke for his brother. He found a kinder tone. "Where'd you get this money, Buddy?"

His brother made a series of exasperated sounds and turned in small half circles. Then he stopped and pointed at Cody. "I worked, Brother. I worked for that money."

"Doing what?" Cody hated his tone, hated that this would be yet another time when he and Carl Joseph would struggle to find the friendship that had always come so easily for them. But he had to make a point. He had never heard about his brother holding a job.

He softened his tone again. "Are you lying, Buddy

"No!" Carl Joseph shouted the word.

Cody hesitated. "Let's get a cab." They crossed the street at the light, and Cody scanned the traffic in either direction. As he did, a soft rain began to fall.

"Buddy . . ." Cody couldn't believe it. Less than a hundred days of rain a year, and today had to be one of them.

"Rain!" Carl Joseph gasped and looked up at the sky. "Daisy! Daisy might get wet!" He reached his hand out toward the church across the street. "Daisy, don't get wet!" Then, before Cody could stop him, he lurched off the curb and straight into oncoming traffic.

In a blur of motion, a van swerved to miss Carl Joseph, but its rear view mirror caught him by the arm and knocked him to the ground. Traffic screeched to a halt, and several drivers laid on their horns.

"Buddy!" Cody ran into the road. Carl Joseph lay on his stomach, sprawled out and unmoving. His arm was bleeding where the vehicle had hit it. "Buddy!" Cody dropped to his knees next to his brother. "Talk to me, Buddy."

The driver of the van, a young guy, was walking toward them, his face pale. "I'm sorry. . . . He jumped right in front of me."

Cody screamed at the guy. "Call 911! Now!"

He lowered his face close to Carl Joseph's. "Buddy, I need you to talk to me."

The rain was falling harder, and after a few terrifying seconds Carl Joseph lifted his head and looked at the church. His cheek was scraped, but otherwise he looked okay. This time he held out his good arm, the one that wasn't bleeding. "Daisy hates the rain."

Cody's eyes filled with tears. "Where are you hurt, Buddy? Tell me."

"In my heart." Carl Joseph heaved himself into a sitting position, oblivious to the traffic stopped all around him. He put his hand over his chest and gave Cody a condemning look. "I hurt in my heart."

Cody carefully helped his brother to the curb. By the time the ambulance arrived, Cody was pretty sure his brother was going to be okay. Physically, anyway. He was given permission to accompany him to the hospital, and the last thing he saw as they closed the door was Elle Dalton and several students on the front steps of the church.

His eyes met hers, and there was no need for explanation. Carl Joseph had been hit by a car, the very thing Cody had feared. But it hadn't happened because of anything Elle Dalton had taught or failed to teach. It was his fault, entirely. Why had he overreacted? So, his brother gave a hundred dollars. . . . They could've talked about it later, at home. Carl Joseph had been having the time of his life—sitting next to Daisy, surrounded by his friends, praying to a God he believed in. What was Cody thinking pulling him from the service like that?

The ambulance took a sharp turn. Cody was thankful that they kept the sirens off. He put his hand on his brother's foot. "You okay, Buddy?"

"Daisy . . ." He covered his face and shook his head. "Daisy needs my coat."

Cody silently cursed himself. "I'm sorry, Buddy."

He lowered his hands and slowly lifted his head enough so that their eyes met. Hurt and betrayal filled Carl Joseph's expression. "I didn't lie, Brother." He rested his head back on the stretcher and began whispering, "Sorry, Daisy. . . . Sorry about the rain."

Cody hated this, hated what he'd just done. Since he'd been home he'd only worked to make Carl Joseph unhappy and uncomfortable. Maybe he belonged back on the circuit, after all. He closed his eyes. If he hadn't pulled his brother from the service, Carl Joseph would be fine. Instead, the accident would likely sway his parents that the doctor was right. Carl Joseph was not suited to a life of independence. And in the big scheme of things, the doctor was probably right. Carl Joseph was safer at home.

After today, the answer would be obvious to everyone in his family. Carl Joseph's days at the Independent Living Center were over.

Chapter Fifteen

Carl Joseph was lying in a big white hospital bed. He stared out the window at the rain. It kept falling and falling but he couldn't help Daisy. He couldn't give her his coat. He didn't even know where she was.

Brother was sitting next to him, but he didn't want

alk to Brother, except sometimes. He looked at him
w. "I didn't lie."

"I know." Brother put his hand on the bed. "I'm
sorry, Buddy. I know you didn't lie."

"I didn't." He looked out the window at the rain
again. "Mom gave me jobs, and I worked for Mom.
'Cause all winter I brought in firewood. Every time
she asked. And I stacked firewood."

"Mom and Dad will be here any minute, Buddy.
Everyone's glad you're okay."

Carl Joseph turned to Brother again. " 'Cause my
heart is not okay. Daisy might get wet."

"I know what you're thinking." Brother stood up
and walked to the door. Then he came back again. His
eyes looked red. "You think this is all my fault, Buddy,
and you're right. It is my fault. I didn't understand
about the gift for Jesus." He breathed hard. "I'm sorry.
I should've let you stay."

"Yes." Carl Joseph nodded. His cheek hurt and it
hurt to turn his neck. "The field trip was not done."

"I know." Brother sat back down in the chair near
the bed. "You didn't want to leave yet."

Carl Joseph touched the owie on his face. He looked
back at the rainy sky. "Daisy might get wet. 'Cause I
tried to get her, but the traffic . . ."

"Daisy is fine. I talked to your teacher. She wanted
you to know that Daisy is not wet, okay?" Brother
sounded sad. "Remember?"

"Yeah, 'cause Daisy might want my jacket." Carl
Joseph saw his parents in the doorway.

His mother took a deep breath and ran to him. "C
Joseph!" She leaned over and hugged him. "I was
worried!"

"Be careful. He has a bruised sternum, Mom."
Brother crossed his arms. He stepped back so Dad
could get in close. "No internal injuries, though. Just
a few bruises."

Carl Joseph looked at his mother. He felt glad to see
her. " 'Cause my heart hurts."

"He's talking about Daisy." Brother leaned in and
looked at her. His voice had a lot of sorry in it. "The
doctor said he's going to be fine."

" 'Cause Daisy might get wet." He pointed at
Brother. "He took my gift for Jesus."

Brother didn't say anything. He just hung his head
down low.

"Carl Joseph"—Mom hugged him again—"I was so
worried about you."

"Me, too." Dad touched his face. The good side.
"Thank God you're okay."

"Yeah, 'cause Brother took my gift for Jesus."

"Okay, well, we'll talk to Cody about that." His
mom kissed his head. She gave Brother a look, and
Dad did, too. Then Mom pointed to the hall and
Brother nodded. She turned back to him. "We need to
talk to Cody. We'll be right out in the hall, and then
we'll come back, okay?"

Carl Joseph didn't want to say it was okay. He didn't
want Mom and Dad to talk to Brother in the hall
'cause that's where they might think of bad news.

Very bad. He felt tears, and he blinked four times fast. Then he looked from his mom to his dad. "Hurry."

They said they would, and they followed Brother out into the hall. Carl Joseph tried to stop the tears, 'cause sometimes kids at school said, "Baby, baby," if he had tears. He looked at the rain and the tears came harder. 'Cause Daisy might get wet and she might need his jacket.

And 'cause Mom and Dad and Brother had bad news in the hall.

Very bad.

HIS PARENTS WAITED until they were far enough away from Carl Joseph's room that he couldn't hear them. Then Cody's father stared at him. "Tell us what happened."

"Was it a seizure?" His mom's face was pale. She gripped his father's arm, and there was a cry in her voice. "The doctor warned us about this."

And like that, Cody had his chance. His parents were afraid, the way he knew they'd be. A week ago, he would've been grateful that finally they had their proof. Evidence that Carl Joseph couldn't make it on his own.

But that wasn't the truth, not now, anyway.

"It wasn't a seizure." Cody folded his arms and looked at the floor. "It was my fault." He lifted his eyes, but instead of finding his voice, he was seized by sorrow. Because of his careless actions, Carl Joseph had nearly been killed.

His father took hold of his shoulder. "Son, it's okay."

"No, it's not." He gritted his teeth. "I've been wrong." He searched his parents' eyes and the entire story tumbled out, every honest detail.

He explained about the incident in the church, how Carl Joseph had placed a hundred dollars in the collection basket. "Which is crazy." He held up his hands. "A hundred dollars?"

Something came over his mother's expression. "Oh, no . . ." She covered her mouth with one hand and shook her head. "I knew about that." Her face was ashen. "I forgot to tell you."

His father looked confused. "I didn't hear about this."

Mary sighed and absently massaged her neck. "Carl Joseph worked for me all winter, bringing in firewood, stacking it, making sure we always had enough to keep the house warm. He made four hundred dollars."

Cody felt his heart sink another notch. "Still . . . he doesn't understand the value, Mom."

"He does." She smiled, but another layer of tears filled her eyes. "He said his gift was half an iPod, fifty bottles of milk, or about four bags of groceries. He told me it was four pairs of jeans or ten T-shirts. He knew how much money it was."

Cody moaned. He let his head fall back against the wall and stared at the ceiling. Why did everything have to be so confusing? No matter how kind Carl Joseph's intentions, a person with so little income-earning potential should never throw a hundred dollars in an offering plate. But did that mean he couldn't live on his own? If living on his own was what he wanted?

"I think . . ." He drew a slow breath and tried to put his thoughts in order. He'd been thinking about this moment since they arrived at the hospital, since he'd known Carl Joseph was okay, and he'd had time to analyze the situation. He looked from his father to his mom. "I see what you mean about the center. I think it might be good for Carl Joseph."

For half a minute his parents only stared at him, mouths slightly open. Then his mother exchanged a worried frown with his dad. "Cody"—she turned her attention back to him—"we've made a decision. Carl Joseph's health is too unsteady."

"We're pulling him from the center."

Cody could hardly believe it. The tables had turned, but after Carl Joseph's accident and the doctor's advice earlier that week, there wasn't much to say. "I don't know about independent living"—he shifted his weight—"but that center's good for Carl Joseph." Angry tears clouded his vision. "He loves it there."

"We've made up our minds." His father's voice was calm, but certain. "Your mother and I have talked about having you work with Carl Joseph."

"You were looking for a way to be more involved, remember?" His mother touched his elbow. "That's what you said when you came home."

Cody didn't respond. Anything he might say would

make him sound delusional. After all, he had wanted safety for Carl Joseph whatever the cost.

They went on about how Cody could teach his brother ranch work, how to help with Ace and how to keep the fence around the property in working order. How to clear land and trim hedges—that sort of thing.

"Eventually he could take over for one of our ranch hands." His father sounded as if he'd been thinking about this for a while. "Carl Joseph could make a living right at home."

"Yes." His mother's tone was hopeful. "I found a program at the park for people with Down Syndrome. Something social, without the goal of independence. Something to help replace the center."

Nothing would replace the center. Cody understood that now. The idea sounded safe. Constructive. But would it give Carl Joseph a reason to look forward to Fridays? Cody's heart ached. He pictured Carl Joseph, the way he'd looked earlier today, basking in the light of his special friend. He peered back toward the hospital room and then at his parents. "What about Daisy?"

"She can visit." His mother's answer was quick. "Her parents can bring her over any time."

"He has friends at the center." Cody's argument was only half-hearted.

"He'll make new friends." His father sighed. "We have no choice, Cody."

Defeat settled in around Cody's soul. He could hardly argue. After the accident, Carl Joseph might need a month before he was stable enough to leave the house. Based on the doctor's advice and today's accident they had little choice, really.

Cody felt his determination build. If this was a season in Carl Joseph's life when Cody could help him get stronger or teach him how to be a ranch hand, so be it. He'd take him to the new classes and help him get stronger. He'd do it to the best of his ability. He owed Carl Joseph that much. Especially after today. His parents' plan might work, even if it wasn't what his buddy wanted.

Now it was only a matter of breaking the news to Carl Joseph.

Chapter Sixteen

Mary Gunner hovered over a stack of dishes in the kitchen sink and watched Cody pound out of the barn on Ace. His frustration was at an all-time high. Mary watched him go, and she felt her anxiety grow. So far the new plan wasn't coming together the way any of them had hoped. She sighed and adjusted the drain plug so it was tight against the base of the sink. Then she squirted dish soap in and around the plates and cups and turned on the hot water.

The old farmhouse didn't have a dishwasher, but Mary had never minded. She enjoyed washing dishes. It gave her time to look out the window at the distant fields and foothills. Here, with her hands in warm, soapy water and her eyes on the endless ranchland, she always believed that somehow everything would work out.

But today she had her doubts.

Carl Joseph had stayed in the hospital overnight while they watched his heart. It had slipped into a weak rhythm after the accident, and his doctor wanted to be sure he was completely back to normal before he came home. By the time they released him, all his tests were fine, and Carl Joseph was ready to go home, ready to get back to his life.

His new life.

That afternoon, she and Mike and Cody sat down to explain the situation to Carl Joseph.

Mike had started the conversation. "We're proud of you, son. You know that." He leaned over his knees and rested on his forearms. He never broke eye contact with Carl Joseph.

"'Cause I'm growing up and Teacher is teaching me." Carl Joseph looked nervous. He shifted his attention from Mike to her, and finally to Cody. "I was on a field trip."

Mary could see the accusation in Carl Joseph's eyes. He might not have confronted Cody, but he was angry. He hadn't acted the same around his older brother since the accident. Cody stared at the old wooden table. Mike cleared his throat. "We have some new ideas for you, son. All of us think they could be a very good change for you."

"Change?" Carl Joseph pushed his glasses up his nose and knit his brows together. "At the center?"

Mary couldn't bear to drag the inevitable out any longer. "Carl Joseph, you're not going back to the center. Not for now, anyway."

"What?" His mouth hung open, and he took a few seconds to stare at each of the faces around him. A loud exasperated sound came from him. He stood and walked a few steps, then he came back and sat down. All the while the shock never left his face. "I like the center."

"But it might not be safe." Mary reached out and held Carl Joseph's hand. "You were nearly killed on Friday."

Carl Joseph stared at Cody for a long time. Then he turned back to his mom and said, "'Cause Daisy might get wet."

"I know." Mary felt her throat get thick. If only there was a way to make Carl Joseph understand.

Mike took over then. "We thought maybe Cody could work with you, teach you how to be a cowboy here on the ranch. That would be a great life skill."

"Brother. . . ." Carl Joseph turned a blank look at Cody. "Brother is not Teacher."

"But I can teach you a lot about working a ranch, Buddy." Cody's voice was tender. "Give it a try, okay? I have some good ideas."

Carl Joseph seemed to sense defeat. He nodded and his shoulders slumped forward. Then, without saying another word, he stood and headed slowly down the hall toward his room.

Mary had replayed the scene a hundred times since then.

Since that day, Carl Joseph had spent a few hours each afternoon learning ranch skills, but his heart wasn't in it. That much was clear to everyone. Mary blew at a wisp of hair. So what was the answer?

She heard the pounding of hooves across the grass out back. Cody came into view, he and Ace flying across the ranch toward the old farmhouse. As they drew closer to the barn, they slowed and came to a stop. Cody was breathing hard, Mary could see that much through the kitchen window. He leaned close to the horse's mane, the way he often did.

All last week, he'd been a different person. Happier, more engaged in conversation. But now . . . now he was the same sad Cody he'd been for the past four years. She studied him, the way he held himself, the way grief still tugged at his shoulders and his jaw line. Poor Cody. He missed Ali so much. The day she died, she took with her so much more than his lung. His excitement and love and laughter. She took those, too. He was lost without her. He wore his sorrow like a thick cloak—especially when he was on Ace.

Mary watched Cody and Ace head back out toward the far fence again. Cody was struggling with more than missing Ali. No matter how he tried, he couldn't find the familiar friendship with Carl Joseph. They hadn't visited the park program yet, but Cody had his doubts. They all did.

She drew a breath and returned to the dishes. Something would have to give soon, because neither of her sons was happy. Carl Joseph mostly kept to his room.

Once in a while Mary would catch him at the computer trying to compose a letter to Daisy. But his frustration generally won out before he finished.

He was missing her badly, and though Cody had called Elle Dalton to inform her of the family's decision to remove Carl Joseph, so far Daisy hadn't been able to come for a visit. Too soon, Elle told Cody. Daisy needed more time to get used to the idea that Carl Joseph wasn't coming back. A visit now would confuse her.

And so these days Mary Gunner didn't stand at the kitchen sink looking out the window admiring the view. She spent her time doing something she'd learned from Carl Joseph.

She prayed.

For healing and hope and love. And most of all she prayed that God would allow the sunshine to break through the clouds that had gathered around their home. Before the sad changes in her sons became little more than a way of life.

As MUCH AS Elle wanted to believe Cody and his parents would change their minds, by Monday there was no denying the obvious. Carl Joseph wasn't coming back to the center.

Elle had asked for a week to convince Cody Gunner, but she'd failed. She could see that when her eyes met Cody's as he sat in the back of the ambulance moments before it pulled away with Carl Joseph inside. Cody had probably convinced his parents before sundown that Carl Joseph couldn't return to the center.

Carl Joseph's accident had been deeply traumatic for Elle's students. She was still trying to reassure them that Carl Joseph was okay, that the accident hadn't done serious damage. The questions about his condition came every hour at first, but by Friday—a week since they'd seen Carl Joseph—the questions had stopped. Even so, nothing was the way it had been. The students entered the classroom more slowly, and the first thing they did was look around and take stock. When they saw that once again Carl Joseph wasn't there, they frowned, wrinkling their brows and muttering his name under their breath.

Of course the one most affected was Daisy.

It was Monday morning and Elle was in the break room, waiting for the students to arrive. Her sister was sitting at the art table, coloring a picture. For a week she'd done almost no talking. She didn't volunteer information when Elle asked a question, and she wasn't enthused about their latest field trip to the bowling alley.

The coffeemaker needed cleaning, so Elle took it to the sink and began rinsing it out. She could remember every detail of her conversation with Cody Gunner, the one that had taken place the day Carl Joseph got out of the hospital.

"We've made a family decision," he told her.

At first she'd been distracted, trying to hide the effect his voice had on her. But then she realized what he was saying. His tone didn't sound harsh or judgmental, the way he'd come across at times before. If she hadn't known better, she'd have thought she heard regret. "Carl Joseph won't be coming back to the center."

And that was that. It served her right, because there was no denying the feelings she'd developed for Cody Gunner. What sort of woman was she? Looking forward to the company of a guy whose wife was sitting at home waiting for him? Elle was disgusted with herself because after a week with Cody, she was doing it again, letting herself fall for the wrong man. Now he would no longer be a temptation. He wasn't coming back, and neither was Carl Joseph.

But where did that leave Daisy?

Her sister still looked at the door every fifteen minutes, longing for Carl Joseph. When the music played, Daisy sat in her seat staring at her hands or looking at a blank part of the wall. All the while Elle allowed her sister to believe that maybe her friend would return

But it was time to tell her the truth. No matter how much she hoped the Gunners would change their minds, they clearly weren't budging. Carl Joseph wasn't coming back.

Elle studied her sister. She would tell her today, after class.

The students were arriving, and Elle went to meet them. But as the day progressed, an undeniable cloud of sadness hung in the air. Even bad-tempered Sid was concerned about Carl Joseph. Sid raised his hand in

219

the middle of an explanation on the new bus route. He didn't wait to be called on. "Has anyone seen Carl Joseph?"

Elle didn't give the others a chance to answer. "He's getting better, remember? He had an accident."

"So . . ." Sid held up his hands. He squinted, the confusion written across his face. "Is he still on the orange bus?"

"No, Sid. He's home getting better."

"He could get better here." Gus looked around for approval. Several of the students nodded and started a chorus of voices agreeing that yes, certainly he could get better just as easily at the center as he could at home.

The rest of the day Elle had trouble keeping them focused. Finally when the last student was gone, she looked around and found Daisy back at the art table. *God . . . how am I going to say this?* Sadness filled her heart and stung at the corners of her eyes. Dear sweet Daisy. She would be devastated by the news.

Her sister didn't seem to notice her approaching, and Elle had a moment to stand behind Daisy before beginning the conversation. Her sister was drawing a picture of Mickey Mouse, each line meticulous, the colors exactly the ones used in the real Mickey.

"Nice, Daisy." She took the seat beside her sister. "I like it."

"Thank you." Daisy didn't look up. She switched the black crayon for a red one and kept coloring. "It's for CJ."

"Oh." The pain in Elle's heart doubled. "I'm sure he'll like it."

"When he comes back." She paused and looked straight at Elle. "For when he comes back."

"Yes." Elle turned her chair so she was facing her sister. "Daisy, I have to tell you something. It's not something I want to say."

Daisy didn't answer, but her head began to bob ever so slightly. When Daisy was frightened, this was always the first sign, long before she was able to articulate what she was feeling. Elle put her hand over Daisy's. "Stop for a minute, okay? I need you to look at me."

Daisy put down her crayon. She turned to Elle, but she didn't lift her eyes. She was still rocking, and now a soft humming came from her throat. Everything about her mannerisms told Elle that she wanted to shut out whatever was about to be said.

Elle wanted to tell her to look up, but instead she took her sister's hands and held them softly. "Carl Joseph is going to stay at home for a while." She had decided this was the best way of putting it, better than to say that her friend was gone for good. She leaned down so she could see her sister's face better. "His brother told me we can visit him."

"CJ wanted to entertain me." Finally she lifted her head. Tears left a shiny layer over her eyes. "He wanted to entertain me at Disneyland. With shortcake." She sniffed. "And dancing at Disneyland."

"I'm sorry, Daisy. Maybe you can still go to Dis-

neyland one day." Elle wanted to hold her close, bu
she needed to be clear at the same time. "Do you
understand? About Carl Joseph?"

Daisy looked around and nervously twirled a piece
of her blonde hair. "CJ isn't here. He's at home."

"Yes. Right." Elle felt her own tears gathering. "He
needs this time."

Daisy cast her eyes back at the picture she was coloring. As she did, a single tear landed with a splash on
Mickey's nose. Daisy tried to rub it, but it only
smeared the black, leaving a smudge at the center of
her artwork. Daisy put her hands to her face and
pushed her chair back.

"Honey." Elle put her hands on her sister's shoul-
ders. "It's okay. Everything's going to be fine. Your
Goal Day is coming, and then you can go visit Carl
Joseph any time you want."

Daisy shook her head. Anger was clearly throwing
itself into her hodgepodge of emotions. She stood and
went to the window, wobbling more than usual as she
walked. When she reached the sill, she braced herself
and stared out at the overcast sky. "Why, God?" she
whispered in a voice that was loud and slurred.
"Why?"

The moment was too heartbreaking. Elle made her
way next to her sister and slipped her arm around her
shoulders. "What, Daisy? Talk to me."

She was crying harder now. She pointed at the sky.
"Sunshine . . . just beyond the clouds." Her eyes found
Elle's. "That's what CJ says."

"He's right." Elle put her fingers to her throat. The lump there made it almost impossible to talk. "In a rainstorm and in life."

Daisy hung her head then and cried like a little child. The sort of gut-wrenching tears that only time could comfort. After five long minutes, Daisy wiped her eyes and pulled away from Elle. She went to the desk, took a tissue, and blew her nose.

Then she moved across the room to the CD player and pushed a few buttons. Glenn Miller's "In the Mood" broke the silence, its rhythmic horns and strings filling the room. Daisy held out her hand the way she'd done when she danced with Carl Joseph on a number of occasions.

This time, though, she kept her eyes on a vacant spot just in front of her. She smiled and took a step forward. Her feet began to move in time to the music, and with both hands up around her pretend partner, she danced across the floor.

They needed to get home, and Elle couldn't take much more. The day was sad enough without watching Daisy dance by herself. She went to her sister and touched her elbow. "Daisy . . . it's time to go."

"But"—she was out of breath—"I'm finding something."

"What, honey?" Elle was about to turn the music off. "What are you finding?"

Daisy stopped, her chest heaving. "Sunshine." She pointed toward the window. "I'm finding sunshine."

Chapter Seventeen

Nothing about his parents' plan was working, but after only two weeks, Cody wasn't ready to give up. Carl Joseph was sulking, missing his friends at the ILC. That was to be expected. Cody missed the routine, too. But maybe if he realized the joy of working outdoors, helping with Ace and checking the fence around their ranch, the pain of missing the center would ease a little.

Working so hard with Carl Joseph had brought about only one benefit so far.

Cody was thinking of Ali less.

Not that she wasn't still there in his heart. She was. But now when he found himself missing someone, more often it was Elle. Her sweet and subtle sarcasm, the way she held her own with him. And her eyes— the way he could get lost in them without meaning to.

It was Monday, start of the third week. Cody walked from his house to his parents', and as he reached the back door he dug down deep for another dose of patience.

Inside, Carl Joseph was sitting at the dining room table. His face almost touched his plate of scrambled eggs.

"Hi, Buddy."

Carl Joseph mumbled something, but he didn't look up.

Maybe it was Cody's imagination, but it seemed that

Carl Joseph was regressing on purpose. As if he were smart enough to know that if he acted disengaged, maybe someone would decide to take him back to the center where he'd been doing so well.

Cody sucked at the inside of his cheek and studied his brother. "I'm going to teach you how to stack hay today, Buddy."

"It might rain." Carl Joseph poked at his eggs. "It might."

"That's okay. Guys who work on ranches have raincoats." Cody had wished more than once that the weather would go ahead and clear up. It was one of the rainiest late springs the area had ever experienced. And every drop reminded Carl Joseph of Daisy and his friends back at the center.

They headed out to the barn, where a neighbor had dropped off twenty bundles of hay. All of it lay in a heap near the entrance to the arena. "Okay, first I'll teach you how to pick up a bale of hay."

Cody positioned himself in front of one of the bales. "Always bend like this, Buddy. You don't want to hurt your back."

"Gus hurt his back one time in cooking class." Carl Joseph turned toward the door, his back to the hay. "One time he did that."

"I'm over here." Cody held his breath. He didn't want his frustration to show in his voice.

Slowly Carl Joseph turned toward him and moved behind a bale of hay. " 'Cause not to hurt my back." He pushed his glasses back into place, spread his legs wide, and bent at the knees. But as he did, he rose up on his toes and lost his balance. He toppled forward and didn't get his hands out in front of himself in time. He hit the hay face-first and fell to the ground. He had hay sticking in his hair and small cuts across his cheeks—including along the newly healed section where he'd gotten hurt in the car accident.

Cody hurried to his side and helped him brush the hay off his shirt and out of his hair. "Not that wide, okay? You can't spread your legs that wide." He helped his brother to his feet. But by then, Carl Joseph was shaking from the fall.

"Fine, let's try something else."

CARL JOSEPH DIDN'T want to learn about the ranch. But he didn't want to say that to Brother or Brother might get mad at him. Also, this was his home, and Brother said boys should help out at home. He would get paid if he could learn all the jobs.

But he didn't want to.

Brother said it could be a break from the prickly hay, but Carl Joseph didn't clap or smile or laugh. 'Cause what about Daisy? What about Gus and Tammy and Sid? What about Teacher and the bus routes and the field trips?

Brother said they were going to fix a fence. So Carl Joseph walked with Brother out across the dirt where Ace liked to run, to a fence at the far back. Brother pointed to a broken part. "See that, Buddy?"

"Yes." He squinted through his glasses. They still

had hay on them. He took them off and rubbed them with his shirt. Then he put them back on. There. "I see that now."

"First thing we have to do is cut a piece of wire." Brother had a roll of something and he knelt on the ground and took cutters from his pocket.

Carl Joseph didn't care about the wire. He sat down on the ground while Brother worked, and he dragged his finger through the soft sandy dirt. Where was Daisy right now? He looked at the sky. It was darker than before. He studied the dirt again. He could write in the dirt. He'd done it before.

"Then you take the wire," Brother was saying, "and you wrap it several times around the post and . . ."

The dirt felt good on his fingers. Better than the hay. Carl Joseph drew lines one way, and then another. Then he erased the lines with his whole hand. Then he had an idea. He began drawing letters in the sand. All the letters he knew how to spell.

"Buddy?" His brother was standing beside him. He sounded upset. "What are you doing? You're supposed to be watching me fix the fence. So you can learn how to do it."

Carl Joseph leaned back so Brother could see better. "I'm writing my favorite letters."

"You are?" Brother moved around so he could see the letters better. "What's it say?"

Carl Joseph felt sadness deep inside. "D-A-I-S-Y. . . . It spells D-A-I-S-Y."

Brother tossed his cutters onto the ground and he

dropped onto his behind. "I know you want to be back at the center, Buddy. I want that, too." He took off his hat and wiped his forehead. "But the doctor says no, and Mom and Dad say no. You need to understand."

"D-A-I-S-Y."

His brother was going to say something, 'cause his eyes looked tired. But then the rain started hard and fast. Carl Joseph gasped and looked at the letters in the sand. He covered them with his body so they wouldn't get wet. So they wouldn't melt.

But then he felt sadder than ever before. 'Cause the rain fell on everything and Daisy might melt. She might get wet and melt. Even if she wasn't the Wicked Witch of the West. Water fell onto his cheeks, but it wasn't from the rain.

"Your teacher will take care of Daisy. She won't get wet."

" 'Cause I'm not there." He covered the whole word "Daisy" with his body. "She might get wet."

"Buddy, what can I do?" His brother breathed out hard. He slid closer on the wet ground. "How can we get you excited about working at home?"

Carl Joseph wasn't sure what Brother meant. He thought and thought, and then he knew what to say. He kept his body over her name, but he looked at Brother's eyes. "Remember Ali, the horse rider?"

Brother pulled up one knee and laid his forehead on it for a minute. "Yes." He lifted his head. "I remember her."

"You miss her, Brother. You said so."

"I do." His brother's voice was quiet. "I miss her a lot."

"That's how I miss D-A-I-S-Y."

Brother looked at him for a long time. Then he said, "I'm sorry, Buddy."

And that's when the rain stopped, and Carl Joseph had an idea. He could pray. So he prayed the rest of the day that maybe sometime soon Brother would take him back to see Teacher and the students and Daisy. Because praying was a life skill.

The most important of all.

ALL ALONG—FROM the start of his parents' plan—Cody figured the club meeting at the park would be a highlight for Carl Joseph. The day dawned warm and sunny, but no amount of small talk about the weather on the ride to the park lifted Carl Joseph's dark mood.

"Are you excited, Buddy?" Cody tried again as they reached the front door of the park building.

"I don't know." Carl Joseph kept his gaze straight ahead.

The two of them walked inside and saw an older man at the front desk. He was busy writing something, but when he noticed them he smiled and stuck his pencil behind his ear. "Can I help you?"

"Yes." Cody wasn't sure where to begin. He decided to keep the explanation simple. "My brother's name is Carl Joseph Gunner. He'd like to take part in the club meeting today."

Next to him, Carl Joseph folded his arms in front of his chest and scowled.

Cody managed a weak smile. "Are we on time?"

"Yes. The others are all here, but they always come a little early." The man was kind; his expression and voice were warm and welcoming. He took a piece of paper from a stack on his desk and handed it to Cody. "Fill this out for him"—he pointed beyond his desk around a corner—"then take him in with the other adults."

Cody took the piece of paper and a pen from the counter. The questionnaire was simple and straight-forward. Name of club member, condition of club member, any health or allergy problems, any behavioral problems, any triggers. Cody answered as quickly as he could.

"Teacher says I should write the words," Carl Joseph mumbled under his breath. The man at the counter took a phone call and didn't notice.

Cody stopped writing and looked at his brother. "The man asked me to fill it out, Buddy." Cody returned to the paper.

At the bottom of the sheet was a contact list, where Cody provided their home number, his cell phone number, and his parents' cell phone numbers. The man was off the phone by then, and he smiled as he took the paper from Cody. He studied it and nodded. "Looks good." He reached out his hand to Carl Joseph. "Welcome to Club!"

Cody held his breath and willed his brother to respond the way he should. Carl Joseph was the kindest person Cody knew. He wasn't used to this new depressed, sulking Carl Joseph. Cody did a nervous laugh to ease the tension of the moment.

The internal struggle Carl Joseph was going through played out on his face. With his arms still folded tightly in front of him, his scowl became a mild frown, and then more of a fearful look. Finally he relaxed his shoulders and his arms released to his sides. He found a tentative smile for the old man. Then he took the man's hand and shook it.

"Good." Relief filled Cody's voice. He gave the man a grateful look. "Thank you." He put his hand on Carl Joseph's back and guided him around the corner. "Come on, Buddy. It's this way."

In the next room, art supplies were set up at a number of tables. Molding clay took up one, paints and paper another, and yarn and felt another. Moving around the room and between the tables were maybe fifteen Down Syndrome people, all ages and sizes.

Sitting at a desk near the back of the room was a woman who looked familiar. Cody led Carl Joseph to her desk, and as he came closer she looked up. In a rush he remembered where he'd seen her before. She was his mother's friend, a woman who used to work at the bank near his parents' house. Her name was Kelley Gaylor, and she and Cody's mom had done volunteer work together over the past few years.

"Mrs. Gaylor . . ." Cody reached out and shook her hand. "My brother's joining the club for today."

"Cody! My goodness. Your mother said you were taking a break from the rodeo circuit. I keep wishing we could hire you to help run our family's thorough-bred farm." She stood and a smile brightened her eyes. She looked at Carl Joseph and came around her desk to greet him. "Carl Joseph, I'm glad you're here."

Cody tried to remember what his mother had said about her friend. She was much younger than his mom, maybe in her late thirties, and very pretty. She was married with three kids, and very involved in charities for children.

And now she was here helping with handicapped adults.

"Did you leave the bank?"

"Yes." She leaned on the edge of her desk. Her blue eyes were filled with a warmth that put Cody at ease. "I'm doing some accounting work for my parents, and spending more time with my kids, and volunteering. Actually this is only my second day working with the club. I was going to tell your mother about it, but . . ." She hesitated. Clearly she didn't want to talk about Carl Joseph with him standing there. She motioned to him. "Why don't you follow me, Carl Joseph? Let's start you off at the painting table."

Cody looked at her desk. There were framed photos of her and her husband, and another of a daughter and two young boys. On the other side of the desk were two framed pictures of beautiful horses. He had finally found the perfect place, led by someone he knew and was comfortable with. What could be better?

He turned his attention to Kelley and Carl Joseph,

making their way to the paint table. Things had been rocky until now, but this place, this club, was exactly what Carl Joseph needed. Maybe his parents were right. Tuesdays here would give him a safe way to be creative and social.

Carl Joseph didn't resist. Maybe because of the woman's gentle approach or because of her compassionate voice. He followed her to the table where the paints were, and she introduced him to another young man who was deciding on a color. Carl Joseph's expression was blank, but he took a piece of paper and a small jar of red paint. Then he sat at a nearby table and began to work. For a long moment, Kelley stayed with him, helping him and making him feel comfortable.

Kelley waited until Carl Joseph was working on his own, then she came back to Cody. She kept her voice low. "Your mother told me Carl Joseph was working with the ILC, heading toward his Goal Day." She looked concerned. "Did something happen?"

Events from the past few months flashed in Cody's mind. Cody explained about the accident and the doctor's suggestion—that Carl Joseph be kept at home where he would be safer in light of his epilepsy.

Kelley was quiet for a moment, but her eyes never left his. "What about Carl Joseph? Does he like being home?"

"He misses the center." Cody's answer was thoughtful. "He's always been the happiest kid. But now he knows about life away from home." He narrowed his eyes and looked at his brother. "The risks are just too great."

Kelley smiled. "All of life is a risk, Cody. Bull riding and loving a sick barrel racer. Giving up one of your lungs." She paused. "You, of all people, should know that."

Her words cut him deep. It took a few seconds for him to catch his breath, and when he did, he no longer wanted to talk. He had figured Kelley would be on his parents' side, but instead she sounded just like Elle Dalton. The way maybe he should've sounded if he'd tried harder to convince his parents that Carl Joseph still needed the center. Cody exhaled. He felt as if he'd aged a decade in the past week. "The club meeting is three hours?"

"It is." She touched his arm. "You can come back then. Don't be upset by what I said. Whatever you and your family decide for Carl Joseph, I'm sure you'll all be fine." She angled her head and looked at the club members. "This sort of outing is the answer for many of them. But for some"—she met Cody's eyes again—"independent living is a very real possibility."

He hesitated. "Thanks."

Cody wasn't sure how he made it out to the parking lot and climbed into his car. He didn't remember any of it. All he could think about was what Kelley Gaylor had said. Cody, of all people, should know that life took risk. So why wasn't he trying harder to be his buddy's advocate? The way Elle Dalton would be if she had a voice in the matter. He started his engine and headed to the mall. He needed a pair of jeans, and he wanted to pick up a few CDs for Carl Joseph. Even when all he wanted to do was get his brother back in the car and head to the center. Because Buddy was going crazy missing the people there.

And just maybe Cody was, too.

Chapter Eighteen

Cody was pulling into a parking spot at the Citadel Mall when his cell phone rang. He checked the Caller ID. *Park and Rec Dept*, it read. His heart skipped a beat. Carl Joseph was fine when he left, but maybe he was having a meltdown, weeping for his friends at the center. He flipped open his phone. "Hello?"

"Cody, it's Kelley." She sounded frantic, breathless. "Carl Joseph's disappeared."

"What?" Cody shouted the word. He felt the blood leave his face. "How could that happen? Have you searched the building?"

"Everywhere. I've called the police. They're on the way." She let out a single sob. "Cody, I'm so sorry. He painted a picture of Minnie Mouse, and he wrote the name Daisy at the top." Her words were choppy, mixed with panic. "Then he asked if he could go outside and look at the park. We have a special yard for our disabled club members. Normally the gate's locked, but today . . . today the maintenance man left it open."

"So he's gone? No one saw what direction he went?" Cody's heart tripped into a crazy fast rhythm. He started his truck and backed out of the parking space. In a frenzy he headed back the way he'd come. "Where have you looked?"

"Around the perimeter of the park." She moaned. "I can't believe this. When he didn't come back after a few minutes, I followed him. The gate was open. How far could he have gotten?"

Suddenly Cody felt an awful possibility explode in his mind. "Is there a bus stop near the park?"

"Yes, of course. Right out—" She gasped. "You don't think . . ."

"Just a minute." Cody jerked the car into the nearest gas station parking lot and did a U-turn. There was only one person who would know the bus routes Carl Joseph might take. He tried to concentrate. "Carl Joseph had his wallet with him. I'm sure he had his bus pass and probably ten dollars."

"What should I tell the police?" Kelley's words came fast, filled with fear.

"Tell them Carl Joseph probably took the bus. I'm heading toward the ILC. Carl Joseph was probably trying to get back to the center."

"How would he know which bus to take?"

Cody forced his head to stop spinning long enough so he could think straight. "His former teacher would know."

"Anything else? I want to get this to the police right away."

"Yes." Cody felt the first tears. His brother was lost somewhere on a city bus. What if he got off and ran into traffic again? Or had a seizure? He pinched the bridge of his nose. "Please, Kelley. Pray for Carl Joseph."

When the call ended, Cody reached the center in record time. They never should've pulled Buddy from his friends. Never. Whatever the consequences of this ordeal, they'd have to sort through them later. In the meantime, Cody was grateful for one very good thing.

There wasn't a cloud in the sky.

He hurried inside, but before he reached the door, he stopped himself. He couldn't disrupt Elle's class. Not after all the damage he'd already caused them. Despite his racing heart, he forced himself to exhale. He opened the door slowly, and immediately his eyes found Elle's. Almost on cue, the students turned their attention to him. Shock filled their faces. Two of them cheered out loud and clapped.

Gus pointed at him. "Carl Joseph's brother!" He grinned big and looked at the others. "Hey, everyone—Carl Joseph's brother! That means Carl Joseph is coming in next!"

"No." Cody kept his tone as gentle as he could. Panic was making it hard to draw a breath. Carl Joseph was missing; he couldn't think of anything else. "Sorry, guys. Carl Joseph isn't here." He shot a desperate look at Elle. "Please . . . can I talk with you outside?"

Elle didn't look pleased, but she must've sensed the

urgency in Cody. She motioned to her aide, and the older woman came to the front of the room. The students were talking all at once, guessing where Carl Joseph might be hiding and whether he was still hurt and why Cody would come without his brother.

"Listen." Elle held up her hand. "I need your attention up here. I'll speak to Mr. Gunner and I'll be right back."

She followed Cody outside the classroom. When the door was shut she turned to him, her expression a mix of confusion and concern. "My students have only today stopped asking every ten minutes about your brother. I've asked if you would call before—"

"Elle, I need your help!" Cody's mouth was dry. His mind was racing, picturing his brother catching a bus to Denver or getting mugged. "Carl Joseph's missing. I took him to the park, to a club meeting, and he left." He paused, horrified. "I think he took the bus."

Her eyes grew wide. "Dear God, no . . ." She took a step back. "Wait here."

Cody stayed outside, but he watched through the window. Elle pulled her aide aside and whispered something.

The moment she was outside, Cody caught her hand and ran with her back to his truck. He tried not to think about how her hand felt in his. All that mattered was his buddy. "You know the bus routes, the ones Carl Joseph knows."

"Yes." She waited until he opened the passenger door. "Get in and drive to Adler Street."

Cody raced around the front of the truck, and as he jumped into the driver's seat he felt a sense of relief. Elle would help him. They'd find Carl Joseph. They had to find him.

Before the unthinkable happened.

CARL JOSEPH FELT bad about what he'd done.

The nice lady, Kelley, was his mom's friend. Carl Joseph remembered her coming to the house. But no one said he had to stay. Cody would come back in three hours. Kelley told him that. Three hours was enough time for a field trip. Teacher said so.

When Carl Joseph went into the yard and out the gate, the bus was just coming. He remembered his wallet. "Every time you go out, Carl Joseph, make sure you have two things with you," Teacher had said. "Your bus pass and ten dollars." So that morning he remembered.

He walked over, and when the bus stopped, he climbed on. All by himself. And the driver was friendly. He asked where Carl Joseph wanted to go. There was no line of people, and no one was pushing him to move along, move along. He licked his lips and pulled his wallet from his jeans pocket. He showed his pass, and then something else. He showed the card from Elle Dalton. The one from the center.

"Here." He pointed at the card. "I want to go to the center."

The man was still friendly. He said to take the bus four stops and then he would say what to do next. Carl

Joseph sat down near a window. 'Cause window seats showed the whole world outside. That's what Gus said every time they had a field trip.

But when Carl Joseph sat down, he felt scared and sad. 'Cause maybe he should ask the driver to call his mom or call Brother. The bus was a big place without any other students. And no Teacher, too. And no Daisy, who knew the bus routes better than all the students put together.

He pushed himself close to the window and tapped his feet. Maybe he would call his mom when he got to the center. She could tell the nice Kelley that Carl Joseph was sorry for leaving. Sorry for not saying good-bye. He pressed his forehead against the glass. It felt hot, so he pulled back.

Then he remembered about the life skill. He closed his eyes. "Dear God, I don't like this." He whispered the prayer. But maybe it was loud because the driver looked back at him.

"You okay, pal?"

"Yes, pal." Carl Joseph sat up straighter. "I'm okay." His heart was pounding hard. "D-A-I-S-Y . . . D-A-I-S-Y." He spelled her name a few times. Very quietly. Then he talked to God once more. "Help me, God. Help me now."

They reached four stops, because the driver stopped the bus. Then he stood up and came back. Carl Joseph was the only person on the bus. "This is your stop."

Carl Joseph stood, but his legs felt shaky. Like after

he rode Ace. He swallowed and pushed his glasses up the bridge of his nose. "What now?"

"Follow me." The driver led him slowly down the middle aisle and slowly onto the steps. On the sidewalk, the driver pointed across the street. "Cross at the light and walk one block. There's a blue bench. Take that bus five stops and you'll be right at the center."

Carl Joseph smiled. See? He could do this. He could take a bus and go see Daisy. He should've done it sooner. Then Brother wouldn't have to work with him so much. It was better when he and Brother were friends. Now Brother was trying to change him. 'Cause he wanted to change him.

Carl Joseph shook the bus driver's hand. "Thank you, pal."

"You're welcome." He hesitated. "You sure you're okay?"

"A-okay." He felt less wobbly. A-okay was what Tammy said. It sounded professional. "Yes, very a-okay."

The bus driver climbed back up the steps of the big bus. Then he closed the door and drove away. Carl Joseph walked six steps, 'cause he counted them. 'Cause counting was a life skill, too. Then he stopped and looked around. Was he supposed to cross straight ahead? Or straight across? He took two steps straight ahead. His heart started to beat faster again.

Then he turned and took three steps toward the other light. He blinked four times. Which way was it? He covered his face with his hands and turned around and around. First one direction, then the other. The bus driver called him Pal. Then what? Which way was he supposed to go?

"Life skills, Carl Joseph," he told himself. "Think of life skills." He parted his fingers and peered out. Two people passing by looked at him. They had scared faces. "Life skills," he told them. "Time for life skills."

The people kept walking. Carl Joseph couldn't hear. His heart was beating too hard, 'cause he didn't like this. He was alone and he was about to cry. But the first life skill was praying, 'cause praying made you remember that . . . that you were never alone! Carl Joseph dropped his hands to his sides and looked up at the sky. Straight up. It was bright blue, no rain at all. "God, I want to go to the center. I forget which way."

He was about to look at the lights again, walk up to each crossing line and decide what to do, when he felt a hand on his shoulder. Maybe it was Brother or his mom. He turned around and right away he covered his face again.

'Cause policemen only came when there was trouble. Big, big trouble.

And right there his eyes started shaking back and forth. Back and forth and back and forth. And his mouth came open and he couldn't say anything. 'Cause his legs and arms were shaking and then he was falling.

And everything, everywhere turned the blackest of black.

Chapter Nineteen

Nearly an hour had passed since Carl Joseph's disappearance, and Elle was out of options. Beside her, Cody was desperate, his eyes wide, terror written into the worried lines on his forehead.

Elle pointed to the stoplight just ahead. "Turn right, there's another bus stop just down the street." Her heart pounded, and she felt sick to her stomach. No matter how hard she prayed, Carl Joseph wasn't turning up. They'd driven three times by every bus stop familiar to Carl Joseph, but there was no sign of him.

"He could be almost to Denver by now." Cody made the turn, and the muscles in his right forearm flexed from the death grip he had on the steering wheel. A raspy sigh slid through his teeth. "It's my fault. I should've stayed with him. Of course he'd try to find a way back to the—"

The ring of Cody's cell phone stopped him cold. He took the wheel with his left hand, grabbed the phone, and flipped it open. "Hello?"

Elle couldn't hear the caller's response, but all at once the tension seemed to leave Cody's body. "Thank You, God . . ." He paused. "We're close. Maybe five minutes."

"He's at the center?" Elle leaned closer, her voice a whisper.

Cody nodded. "Okay . . . yes, we're on our way." He

snapped the phone shut and set it on the seat. Then, as if it were the most natural thing in the world, he took hold of her hand as he sucked in a long breath. "He's safe."

Elle couldn't respond. The feel of Cody's hand in hers burned all the way up her arm, screaming at her to let go. Never mind the high stakes, or how differently things might've turned out. Regardless of the emotion of the past hour, Cody was married. Holding his hand made her the worst of women.

But in that moment she couldn't let go of his hand if her life depended on it. Elle worked to find her voice. "How . . . how did they find him?"

Cody didn't seem to notice her struggle. He focused on the road ahead, and when it was safe he flipped a U-turn. "I guess he boarded a bus and showed the driver your card. Told the guy he wanted to go to the center." Cody glanced at her. Relief shone in his eyes. "He must've gotten confused between buses." He ran his thumb along the side of her hand. The worry was back in his voice. "He had a seizure just as a police officer found him."

Let go of his hand, Elle told herself. But his touch was intoxicating. "He had a seizure?"

"The officer helped him through it. He's with my mom in the parking lot of the center."

Elle tried to picture Carl Joseph on a bus by himself, trying to make a connection without any of the tools or help he was used to. And if he had a seizure, how come the officer hadn't taken him to the hospital? She still had questions, but they would be answered in a minute or so when they reached the center. All of them but one.

Why was she still holding the hand of a married man?

CODY WAS INTENTLY aware of Elle's presence beside him, the faint smell of her perfume, and the way her hand felt in his. In the past hour the underlying connection he'd been feeling toward her, the attraction, had all but consumed him. Even so, while he was still frantic to find Carl Joseph, he didn't dare act on it, didn't consider taking her hand.

Now though, in his relief, he had the overwhelming desire to pull over and take Elle in his arms, hold her, and thank her for caring about Carl Joseph the way she did. But the idea was only a crazy passing thought. Elle seemed uncomfortable, and little wonder. With Carl Joseph's accident, he had never had a chance to tell her how she'd succeeded. How much he believed in her work now that he'd seen it for himself.

In some ways, she must've still seen him as the enemy.

He released her hand as they pulled into the parking lot. His mother was parked in the front row, and Cody took the spot beside her. He turned off the engine and let his head fall back against his seat. "I didn't think it would matter."

"What?" She took hold of the door handle.

He turned so he could see her. "Praying." Awe filled

his heart, his soul. "I prayed from the moment I heard he was missing, and it worked."

She smiled, but it didn't quite reach her eyes. "Praying always works." Her tone was sad, resigned. "Even if sometimes we don't like the answer." She opened the door. "I have to get back inside." She glanced past him to Carl Joseph. "Bring him inside before you go?"

Cody searched her eyes. He didn't want to upset things any more than he already had. "You sure?"

"Yes." She stepped out, but her eyes held his. "Daisy misses him." She hesitated. "A lot. She's become a different person without Carl Joseph."

"All right." He opened his door. "Give us a few minutes."

Elle nodded and then she hurried back inside the center. Cody watched her go, and he realized he'd been holding his breath. She had that effect on him—and there was no denying it. But even with his lack of experience he could easily read her.

She wasn't interested.

He climbed out and knocked on Carl Joseph's car door.

His brother jerked around and his eyes grew wide. He flung his door open, hurried out. Then, all at once, shame and sorrow seemed to hit him. "I'm sorry, Brother. 'Cause I didn't ask first." Carl Joseph shook his head, his mouth hanging open as if he couldn't find the right words. He pushed his glasses back into place. "I'm so, so sorry."

Cody couldn't take another moment. He pulled his brother into his arms and held him tight. "Buddy . . . I'm so glad you're okay." The hug lasted a long time, and when Cody released him, he put his hands on Carl Joseph's shoulders and stared straight into his eyes. "This wasn't your fault, Buddy. I never should've left you."

"No." Carl Joseph shook his head, a little at first and then more strongly. "No, 'cause the driver said, 'You okay, pal?' and I told him yes and then I wasn't sure to cross that way." He pointed straight ahead. Then he pointed out to the side, "Or that way. And so no, Brother, it isn't your fault."

Their mom was out of the car now. She came up and put her arms around both of them. "Did Elle say we could stop in?"

"Yes." Cody wasn't sure what was going to happen next for Carl Joseph. He wanted to hear more about his seizure, and another doctor's visit was already set up for tomorrow morning. His mom had told him that much when she called. But for now, they needed to get inside because that's what his buddy wanted.

Badly enough that he'd risked his life to get here.

The three of them walked toward the center door. Through the window they could hear the sounds of swing music and happy laughter. Clearly the students had been spared news of the ordeal.

"I'll get it." Carl Joseph seemed slower than usual, but he stepped in front of Cody and their mother and held open the door.

A swing dance session was in full progress inside. All except for Daisy. Carl Joseph's friend was sitting at an art table in the far corner of the room, alone. Cody's heart sank. Daisy was the most sociable student in the class. Her solitary behavior could be caused by only one thing.

Elle looked over, and immediately her face lit up. "Carl Joseph!" She smiled and hurried toward him. All signs of the regret and sorrow she'd shown earlier were gone. She took Carl Joseph into her arms and hugged him. "Are you okay?"

"I am now." He grinned at Elle and then at the students, who were one at a time stopping and turning toward him. "I wanted to come here really bad. 'Cause here's where I get my goal one day. Where I grow up like a man." He moved closer to Elle and lowered his voice to what he must've thought was a whisper. "I can't grow up around Brother."

Elle shot a sympathetic look at Cody.

Cody wanted to shout at both of them that he was on their side. But it wasn't the time. Besides, he was still stinging from Carl Joseph's words, playing them again in his mind. *I can't grow up around Brother.* No wonder Carl Joseph had been difficult the last few weeks.

Carl Joseph was going on about how happy he was to be back. "I missed this place bad, Teacher!" Carl Joseph nodded fast. "Really bad."

"That's for sure." Their mother looked exhausted, but she was smiling. She leveled her eyes at Elle. "Thank you . . . for everything."

Elle's smile softened. She patted Carl Joseph's shoulder just as someone turned off the music. A chorus of voices began talking all at once, the students calling Carl Joseph's name and clapping their hands. Elle raised her voice so she could be heard over the noise. "Your classmates have missed you. Especially one of them."

Carl Joseph laughed, the loud lovable open-mouthed laugh Cody hadn't heard around the house since the accident. "D-A-I-S-Y!"

"Yes, that's the one." Elle led the way to the back of the classroom.

Cody was drained from the scare. He hung back with his mother while Elle linked arms with Carl Joseph and walked him to the students. It took a few seconds, but a chain reaction started.

Gus covered his mouth with both hands and then slid them along the side of his face to the top of his head. He danced in a circle and raised both arms high. "Carl Joseph is back!" He looked at the others and motioned for them to follow. "Carl Joseph is back, everybody!" He ran toward Carl Joseph so fast he tripped. Three other students helped him up, and just like that, Cody watched his brother become sur-rounded by the support of his friends.

Sid frowned at Carl Joseph. "You should never go that long without coming to class." But after a few seconds, he smiled, too. "Never again, Carl Joseph."

Some of the students were jumping in place, clap-ping and laughing and talking all at the same time.

"We have a new bus route! You have to know the new bus route."

"Look at my haircut, Carl Joseph. Hair-cutting is a life skill!"

"We cooked asparagus, so now you can cook asparagus if you want asparagus."

Those who weren't shouting came up and patted Carl Joseph's back. A few of them thanked him. "Finally our class is together again." Tammy swung her long braids one way and then the other. "Thank you for coming back, Carl Joseph!"

Only then did Cody see Daisy. She had left the art table, and now she was walking up to the group. Her mouth hung open, and tears streamed down her face. At the same time, Carl Joseph seemed to take inventory of the faces around him, and he must've realized who was missing. In a sudden frantic burst of motion he made one half turn and then another, until finally he saw her coming closer. He smiled bigger than Cody had seen since he'd been home.

"Daisy . . ." He parted the circle of friends and ran to her, arms outstretched, big oaflike steps, all the way across the room.

But Daisy didn't run to meet him. She hung her head and kept crying, stifling quiet sobs as Carl Joseph made his way to her. Cody and his mother drew nearer so they could hear.

"Daisy, what's wrong?" Carl Joseph put his hand on her shoulder. "I'm here now."

"You . . . left me." Her words were hard to understand through her deep emotion. She looked up and her nose was red, her cheeks wet. "I didn't know where you were. Even when it rained."

Carl Joseph's eyes grew wide and his lips parted. Cody understood the shock and regret in his expression. He had let his friend down and he felt terrible, wracked with guilt. He released a quiet gasp. "I'm sorry, Daisy. I wanted to be here. I did."

She seemed to grow calmer in light of his explanation, but still there was something in her expression. Hurt and betrayal. And it was then that Cody felt the pain of Carl Joseph's last several weeks worst of all. What had they done, keeping him away from the center? Away from Daisy and Elle and Gus and everyone here?

Elle caught his eye. Then, dabbing at her own cheeks, she approached him and his mother. "I know you don't agree, but"—she looked at Carl Joseph and Daisy—"he belongs here." She hesitated, clearly struggling with her emotion. "He needs this."

Their mother looked at Carl Joseph, at the way he had both his hands on Daisy's shoulders now, how he was looking straight into her eyes, trying to convince her that he hadn't meant to be gone, that he had missed her as much as she missed him. The wounded look in Daisy's eyes was fading. She gave Carl Joseph the slightest smile. Mary touched her fingers to her throat and turned her attention back to Elle. "You're right." Her voice cracked. "But his health . . . I don't know how we can do it."

The other students made their way over to Daisy and Carl Joseph. By then Daisy was smiling, and Carl Joseph was doing a silly dance trying to make her laugh.

"Please, Mrs. Gunner. I know of other doctors you can talk to." She swallowed, as if she didn't want to overstep her bounds. "Please consider it."

His mom seemed overwhelmed by the idea. But she nodded. "We will."

Cody could've kissed Elle Dalton right there. That was the answer! Another doctor, one who was more open to advancements for sick people with Down Syndrome. He didn't say anything, because he couldn't. He was too mesmerized by the young teacher standing there, talking to his mother.

Before they left, Cody pulled Elle aside. "Thank you." He studied her. Something in her eyes closed off whenever they were close like this. He swallowed a ripple of frustration. "For helping me look, but also for caring."

"Of course." She took a step back and motioned to her students. "I need to go. Maybe . . . maybe we'll see Carl Joseph sometime soon."

"Maybe." He wanted to ask her what was wrong, but he resisted. "My parents . . . They have a meeting with his doctor tomorrow."

"Well, then . . . I guess, have them call me." She gave him a professional smile. Then she returned to her students.

On the way home that afternoon, while Carl Joseph

rattled on about Daisy and Gus and Sid and Teacher, Cody couldn't stop thinking about Elle. His feelings weren't caused only by her eyes or the way he felt when he was near her. More than that, it was her love for her students. Her dedication and concern for Carl Joseph. In the hour they'd spent together looking for his brother, she'd taken hold of Cody's heart with an intensity he'd known just one other time in his life. He didn't have to wonder about his feelings for Elle Dalton, not anymore. Today they were as clear as the sky over Colorado Springs. There was only one problem, and it consumed him the rest of the day and into the evening. He'd left a first impression bigger than Pike's Peak.

And now—no matter what he tried—he wasn't sure there was any way around it.

Chapter Twenty

The appointment with the specialist brought more bad news.

When the three of them got home from Denver that evening, Cody's father found him out back in the barn and told him the details. An MRI proved that a degeneration was happening in Carl Joseph's brain. He would be prone to more and stronger seizures, and worse, he was at high risk for a stroke.

"Between that and his heart disease, he might not have long. A few years. Five, maybe." His father's eyes were red and swollen. "So we've made our decision. Carl Joseph has to stay here, where we can care for him." His dad took a quick breath and looked up, fighting a wave of emotion. When he had more control, he searched Cody's eyes. "We want to talk to Elle about having him visit the center. Maybe once a week."

Cody reached out and steadied himself against the nearest wall. This couldn't be happening, not to Carl Joseph. Losing Ali was enough loss for a lifetime. They couldn't give up, couldn't simply accept the diagnosis when maybe there was something they could do. He swallowed his disbelief and let his hands fall to his sides. "Elle says she knows another doctor . . ."

"The tests don't lie, Cody." His father gave a sad shake of his head and then moved toward the barn door. "I'm going back inside. Your mother's having a hard time."

When he was gone, Cody tried to draw a full breath, but he couldn't. His one lung fought against the news, against the shock ripping through him. So that was it? Carl Joseph was doomed? There had to be another answer, a way for his buddy to accomplish the goal that mattered so much to him.

The one Carl Joseph didn't think he could reach working alongside Cody.

There was only one place Cody could take all the feelings crowding his heart. Out to the fields with Ace. He hadn't been on the horse in three days, too caught up with Carl Joseph to find even an hour to ride. Now he straightened and adjusted his baseball cap, saddled the horse, and climbed on.

"Let's go, Ace." He blinked back tears. "I need you to run today."

A warm wind blew over his parents' ranch, and it carried with it memories of everything that was gone from his life. Everything that would never be again. His days of bull riding, and his time on the rodeo circuit, and Ali. He breathed deep and peered at the still blue sky. He stopped and let his sadness come to the surface.

He walked Ace out to the trailhead. June evenings in Colorado Springs were always beautiful and this one was no exception. It was eight o'clock and he still had half an hour before sunset. The old horse was still as strong and proud and faithful as he'd been when Ali rode him at one barrel-racing event after another, week after week, season after season. The vision of Ali tearing around the barrels on Ace stayed with him still. The way it would forever.

Cody patted the horse's neck. "Atta boy, Ace." He leaned forward and in a sudden rush he shouted, "Giddyup!"

A strong whinnying came from the horse and Ace set off at a trot that quickly became a full run. The pace fit his mood, made him feel that somehow they could outrun the bad news about Carl Joseph, outrun the ways things had gotten worse for his brother in the weeks since he'd been home.

Usually, riding like this made him think only of Ali,

but not so today. With the wind in his face and Ace pounding out a timeless rhythm beneath him, Cody could only think of his brother and the teacher who had given his buddy a chance to truly live.

Elle Dalton.

The sun was making its way toward the mountains, casting that surreal final splash of light against the cactus and shrubs that dotted the back acreage of the property. Cody leaned back and let the rays hit his face, as if the warmth might find its way to the cold dark places of his heart. Gradually, Ace slowed to a walk.

"So, Ace . . ." He rubbed the horse's mane. "Carl Joseph, too."

The horse took a few steps, then stopped and ate from a patch of grass.

Carl Joseph was dying. Not today, but soon. Cody stared as far as he could toward the horizon. Carl Joseph, his buddy. The kid who had adored him since he was old enough to crawl. The one who wanted to be a bull rider so he could be a little more like Cody. Dying from something Cody couldn't understand, let alone help.

If he was at risk for a stroke, then every day would represent danger to Carl Joseph. Cody settled back in the saddle and drew a full breath. What had Kelley Gaylor said yesterday morning? Cody of all people should know about taking risks.

At least a hundred times since the nightmare of losing Carl Joseph, Cody had played one particular noment over in his mind. Yesterday as he walked into the recreation center, he had been struck by something that hadn't dawned on him until after Carl Joseph disappeared. The young adults at the club meeting were entirely different from the students at Elle Dalton's Independent Living Center.

At the club meeting, people with Down Syndrome were given crafts and simple books and time to visit. But they wore blank expressions on their faces and seemed almost despondent. No challenge was presented, no learning. Just a way to pass the time together. Something to set apart Tuesday from Wednesday. It wasn't Kelley Gaylor's fault. The club wasn't designed to teach independence or give its members a goal.

Cody stroked Ace's neck again, and the horse lifted his head. There weren't many horses like Ace. He could sense a person's feelings, a person's mood. Now, for instance, when Cody wanted to wrestle with his feelings, Ace was content to graze and take only a few small steps in either direction. And when Ali was sick, when Ace could tell her breathing wasn't right, he would lift his head high, giving her something to rest against until she caught her breath.

Cody looked at his wedding ring, the simple white gold band he still wore. If Ali were alive today, if she were here with him, well enough to ride across the back field with him, he knew without a doubt what she would say about Carl Joseph's situation.

Ali and her sister were both born with cystic

fibrosis, and for the first decade of their lives they stayed indoors. Their parents bought special air filters and did everything possible to keep allergens and dust from entering. Ali and her sister would sit by their bedroom window and dream of running across the grassy hills and over to the neighbor's barn and the horses he kept there.

Ali rode horses even after her doctor told her it would take years off her life to do so. She rode because she wanted to live her life, not sit it out. Ali was a dreamer and a doer, and if she had known Carl Joseph longer, she would've been supportive of the ILC from the beginning, and she would've cheered its purpose.

Even when she knew her death was coming, she lived every day, every final moment to the fullest. He pictured Elle Dalton and her tireless work with Carl Joseph and the other students. Elle wasn't so different from Ali, really. They both understood that risk was a necessary part of living.

Cody gave a light nudge with the reins, and Ace started walking back to the barn. One autumn, a year before she died, Ali was walking beside Cody in the mountains when she stopped and stared at a tree whose leaves were brilliant red with just a hint of gold.

"Funny, isn't it?" She picked up a red one from the ground. "A leaf's most beautiful days are at the very end, just before it dies."

He had listened, watching her, memorizing her.

"Sort of like me." She met his eyes, leaned up, and kissed him. "These are the most beautiful days of all, Cody. The ones I want you to remember."

The sun was behind the hills now. Streaky pinks and pale blues filled the sky. He'd had enough loss to last him a lifetime, without having something happen to his younger brother. But it would be worse to watch him waste away at home, having never done even the simplest things he dreamed of doing.

Maybe he could move out with Carl Joseph, and the two of them could live together. That might make things a little safer for Carl Joseph. But as soon as the thought crossed his mind, his doubts overshadowed it. He and Carl Joseph were better off with the friendship they used to share. His buddy didn't want him acting as the teacher. He wanted to do things on his own. Cody would only hold him back.

Cody sucked in another breath of sweet early night air.

Then there was the phone call he'd gotten earlier today. A vice president from the network had phoned. Apparently, Cody's agent had given a verbal commitment that Cody would return to the circuit.

"We could use you, Gunner," the man told him. "The fans love you. I need an answer by the end of the week."

An ache filtered through his chest. In the end, it probably made the most sense to go back. Bull riding was what he knew, what he was good at. And it would take him away from Elle Dalton—a woman who clearly wasn't interested. Either way, his decision about the circuit didn't matter nearly as much as the one his parents needed to make, the one about Carl Joseph's future.

Cody pressed his heels lightly to Ace's side, and the horse began to gallop. He released the tension on the reins, and Ace moved into a full run. The details weren't clear, but somehow he had to change his parents' minds. Cody leaned down close to Ace's neck and squinted against the wind. Carl Joseph would tell him to pray about it. And prayer had certainly helped yesterday. He was getting closer to the barn, and in the fading sunlight he could see someone standing near the back of the house. As he came nearer, he saw it wasn't one person, but three. Carl Joseph and . . . He strained forward, trying to make them out, until finally, he knew. His heart skipped a beat and he sat up straight in the saddle.

It was Elle Dalton and her student, Daisy.

Chapter Twenty-one

Elle couldn't take her eyes off Cody. The way he looked in the fading sunlight, flying across the field on the beautiful palomino. Together they made a picture of strength and grace and beauty. She wasn't here to see Cody, but it was impossible not to look.

She turned away and watched her sister and Carl Joseph, slow dancing on the fresh-cut grass. Carl Joseph's mother had called with the news, and Daisy had heard her half of the conversation.

"CJ is sick?" Daisy had tugged on her arm. "Is he sick, Elle? Tell me if he's sick."

Elle held her finger to her lips and gave her sister a sharp look. But Daisy wouldn't be ignored. Finally, Elle had to ask Carl Joseph's mother to hold on while she explained to her sister that CJ was okay. A discussion of epilepsy could come later.

"Take me to him, Elle . . . I have a Minnie picture for him. Please!" Daisy tugged on her again. "Please, Elle!"

Finally, Elle relented. "Would you mind if Daisy and I came by after dinner?"

Carl Joseph's mother sounded tired, but she said she was grateful for the offer. "We could all use a reason to smile."

Elle had another reason for coming to the Gunner house tonight. She wanted to meet Cody's wife. She scanned the area adjacent to the driveway. Was his wife here? According to Carl Joseph, Cody was home for six weeks. So where was his wife? Did she stay back in whatever city Cody had come from?

The pieces of his story didn't add up.

She heard Cody's horse getting closer, so she shifted back toward the pasture and watched Cody ride into the barn. The news about Carl Joseph must've been devastating for him. If he was hurting, she had to be especially careful. His behavior yesterday when he held her hand, and the way she enjoyed it, still burned in her conscience. She wouldn't cross that line again today.

A few feet away, Carl Joseph was explaining the situation to Daisy. "Brother has to put Ace in there 'cause it's bedtime." He was talking loudly, probably trying to impress Daisy with his horse knowledge.

"But horses don't lay down to sleep, right?" Daisy was standing next to Carl Joseph, leaning against his arm.

"'Cause they don't have beds." He laughed hard, and she did, too. "Isn't that funny, Daisy? 'Cause horses don't have beds."

Cody came out of the barn toward them. The closer he came, the more Elle was sure she could see something different in his eyes, something that hadn't been there before. A compassion and empathy that seemed directed straight at her. She felt her guard go up. *He's married, Elle . . . Don't be crazy. God, help me keep my head.*

"Hi." He folded his arms and looked at Daisy. "I see your teacher took the long way home."

Daisy laughed. "I'm not allowed to call her Teacher after class."

Suddenly Elle realized how little Cody knew about her. She moved closer to Daisy and took her hand. "Daisy's my sister." She looked at Cody. "You didn't know that?"

Cody's expression went blank, and then filled with wonder. "You're her . . . she's your . . ."

Cody was clearly shocked by the news, but more than that, he seemed touched by it. Elle allowed a nervous laugh. How had she missed telling him this detail before? They would've found common ground on the issue of independent living so much sooner.

He was still looking at her, searching her eyes, when Carl Joseph walked up to him and tugged on his denim shirtsleeve. "Brother, look at this." He held out a painted picture. "She drew me Minnie Mouse." The painting was meticulously done, and at the top, Daisy had written, *Daisy wants CJ to come back.*

A smile lifted the corners of Cody's lips. "It's beautiful." He winked at Daisy. "Nice work."

"Thanks." She was beaming. Whatever ill feelings she had had toward Cody Gunner, they were gone now. Daisy pulled a picture from behind her back. "And look what CJ gave me. Mickey for D-A-I-S-Y. And that's the very best gift of all."

Again Cody appreciated the artwork, and the painstaking way that Carl Joseph had spelled out Daisy's name across the top. Her name was still one of the few words he could consistently spell correctly.

Carl Joseph said something quiet to Daisy, and the two of them laughed again. Elle took the moment to approach Cody. *Keep it professional*, she told herself. She crossed her arms. "Can we talk?"

"Sure." He walked a few yards away from their noisy siblings, and she followed. "My mom told you, huh?"

"Yes. His diagnosis isn't good." Elle kept her distance.

Cody put one foot up on the split-rail fence. It wasn't dark, but shadows were falling across the yard.

Cody stared into the distance, heartbreak glistening in his eyes. "Just when he was starting to really live."

The back door of the house opened, and Mrs. Gunner stuck her head out. "I sliced up some apples," she called. "Carl Joseph, maybe you can bring your friend in for a snack."

Carl Joseph cupped his hands around his mouth. "Apples all alone or with peanut butter?"

"Peanut butter." There was a laugh in Mrs. Gunner's voice.

"Goodie!" Carl Joseph clapped loudly and took Daisy's hand. "Come on, Daisy . . . 'cause my mom makes the best apples and peanut butter in the whole Rocky Mountains."

Elle watched them skip toward the back door and disappear into the house. She moved a step farther away from Cody. Though the night was warm, a shiver passed over her arms. The song of faraway crickets mixed with the breeze and heightened her awareness of Cody a few feet away. She tried to concentrate. "The other doctor . . . he has methods for helping patients remember to take their medicine. Ways an epileptic patient can be certain not to forget."

Cody studied her, and for a while he said nothing. Then he leaned back again on his elbows. "You're uncomfortable around me."

It wasn't a question, so at first Elle wasn't sure how to respond. But anger mixed with her curiosity and she put her hands on her hips. "Which might be a good thing, don't you think?"

Cody wiped his brow with the back of his hand, but his eyes stayed locked on hers. "Because you still think I'm your enemy?"

"No." A sound came from her that was part laugh, part frustration. "Because of your wife."

Disbelief flashed in Cody's eyes, and then faded. He opened his mouth to say something, but then he must've changed his mind because he pushed away from the fence and took three steps toward the barn. He stopped and slowly faced her again. "You're serious?"

Elle prided herself on being in control of a situation. But she had clearly lost all sense of it here. What was he implying? That he wasn't the least bit interested, or that it was okay for the two of them to have feelings for each other despite the fact that he was married?

She exhaled in a huff and moved a few feet closer. "Of course I'm serious. I never hear about her, Cody." She looked back at the house and tossed her hands. "So where is she? What's her name?"

This time an undeniable sorrow colored his expression. "Her name's Ali." He stuck his hands in his jeans pockets and his voice fell a notch. "She died four years ago."

Elle felt her heart sink to her knees. "What?" Her voice was a whisper, the news hitting her in waves. All these weeks? The whole time she'd been assuming he was married, when . . . "Cody . . ." She covered her face, mortified and humiliated and broken because of the loss the man across from her had faced. She let her hands fall slowly to her sides. "I'm so sorry."

Absently, he rubbed the ring on his left hand. "Maybe you and I need to take a ride."

Elle wasn't sure where to or how long they'd be gone. But she wanted to go wherever Cody Gunner might take her, and she wanted to know his story, wanted to understand every detail.

Because maybe then she would understand the man behind it.

CODY WASN'T SURE whether to laugh or cry.

It was his wedding ring, obviously. That and maybe something Carl Joseph had said. But either way now he finally understood the way she'd felt around him. She thought he was a married man. Of course she hadn't acted interested. Not that it mattered much now, because he was going back to the circuit. His life would be on the road, and hers would be here with her students.

But he still wanted the next hour or so to clear the air.

He led her to his pickup and opened the passenger door. When he was behind the wheel, he started the engine and drove through a gate on his parents' property. "There's a road along the side of our ranch. . . . It leads to a bluff." He drove slowly along the dirt road. "From there you can see a million stars."

The ride took only a few minutes, and then Cody parked and grabbed a flashlight from his glove box. As he did, his hand brushed against her knee. He tried not to notice, but it was impossible. They climbed out and he took her hand, using the flashlight to navigate the path the last fifteen feet to an outcropping of rocks at the top of a small hill.

He waited until she was seated before releasing her hand and turning off the flashlight. For a few seconds he said nothing, just let the warm breeze wash over him, clearing the air between them. He leaned back on his hands and looked up. A carpet of stars covered the sky. "See . . . the first time I found this place at night— about a year ago—I thought it must be a little bit what heaven's like." His voice was quiet, gentle.

"It's beautiful." Her teeth chattered and she rubbed her arms.

"Cold?" He started to get up. "I have a sweatshirt in the back."

"No . . ." She touched his arm. "I'm fine . . . just . . . just shocked." She pulled her knees up to her chest. "About your wife."

"You saw my ring?"

"That. And Carl Joseph told me you were married." Her sad smile was just barely visible in the light of the stars. "He said your wife was a horse rider. Of course he said you were a bull rider."

"Ali was a barrel racer." His voice grew softer. "One of the best ever."

Elle shifted so she was facing him. "Really? Professional rodeo?"

"Yes." He tried not to picture her, the way she had looked tearing around the barrels. "Buddy was right about me, too."

"You're a bull rider?" Elle sounded embarrassed, frazzled. "Wow . . . what else have I missed?"

"I rode bulls full-time for a while. Gave it up a year after Ali died." He smiled. "Carl Joseph will always see me as a bull rider, but these days I work the shows. Keeps me involved."

"So . . . you met her through the rodeo."

"I did. I was the first person outside her family who knew she was sick." The sound of an owl drifted on the breeze from a few hills over. Cody felt Elle shiver again, and this time he didn't wait for her to refuse. He popped up, turned on the flashlight, and took long strides back to the truck. He grabbed the sweatshirt, jogged back up the hill, and handed it to her. "Wear this."

She slipped it on, and in the process she moved closer to him. "She was sick? That's how she died?"

"She had cystic fibrosis." He hadn't told Ali's story for a long time. Doing so now made his time with her seem far removed. Almost as if it had happened to someone else.

"CF." Elle sighed, and for a few seconds she was quiet. "I did a paper on it in college." She faced him again. "You knew, then, when you married her . . ."

"Yes." He wasn't sure he wanted to tell her the rest of the story, but he'd come this far. He drew a steady breath. "I gave her one of my lungs."

"Cody . . ." A quiet groan came from her. "You gave her a lung, and it didn't work?"

"It worked." He had no regrets; he never would. "The

268

doctors told us the transplant would buy her three years, and it did." He paused. "About a thousand tomorrows."

Elle's eyes glistened. "The way you love your brother . . ." She sniffed, sadness spilling into her voice. "I understand better now."

"I can't imagine losing him." Cody turned his gaze up toward the stars. "But I can't imagine him spending his last years at home watching Nickelodeon, either." He reached for her hand. "He has to get back to the center, Elle. Help me find a way."

"I will." She didn't sound convinced. "I guess I had that wrong, too."

"You thought it was me—that I was standing in Buddy's way?"

"Yes. I mean"—she seemed flustered again—"I knew it was your parents' choice, but I figured after the accident you talked them into pulling him out."

"No." He nudged her shoulder, playing with her. "You asked me for a week, and you did it."

"Really?" Their arms were touching again.

"Yeah." The feeling was back, the intoxicating sense of her nearness. "You proved that my brother needs to be there. Whether he's sick or not."

"Think your parents will let him go?"

"I'm not sure." Cody remembered his father's tone from earlier. "They're worried. I even thought maybe I should stay and live with him."

"Hey"—she angled her head—"that's a great idea."

"Except Carl Joseph's never been more frustrated with me than in the last few weeks." Cody gave a single laugh. "He basically told me I wasn't you."

"Oh." Her tone was lighter than before. "I think there's a compliment in there somewhere."

"There is." He tried to look deep into her eyes, but the darkness wouldn't allow it. "You're amazing with your students, Elle. It makes sense now that I know about Daisy."

"Mmm. There's a special sensitivity that comes with having a sibling with Down Syndrome."

"Definitely."

A quiet fell between them again, and Cody broke it first. "I'll be going back on the road again in a week or so. That way Carl Joseph won't feel like I'm watching over him."

"Oh." Her disappointment was subtle, but clear. "I'm not sure about that. I mean . . . I think he needs you more than you know."

"He needs you and your center." Cody smiled. "I know that much." It was getting later, and Daisy and Carl Joseph would be wondering where they went. He stood and took her hand, helping her to her feet. "Thanks for talking."

She faced him, her hand still in his. "I'm sorry about Ali."

Cody gave a slow nod. He shifted his lower jaw and looked away for a moment. "We all are."

"It's why . . . you're so protective of Carl Joseph."

"It is." His eyes found hers again. "I guess we both understand each other a little better now."

"I guess we do."

・ ・ ・

CODY HELD HER hand all the way to the truck before letting go. Elle was quiet, leaving some space, some time. They rode back to the house, and when they went inside Daisy and Carl Joseph were dancing, humming something that didn't sound like any swing music Elle had ever heard. She smiled. "I like seeing them together."

Cody didn't say anything, but his eyes shone a little brighter as he watched their siblings. "He missed her."

"Same at our house." She drew a deep breath. She could hardly believe the turn of events tonight, or the rollercoaster of emotions she felt. The man she could feel herself falling for wasn't married, but single. Only now he was determined to stay on the road working for the rodeo? She couldn't imagine telling him good-bye in a week.

The idea hit her on the way back to the house. Actually, it was Daisy's idea, something she'd mentioned earlier today after school: "CJ wants to entertain me at Disneyland. But here's what I think." Her voice was determined, as if she'd given a lot of thought to whatever was coming next. "I think a hike first. First a hike, Elle. Wouldn't that be nice?"

Elle stayed by Cody's side, watching her sister. *Come on, Elle . . . You can do this* "So, I have this favor to ask you."

He angled his head, and she saw a teasing in his smile. "Elle Dalton . . . asking a favor of me?" He took off his baseball cap and tucked it beneath his arm.

271

His reaction set her at ease. "Yes. Actually, I have this sister who's practically desperate to go hiking with her friend CJ." She raised her eyebrows. "And my guess is they'll both need a little help for a trip like that."

He laughed. "So maybe the four of us might be better?"

"Exactly."

"Well, I'll tell you what." Cody's smile was easy-going and tinged with just a hint of sadness. "If the doctor says my brother's up for a hike—even from the parking lot to the first trail sign—we'll do it this Sunday afternoon." He gave her a light nudge again. "How's that sound?"

"Like I'm going to have one very happy sister on my hands."

He led the way over to Carl Joseph and Daisy. For a few minutes more, the four of them talked and laughed about horses' having beds and whether—if they did—they would have to take off their shoes. Finally, Elle put her arm around her sister's shoulders. "We'd better get going. It's late."

Long after they left that night, Elle replayed her time at the Gunner house. She saw Cody riding in on the palomino, the look in his eyes when he saw her, and the way he treated her with a new level of camaraderie once he understood that Daisy was her sister.

She had felt more emotion sitting on the bluff next to Cody than she'd felt in years. She couldn't get over his story, the way he'd sacrificed out of love for Ali, and all he'd given up, all he'd lost along the way.

As she pulled into the driveway, she was practically desperate to keep her strange new feelings from her mother. Daisy was perceptive, but she didn't recognize more than the fact that her big sister was happy. Her mother would be harder to fool.

She couldn't talk about Cody with her mother, not when she could barely identify the way she was feeling. Was she falling for him? And what was the point if he was leaving? She didn't want to have feelings for a man she could see only a few times a year. But maybe—if God allowed it—Cody might stay. She could ask God every night for the next week to keep him here, to convince him that he should run the fitness center when it opened adjacent to the center.

But what then? Could her heart even remember how to take this walk? If so, she wasn't sure she'd be brave enough to follow.

All she knew was that the stars shone a little brighter tonight and the place on her arm where he had touched her felt a little warmer. Her heart felt lighter, and she could practically hear the hope in her own voice. All because she'd spent a few minutes talking with a man who was more than she had ever imagined him to be.

A rugged, brokenhearted bull rider named Cody Gunner.

Chapter Twenty-two

The doctor didn't endorse a hike in the foothills for Carl Joseph, but he didn't forbid it either. Early Sunday morning, Cody found Carl Joseph in his room before breakfast and poked his head inside. "Hey, Buddy. What're you doing?"

Carl Joseph lifted his eyes and his face lit up. "Writing my hundred words! 'Cause today is hike day so no time later. 'Cause of the hike." He laughed a few times, his excitement spilling into his voice.

The smell of cologne saturated the room. "You smell pretty good for a hike, Buddy."

A shy sort of laugh came from his brother, and he shrugged his shoulders. "'Cause D-A-I-S-Y." He wore khaki pants and a polo shirt—not exactly hiking attire. But he had on sturdy shoes. "I dressed up for Daisy 'cause that's called entertaining." He sat back down at his desk and pointed at the piece of paper there. "Look at this, Brother."

Across the top it read, "One Hundred Most Common Words." Painstakingly, his brother had printed two of the words five times each. Remorse rained on Cody's heart as he came up behind his brother and looked over his shoulder. His parents were debating whether to see the doctor Elle had told them about. In the meantime, Carl Joseph had made a decision. He would keep up on his work at home until the doctor said he could go back. In his buddy's mind, it wasn't a matter of *if* he returned, it was a matter of *when*.

"Watch this, Brother!" Carl Joseph covered his eyes with his hands. "No peeking."

Cody came around to the side so he could see better.

"*At*. A-T. *At*." He took his hand from his eyes and stared at the word. Then he clapped and bounced a little in his chair. "*At*, Brother. I can spell the word 'at.'"

Cody put his hand on Carl Joseph's shoulder and gave it a gentle squeeze. "Good work, Buddy. I'm proud of you."

With those words, Carl Joseph made a slow turn in his chair. He pushed his glasses up a little higher on his nose and stared at Cody. Then, like a gradual drip from a faucet, tears filled Carl Joseph's eyes. "Really, Brother? You're proud of me? Even if I'm not learning new things right now?"

Cody felt his heart breaking all over again. "C'mere, Buddy. I'm so proud of you." He held out his arms and Carl Joseph stood. Slowly, he came to Cody, and the two of them hugged the way they hadn't done since Cody's first day home. "Hey, I have an idea." Cody took a step back and smiled. "Let's go to breakfast before the hike."

Joy flashed in Carl Joseph's eyes, but then just as quickly his smile faded. He looked at a calendar on his wall where each day of the week was represented in a different color. Carl Joseph had crossed off every day of the month that had gone by. He moved his finger

275

along the small boxes until he reached the first one not crossed off. Today's date.

"Uh-oh." He straightened and turned back to Cody. "Blue means Sunday. Sunday means church."

Once more Cody felt seized with guilt. He had discouraged his brother from giving money to the church, and Carl Joseph hadn't mentioned attending a service since. But here was further proof that Carl Joseph still knew what Sundays were about. What they were supposed to be about. "Yes, Buddy, today's Sunday. But we can still have breakfast out. Restaurants are open on Sunday."

Carl Joseph's expression fell flat for a moment, and he looked at the dresser next to his bed. He reached down and opened the top drawer, then he lifted an envelope from inside. Across the front in their mother's handwriting it read *Carl Joseph's gift for Jesus.* He studied it, then set it back down and shut the drawer again. "Not church today?"

"No, Buddy. Just breakfast. Is that okay?"

He bit his lip, as if the question was perplexing. Then he nodded, and a hesitant smile lifted his lips. "Okay. On Sunday me and Brother have breakfast."

"At Denny's."

"'Cause Denny's has pancakes!" Carl Joseph hurried toward the door. "I need a shower, Brother. I'll be right back."

In a rush, Cody felt his defenses fade away. Who was he to tell Carl Joseph how he could spend his money? Carl Joseph lived at home, and if he wanted to give a fourth of his earnings to the church, that was his prerogative. He opened the drawer and took out the envelope with his brother's gift.

Cody thought about his years on the rodeo tour, and the lengths people would go for money. Athletes who would shoot themselves with cortisone or painkillers because they wanted to make a thousand dollars. People did crazy things for money.

Guilt ate at him as he ran his thumb over the envelope. He stared out the window and felt the weight of his earlier decision. How come it had taken this long for him to see the gift as what it was? A gift. A decision. One that Carl Joseph had the right to make.

"Okay, God," Cody whispered. He wasn't good at praying, and nothing about it came naturally. He squinted against the sunlight. "Am I supposed to encourage Carl Joseph to put a hundred dollars in the church plate?"

Cody looked around his brother's room, and his eyes settled on a poster near the bed. The words read, "But seek first His kingdom and His righteousness and all these things will be given to you." Beneath the words was a boy with Down Syndrome sitting at a bus stop.

Chills ran down Cody's arms. The message was unmistakable. Seek God first, and everything else would fall into place. He thought of his lung—the gift he'd given his precious Ali. Lots of people would've thought him crazy to let doctors cut into his chest and take out one of his lungs, all so that a dying girl could have a few more years.

Tears stung his eyes again. It hadn't mattered what anyone else said. His gift to Ali made perfect sense to him. But what if he'd had Down Syndrome? What if he'd wanted to give Ali the gift, and someone had stood in the way and forbidden him from giving it? A piece of him would have died right alongside her, no question. The look in Carl Joseph's eyes a few minutes ago came back to him again.

Was that how his brother felt? His hands tied, unable to do something that was so strongly in his heart?

Cody took a long breath and gathered his determination. He would get dressed—khaki pants and a polo shirt, so his buddy wouldn't feel out of place. He'd take his brother out to breakfast and on the hike they'd planned for today. But first, before they stopped at Denny's for pancakes, he would do what he should've done a long time ago.

He would take Carl Joseph to church.

THEY WERE HALFWAY to Denny's when Cody made a turn onto the main highway. His heart felt lighter, happier than it had felt in weeks. In years, even. He drove through the suburbs and toward the downtown area. The closer they got, the more he couldn't stop himself from smiling. Carl Joseph didn't notice anything out of the ordinary until Cody pulled up in front of the downtown church, the one where the field trip had taken place.

Then he stared at the building and his mouth dropped. He looked at Cody and swallowed. "That's not Denny's."

"No, Buddy." He pulled Carl Joseph's envelope from beneath the seat and handed it to him. "I thought maybe we should go to church first. That way you can give Jesus your gift."

Carl Joseph gasped. He had always been emotional, easily moved to tears, though in the last few months he seemed to have outgrown dramatic shows of his feelings. But here, now, Carl Joseph stared at the envelope and his eyes filled with tears. Once more he gave Cody a curious look. "You mean, it's okay, Brother? My gift is okay?"

"Yes." Cody struggled with the lump in his throat. "It's a beautiful gift." He looked at his watch. "But we'd better get inside. Service is about to start."

The message that day was as if God, Himself, had spoken it straight to Cody's heart. It was about trust and worry, and how it was fruitless to be anxious about tomorrow. No one could tell the future, the pastor said. "We can only trust God and follow His lead throughout this journey called life. Then when the end comes, we will have nothing left to do but celebrate."

The idea filled Cody's entire being. Trust God every day, so that in the end—whenever that was—there would be a celebration, not a wake. Joyful memories, not painful regrets.

And wasn't that Ali's message from the beginning?

People died tragic deaths all the time. The point wasn't how a person died. It was how a person lived.

Cody watched Carl Joseph, the way he knelt and stared earnestly, reverently at the cross up front. Cody struggled with relationships and love, with knowing what his next season in life should be about, and with where God fit in his life.

All the areas where Carl Joseph didn't struggle at all.

When the offering plate came around, his brother took the folded envelope from his pocket, kissed it, and placed it tenderly on top. Then he looked at Cody and grinned. And from somewhere up in heaven, Cody could almost feel God grinning, too.

They each ordered a Grand Slam breakfast, and Cody realized he hadn't enjoyed his brother this much since he'd come home from the rodeo circuit. They talked about bus routes and field trips and Daisy. A lot about Daisy. When the meal was over, though he debated it, Carl Joseph decided against the strawberry milkshake. "Ice cream isn't a healthy choice." He shook his head. "Not very healthy."

"No." Cody stifled a smile. "Water's probably better."

"Probably."

The waitress brought the check and set it at the edge of the table. She was older, their mother's age maybe. Already Carl Joseph had explained that Cody was his brother and that they were just returning from church.

"The pastor said to trust God," he told her when she came to clear their plates. "Do you trust God, waitress?"

Cody was about to interrupt, apologize for his brother's behavior, and let the waitress off the hook. People didn't come out and ask questions like that, not of strangers, anyway. But before he could say anything, the waitress patted Carl Joseph's hand.

"I do." She gave Cody a knowing smile, as if to say they made a nice picture—two brothers sharing a meal this way. She turned back to Carl Joseph. "I trust Him every day."

"Good." Carl Joseph stopped short of clapping, but he was clearly overjoyed that the waitress understood this truth about God.

Again Cody was taken aback. He folded his hands on the table and gave a slight shake of his head. The more he thought he knew about life, the more Carl Joseph redefined it. What was wrong with talking about God, anyway? Carl Joseph's question had given the waitress a reason to smile even in the middle of a Sunday late breakfast rush.

After she left, Carl Joseph took the check and studied it. Cody watched him and wondered again about Elle Dalton's offer. Could he take the next season of his life and devote it to working with adults like his brother? Today, the way Carl Joseph was relaxed around him, made him think it was possible.

He took a twenty from his wallet and set it on the table. Carl Joseph was still studying the check.

"Brother?" Carl Joseph had the check in one hand, and the money in the other. "You need more."

"What?" Cody took the check and looked at the total. Fourteen dollars, eleven cents. "But I put a . . ."

Carl Joseph held up the bill. "This is a ten, Brother. You need a twenty for the food we ate. 'Cause Grand Slams aren't cheap." He laughed at himself. "That's why they're Grand Slams."

Cody was stunned. "How did you know that?"

"I learned it." He grinned and laughed at the same time. "Teacher taught me."

Elle again. The girl with the beautiful eyes and sensitive heart. The one he couldn't wait to spend an afternoon with. "I like your teacher, Buddy."

A quiet laugh came from him. "I know you do."

"What?" A smile pulled at Cody's lips. "How do you know?"

"Because"—he laughed again—"I just know. 'Cause standing close and smiling at her. A lot of smiling."

"Okay." Cody was laughing now, too. He dropped his voice to a whisper. "But it'll be our secret."

"Good." He clapped quietly. "I like secrets."

Long after breakfast and into the rest of the day, Cody felt a peace that hadn't been there since he returned home nearly two months ago. He and his buddy were friends again, that was much of it. But also, the pastor was right. Life really was a matter of trusting God every day so that when it was all over, there wouldn't be sadness over a mountain of regrets.

There would be a celebration.

The sort of celebration that was about to take place on a simple hike with friends.

Chapter Twenty-three

Cody and Carl Joseph would be there in an hour. Elle couldn't find her hairbrush, so she went down the hall to Daisy's room. Her mother and sister were in Daisy's bathroom, working together to put curlers in her fine blonde hair.

Elle stood in the doorway and raised an eyebrow. "Did I get the memo wrong? I thought we were going on a hike."

Daisy peered over her shoulder. "It's a date."

"Oh, it is?" Elle loved this about her sister, her feisty independence, knowing her own mind before anyone could speak for her.

Their mother sent a helpless look back at Elle. "Daisy told me it was a date. She wanted her hair curled."

"It's a date for you, too, Elle." Daisy grinned in the mirror. "You and Cody."

Heat filled Elle's cheeks. "It's not a date for us, sweetie. We're only going along for fun."

Daisy stared at her for a few seconds. "It's a date."

Her mother gave her another look, and there was no denying the twinkle in her eyes. "I don't know, Elle. Maybe you'd better curl your hair."

"Thanks, Mom." She gave an exasperated breath.

"You're a big help." But even as she said the words, her heart reacted to the possibility. She forced herself to stay matter-of-fact. Daisy was wrong. This wasn't a date for her and Cody Gunner. They'd discussed nothing of the sort.

Still, if Daisy could curl her hair, Elle could at least wear a nicer pair of shorts. She ran back to her room and changed both her shorts and her shirt. Was it a date? Was that how Cody saw the afternoon hike? She doubted it. He'd made himself clear when they talked about his Ali. Cody never expected to love like that again. Never wanted to. And Elle was the same way. At least that's what she'd always told herself. Now, though, she had to wonder if her heart had a different agenda altogether.

When she was happy with her look, she left the room to rejoin her mother and sister. As she left, the faintest hint of perfume lingered behind her.

THEY WERE AT a stoplight, and Carl Joseph stuck his head out the window and peered at himself in the side mirror.

"Brother . . . can you help me?"

Cody stifled a smile. He'd never seen his brother so concerned with his looks. "What's up?"

Carl Joseph looked in the mirror again. "I look wrong." He turned an empty expression to his brother. "How come?"

The light turned green, and Cody shrugged. "I think you look perfect."

284

"Good." Carl Joseph hiked up his pant leg. "I wore my best socks 'cause Daisy is my best friend. Best and best, Brother."

"See?" Cody patted his shoulder. "You're just perfect."

"Yeah, 'cause I tell the best jokes. That's what Daisy says. Also I might ask her to Disneyland. 'Cause I might entertain her at Disneyland."

"Let's do the hike first."

"One thing." Carl Joseph held up one finger. "Can we pray? 'Cause this is a big day, Brother, and we have a lot of driving and we have Daisy and Elle and we don't want to get lost. 'Cause also prayin'—"

"Is a life skill." Cody smiled at him. "I was just going to say the same thing." He kept his eyes on the road and one hand on Carl Joseph's shoulder, and he prayed a prayer about protection and direction and open hearts and trusting.

And then, silently, he asked for one more thing.

That God might calm his nerves sometime before they reached the Dalton house.

ELLE HADN'T BEEN this nervous as far back as she could remember. She paced to the front window, peered down the street looking for his truck, and then paced back into the kitchen. "No sign of him."

"He's not supposed to be here for five more minutes." Her mother was making a cup of tea. "Right?"

"Cody's always early." She smoothed her jean shorts.

"Elle Dalton." Her mother's voice was low. "You're falling for him."

Daisy was at the sink filling a water bottle, and she didn't seem able to hear their conversation.

Elle stared at her mother. "What in the world gives you that impression?"

"The way you're acting, all flustered. I haven't seen this from you since . . ." She stopped herself. "I haven't seen it in a long time."

"That's because Teacher likes Cody." Daisy turned around and twisted the lid onto her water bottle. "Right, Teacher?"

"Daisy . . ." There was a warning in Elle's voice. She raised her brow and looked straight at her sister. "You can only call me that in the classroom."

"Okay." Daisy danced around in a circle, twirling and doing a slightly awkward pirouette. "Elle likes Cody." She shrugged and gave their mother a silly look. "Cody likes Elle, too."

Elle could feel the entire day unraveling into a disaster. "You're wrong, Daisy. And please don't say anything about that today, okay?"

Daisy held her finger to her lips. "Shhh. Not a word." She grinned and then danced her way into the front room. "I'm waiting for CJ outside."

"Great." Elle fell into the nearest chair and stared at her mother. "Did you have to ask in front of her? She'll talk about it for sure."

"No she won't." Her mother pulled the tea bag from her steaming cup and tossed it into the trash. She gave

Elle a pointed look. "Daisy's the one who told me. A week ago, Elle. All that time and she hasn't said a word to you or Cody."

"Really?" Elle felt herself relax.

"Yes."

Elle thought about her sister. Of course Daisy would've seen this a week ago. Hadn't they all learned ages ago not to underestimate Daisy's perception, her understanding of social settings?

There was a sound at the door, and Elle jumped up. She grabbed her backpack and kissed her mother on the cheek. For the briefest instant she hesitated, her eyes locked on her mother's. "What if you're right?" she whispered. Her heart beat in double time. "What if you're both right?"

Her mother smiled and took her hand. "Then you pray for wisdom and proceed with caution." She squeezed Elle's hand and then released it. "And you thank God for breathing new life into that very special heart of yours. Even if it all amounts to nothing."

ELLE WAS WILLING to sit in the backseat with her sister, but Daisy made a fairly dramatic show of pointing to the passenger seat, the one next to Cody. By the time Elle slid in next to him, Cody was hiding a sympathy laugh.

"Don't worry about it." He looked in his rearview mirror at Daisy and Carl Joseph. "They're just excited."

"It'll be fun trying to keep them focused enough to

stay on the trail." Elle sat back in her seat. The inside of his truck reeked of cologne, and she sniffed a few times.

"It's my brother." Cody aimed his thumb toward the backseat. "You know . . . two capfuls of cologne."

"Ooops." Elle winced and allowed a quiet laugh. "We haven't talked about that in our social graces class."

Cody blinked, as if his eyes were burning from the smell. "When you do, Carl Joseph can be the poster boy."

They both laughed, and Cody turned up the radio. It was a country song by Lonestar, and Elle found the lyrics fitting. Something about how the Lord gave people mountains so they could learn how to climb. If that were true, she and Cody should be experts by now.

She looked at Cody, but only for a moment. She was keenly aware of every move he made. The muscles in his shoulders as he turned the wheel, and the details of his handsome profile. She'd Googled him last night and found that Cody Gunner was definitely a legend in bull-riding circles. One Web site said, "To this day, no one has ridden a bull the way Cody Gunner rode. He is bigger than life in and out of the arena, and it'll be a long time before someone else takes his place."

Indeed. That's what she was sensing from him today. The larger-than-life part. Being in his presence here made it hard for her to breathe. And yet for all his professional reputation, the world didn't see what she'd seen. What he'd let her see on a starry night sitting on a bluff at the far end of his parents' ranch.

They reached the parking lot, and when they climbed out Elle was suddenly aware of Cody's height. This was the first time she'd been around him in anything but high-heeled shoes.

"Ready?" He gave her a quick grin and then patted his brother's back.

"Ready, over and out!" Carl Joseph saluted.

Daisy laughed and did a salute of her own. "CJ, you're so funny!"

Elle mouthed the words, "Oh, brother," for Cody's benefit. Then they set out for the trailhead.

For the first part of the hike, Cody took the lead and Elle brought up the rear. She wanted to make sure there were no problems with Daisy and Carl Joseph keeping to the trail or falling behind. After an hour they found a clearing and took a break. Carl Joseph and Daisy walked over to a patch of clover.

"Over here, CJ. I have a new move for you."

"Dancing in the clover!" Carl Joseph clapped and bounced a few times. "'Cause I like dancing in the clover."

"Yeah, but this is a dance move from class, CJ. So come here."

Carl Joseph went to her, and Daisy started the impromptu lesson.

"They love to dance." Cody bit into an apple and handed a second one to Elle.

She took it and thanked him. "Yes. Sometimes I

wish when we do the addition to the facility, we could add a dance room, too. That way they could see themselves in the mirror." She angled her head and looked at their siblings. "That could help a lot with body control, just knowing how they look."

Cody sat on a chair-sized boulder. He was quiet for a minute, staring at Carl Joseph and Daisy. Finally he drew a long breath. "They look pretty happy."

"They do." She was standing a few feet from him. "Thanks, by the way."

"For what?" He took another bite of his apple.

"Bringing Carl Joseph today. I'm sure the doctor wasn't crazy about the idea."

"No." A sad smile lifted Cody's lips. "But he told us we couldn't protect Carl Joseph from everything." He turned to her. "My parents are thinking about talking to the other doctor, the one you recommended."

Elle felt a surge of hope. "That's what we're praying for."

"Good." He patted the spot next to him. "Sit down. We won't have another rest until we reach the top." He grinned. "The planner of this hike's a real taskmaster."

She laughed and sat next to him. As she did, her arm brushed against his, and the sensation made her dizzy. She gave him a teasing look. "We can go slower if you can't handle it."

"No, no." He held up his half-eaten apple. "My one lung's better than two of yours. Don't worry about me."

"Ugh." She dropped her head in her hands. How come she hadn't thought of that? Here she was pushing Carl Joseph and Daisy up the hill, encouraging them to keep the pace, and she hadn't once thought about Cody's limitations. She peered at him through her fingers. "I completely forgot. I'm sorry."

"Nah." He dropped the pretense and patted her knee. "I'm fine, really. Just teasing. I went a whole season of bull riding with one lung. I can certainly hike up a mountain."

"I guess." She still felt bad, but before she could say anything more about it, Daisy and Carl Joseph began waving at them.

"So"—Cody searched her eyes—"I told you my story. What about you? Never married?" His expression changed. "Sorry. You don't have to answer that."

"No, it's fine." She leaned back on her hands. She watched her sister and Carl Joseph, still working on the dance step. She took a long breath. "I never dated much through school. My only real love was the principal of the first school I taught at. His name was Trace."

She hadn't told the story often, and it didn't come easily now. She stayed with the main details, how after a year of friendship with Trace, she took a transfer to another school so they could date. Cody listened closely, though her story sounded like any other until she got to the part about the wedding.

"The rumor was that Trace was gay." She squinted

against the glaring pain of her past. "I guess I didn't want to believe it. And after we started dating, I had no reason."

Concern colored Cody's expression. "He backed out of the wedding?"

"On our wedding day." She smiled, but she knew it didn't hide the hurt. "We had three hundred guests waiting for the music to start when I got his call."

"Elle . . ." Cody looked sick to his stomach. He shifted, studying her. "That's awful."

"I should've seen it coming." Elle lifted her chin and stared at a slice of blue through a patch of evergreens.

For a while Cody said nothing. Her story had that sort of effect on people. When he did speak, his tone was softer than before. "So you put everything you have into your work."

"Yes."

"Wow . . ." He anchored his elbows on his knees and stared at the ground. "I'll bet you haven't told that to many people."

"No. Our friends and relatives think he had a nervous breakdown, a serious case of cold feet."

"Whatever happened to him?"

"Last I heard he'd walked away from the gay lifestyle. He was getting counseling at a Christian center in San Francisco."

Cody straightened, the concern still in his eyes. "How'd you get through it?"

"God alone." She smiled at him, but her heart hurt. The way it always would when she talked about

Trace. "I've got a good life. Rewarding. Fulfilling. It's enough."

"Hey . . ." Carl Joseph waved at them. "Come on, Brother. We have to teach you the dance!"

Elle let the sad feelings pass. She smiled at their siblings. "They're quite a pair."

"They are." Cody chuckled. "Looks like it's lesson time."

"Come on!" Carl Joseph tipped his head back and laughed with the abandon of a child. He twirled Daisy, and she ducked to get under his arm. In the process, she tripped and almost fell, but Carl Joseph caught her.

Elle smiled. People with Down Syndrome were limited in so many areas. But in so many of the ways that mattered, they weren't limited at all.

"I'm the teacher this time." Daisy ran up and took Elle's hand. When Elle was on her feet, Daisy motioned for Cody. "Come on." She pointed to the patch of clover. "We all have to dance because that's a good dance floor."

Cody followed along, but he shot Elle a wary look. "I can't dance."

"Yes, Brother, 'cause I'll teach you." Carl Joseph met them halfway and helped lead Cody to the middle of the patch.

"Start like this." Daisy put one hand in Carl Joseph's hand, and the other on his shoulder. "Go on." She nodded to Elle. "Like me and CJ."

Elle turned to Cody and made a face. The moment

was more humorous than awkward, but even so she didn't want Cody to feel forced into anything he wasn't comfortable with. "I don't think we have a choice."

"No." He straightened, feigning a proper look, and he held out one hand. He placed the other on her shoulder. His voice was too low for their siblings to hear. "I warned you. I have two left feet."

"Okay, here's the beat." Daisy was still in Carl Joseph's arms. She used her hand to set the rhythm. "Five, six, seven, eight." Moving slowly and deliberately, they took a step together and then a step apart. Daisy pointed at their feet. She jumped in place a few times. "Do that!"

Cody imitated the steps.

"Do it better!" She laughed at the two of them.

"We're trying." Elle giggled. "Give us a break."

One step after another Elle and Cody played along, following Daisy's instruction. Partway through the number, Carl Joseph began to hum, and Cody dipped his head near Elle's. "I love that kid."

"I know." She spoke low near his face. "Me, too. He's been so good for Daisy."

The humor of the moment faded, and Elle could think only of how good she felt. Her hand was warm in Cody's, and they were close enough that once in a while she could feel his breath on her face. When she wasn't focused on the dance steps, she felt dizzy from the nearness of him. New feelings, brand-new emotions were taking root in her heart and soul, and she could do nothing to stop them.

"How're we doing, Buddy?" Cody looked over his shoulder at Carl Joseph. "Doing okay?"

Carl Joseph stopped and watched them for a few beats. He gave a firm nod and pushed his glasses back up his nose. "'Cause this is your first time."

"Very good for the first time." Daisy smiled. "Keep making music, CJ."

The dance continued, and Elle couldn't help but savor the feel of it. After Trace, she hadn't imagined herself ever feeling this way again. But here she was on a mountainside overlooking Colorado Springs, dancing on a patch of clover in Cody Gunner's arms, and suddenly nothing felt impossible.

"All right now, spin!" Daisy did a spin beneath Carl Joseph's arms again, only this time she added a second spin. The move didn't look smooth, but they managed it without tripping or falling.

Cody wore a look of concentration as he tried to copy his brother's move, but in the process his feet got in the way and Elle tripped over them. She let out a cry and fell forward into his arms. He caught her around her waist, and for a moment it seemed they'd both fall to the ground. But he steadied himself and they burst out laughing.

"Brother." Carl Joseph stopped and stared at them. He gave Cody a mildly disgusted look. "That is not how you do it."

"Really?" Cody leaned his head against hers. He was laughing so hard he still seemed unsteady, and she was doing the same. He had one hand on the small of her back, the other up between her shoulders.

As they caught their breath, their eyes met, and Cody seemed to realize the way he was holding her. The laughter faded, and something different filled his eyes. A mix of desire and unbridled fear. She felt the change, too. What were they doing, standing here this way, their faces inches from each other? At the same time, she felt something brush against her middle finger. She didn't have to look to know what it was.

Cody's wedding ring.

He must've realized what she was feeling, because he took a step back and moved his hands to her shoulders. The laughter returned to his eyes, and the intimacy of the moment passed. Clearly, he wasn't going to talk about the ring or why—after four years—he was still wearing it.

And Elle wouldn't either. She fixed her hair and nodded at Cody's feet. "You did warn me."

"I did." He dropped his hands to his sides. He was back to the confident, easygoing Cody, the one he'd just recently allowed her to know. But at least he wasn't shutting her off, frightened by their moment of intimacy.

And that's what it had been, no question. Even if it lasted only a couple heartbeats, Elle had seen in his eyes, his expression, that he wondered about her as much as she wondered about him. The knowing was enough to take her breath.

"You need work," Daisy pointed out. She looped her arm through Carl Joseph's. "Maybe later."

They all agreed that later would be better for the dance lessons.

"I'm thirsty." Carl Joseph pulled his water bottle from his backpack. "See, Teacher. I know this life skill. Drink your water!"

"CJ knows." Daisy patted him on the back.

Elle took a drink, and so did the others. As she did, she watched Daisy and Carl Joseph, the way Daisy had such pride for every milestone Carl Joseph reached, and how he protected her at every turn. They were so comfortable around each other. Elle couldn't help but feel a little jealous. Which of them were really handicapped if relationships came this easily for Daisy and Carl Joseph?

After they'd packed the water bottles in their back-packs, they started up the trail again. But there was a difference. This time Cody let Carl Joseph and Daisy take the lead, and he fell in beside Elle. The trail was narrow in places, and at times their shoulders touched.

Elle wasn't as perceptive as Daisy, but she could sense a slight hesitation from Cody. He wasn't angry or even distant. But though they didn't talk about it, she was pretty sure he was caught off guard by the feelings that had surfaced during the dancing incident. Just as she was.

As they walked, they talked about other hikes Elle had taken with Daisy, and how Cody wanted Carl Joseph to spend more time getting exercise. When they reached the top of the trail, they had talked about everything from Daisy's childhood to Disneyland. Everything except the most obvious thing.

Whatever was happening between them.

The rest of the hike there were no other close calls between them, nothing but two new friends sharing an afternoon. But when Cody dropped Elle and Daisy off at their house, the four of them climbed out of his truck. Carl Joseph walked Daisy to the door and the two hugged. Elle could hear Daisy telling him about the coming week at the center and Carl Joseph trying to guess where the next field trip would take place.

Elle and Cody stayed near the truck. "Thanks." She looked up at him. "That was fun."

"It was." He looked down at his feet and tried a few in-place steps. "I could still use a little help in the dancing department."

"You'll get it next time." Elle's cheeks felt sunburned from the day on the mountain. A gentle wind blew by them, and Elle wondered what he was really thinking, and whether there would even be a next time.

They were facing each other, and then, as if he were wondering the same thing, Cody took her hands in his. And in as much time as it took her to inhale, the moment became deeper, more intimate, exactly what it had been up on the patch of clover. He searched her eyes. "Elle . . . I don't know."

Her heart skidded into a strange rhythm. "You don't know what?"

The muscles in his jaw flexed and he looked up for

a long time, up at the place where big, puffy white clouds punctuated the clear blue sky. He exhaled, and it made him sound beyond weary. Then he faced her again. "I don't know how . . ." He looked at Carl Joseph and Daisy. They were dancing again, this time on the front porch. "I don't know how to feel or . . ." He pointed at his brother. "Or how to be like that again."

She willed her heart to slow down, pressed herself to find the right words. "Maybe you don't have to." A sad smile lifted the corners of her mouth. "It was just one dance, Cody."

He rubbed his thumbs along the tops of her hands. "No, it wasn't." He looked past her defenses. "You felt it, too." His lips parted. He looked nervous and determined all at the same time. His voice dropped a notch. "You feel it now."

A part of her wanted to run into the house and never look back. Wasn't this how things had started with Trace? It would be better by far to keep things casual, to laugh and joke about dancing and Disneyland so that they never had to talk about anything more. She gripped his hands a little tighter. She steadied herself and met his eyes again. "My mother once told me that God doesn't give us something new unless our hands are empty." She shrugged one shoulder and looked at his left hand, at the ring there. "You know?"

Cody looked at her for a long time. "I have a lot to think about." He pulled her into a hug, the sort of hug he would give his sister if he had one. "You, too."

"Yes." She took a step back. Her cheeks were hotter now, and with the sun hidden behind the clouds she was certain the heat wasn't only her sunburn. There was something she wanted to say, something she wanted him to know before he left. "Thank you, Cody."

He must've understood that she meant more than the hike, because he waited, studying her eyes. His smile touched her heart to the core. "For what . . . other than stepping on your feet?"

"For trusting me enough to tell me that." Never mind that it was a summer afternoon. With Cody a few feet away from her, Elle felt a chill run down her arms. "Let me know about the doctor and Carl Joseph."

"I will." He took a step back and waved. "See ya."

After the guys left, Elle put her arm around Daisy's shoulders and the two headed inside. "That was a fun day."

"Know something?" Daisy grinned and made a few silent chuckles, as if she had the biggest secret in the world on the tip of her tongue. "I love that CJ."

Elle hugged her sister. "I'm glad, sweetie. I think he loves you, too."

Daisy nodded, confident of the fact. "Hey, Mom! What's for dinner?"

How easily Daisy handled love. The feelings were there, and that was that. Nothing to hide or act strange about, no need for caution or pretense. Love simply was. Period. Daisy headed back to her bedroom and their mother appeared from the kitchen.

"Help me chop carrots?"

"Sure." Elle knew what was coming. She and her mother had always talked about everything. Spending a day with Cody Gunner would be no different. Especially since Elle had already told her mom about Cody's past, the heartbreaking loss of his wife, and his decision to give her one of his lungs to buy three more years with her.

"People don't usually love like that twice in a lifetime," was all her mother told her. Since then they hadn't talked about Cody, not even when Elle's mom learned that the four of them were taking a hike today.

Now they took up their places at separate cutting boards, a pot of water between them. For a minute, they sliced in silence. Then her mother stopped long enough to look at her. "I saw you outside with Carl Joseph's brother. You looked . . . very happy."

Elle set down her knife and covered her mother's hand with her own. "We're just friends."

"But what about you?" Her words were gentle. "How do you feel?"

Elle hesitated, and in that single hesitation she knew she was in trouble. She could feel the way her fingers nestled into Cody's hand, feel the way she'd felt safe and protected on the path beside him, and how when she was in his arms she never wanted the moment to end.

"Elle?"

"I'm not sure." She picked up her knife and another carrot and looked back at the cutting board. She grabbed a fast breath and found a smile. "Anyway, you should hear about the hike. Carl Joseph and Daisy were hysterical, dancing on a patch of clover halfway up the trail . . ."

She launched into a lengthy description of the day that told her mother in no uncertain terms that the conversation about Cody, about the heart of Cody, was over. The fact was, she couldn't tell her mother how she was feeling about Carl Joseph's brother until she found some time alone, time to talk to God. Because before she could talk to someone else about her feelings for Cody Gunner, there was something she had to do.

She had to figure them out for herself.

Chapter Twenty-four

After Cody took Carl Joseph home, after he evaded a handful of questions from his mother, he looked at his watch. Four o'clock. Four more hours of daylight. Enough time to visit the one place he wanted to be.

The one place he had to be.

By the time he returned to his truck and set out along the dirt road toward the back of the ranch, his head was swimming with a thousand different thoughts. Images of the hike and his time with Elle filled his heart and mind and soul. His feelings for her were rising to the surface before he was ready for them. What had happened today? And how was he supposed to make sense of it when he never planned on loving anyone other than Ali?

He focused on the road ahead.

He parked where he had the other night with Elle. For a few minutes he leaned against his truck and stared at the evergreens and craggy outcroppings of rock that circled the place. Then he walked up the hill and sat on the bluff. He could see miles of undeveloped foothills from here, and the serenity of the place allowed him to think. Cody had a number of spots on the ranch where he and Ali had gone to talk about her impending death.

But this wasn't one of them.

He felt the tears come, felt them overflow from his heart into his eyes. Was he moving on? Doing the one thing Ali had asked of him before she died? He closed his eyes because the shock and sorrow were the same every time he thought about her. It seemed like just ten minutes ago that she was lying beside him, still fighting the disease, still breathing the same air as him. So how could she really be dead?

"Ali . . ." He sat up straighter and pressed his fists to his eyes. *Dear God . . . will it ever get easier?*

The prayer came unexpectedly, and Cody blinked his eyes open. He looked beyond the foothills, up to the distant horizon. *Please, God . . . can You hear me?*

At that same moment, a warmth came over him, settling his soul and calming his emotions. A knowing filled his heart, one that gave him the strength to consider the thoughts that had been stirring inside him all day. He looked at his wedding ring, and he was overwhelmed with a certainty, one that had never hit him when he'd come here before.

Ali was gone, but more than that, she had moved on. She was in heaven taking on the tasks and joys that God had for her on the other side. And what she'd left behind was a lesson he hadn't wanted to act on until now. Ali believed in life, in living every minute as if it were her last.

So how was it he'd lived his last four years as if his life were over, too? He'd resisted friendships and conversations, and he'd built up a determination never to love again. When that wasn't what Ali stood for at all. She would've been angry with him for what he'd become—a closed-off man, at first afraid even to let Carl Joseph have the wings to fly. He blinked away another layer of tears. Ali wouldn't recognize him.

Elle's words from earlier came back. What was it her mother had told her? That God couldn't give a person something new unless his hands were empty. He looked at his left hand again, at the wedding ring he still wore. Elle had noticed it, no doubt. He had felt the moment when her body stiffened, when she looked away because of it.

Cody twisted it, and for a moment he was back again, standing on a bluff in her parents' backyard, beneath the big open Colorado sky, pledging forever to Ali Daniels. He could see her eyes, feel her hands in his. But then, like the changing direction of a gust of wind, the image disappeared.

Wearing the ring didn't make her any less gone. It served only as a reminder that his life had ended right along with hers. And that—Cody was sure of it—would've made Ali furious. Ali, who had made him promise to love again, and who had grown frustrated when he dismissed the idea.

"You need to live, Cody." She rarely raised her voice, but the last time they talked about his future, she grew angry with him. "I won't stand for you to lose your passion, your ability to love, just because I'm not here anymore."

Ali hadn't just hoped for him to find a new life after her death; she'd demanded it. But for four years, one season after another, he'd ignored her wishes. Not because he didn't care what she thought, but because he could barely get out of bed each morning. Her loss made it hard for him to breathe, let alone consider love. He shifted his gaze to the distant hills.

Until now.

He gritted his teeth. He had tried to keep Elle Dalton out of his heart, tried from the moment he saw her. So what if she was beautiful? He could walk away from beauty. But today, on a hike that was supposed to be nothing more than an outing with their siblings, he had learned something about himself.

He couldn't walk away from Elle Dalton's heart.

Elle was passionate about love and life and people with Down Syndrome. Deep inside her wounded heart was a love for Daisy that rivaled his love for Carl Joseph, and in that, Elle was a kindred spirit.

Part of his attraction to Ali, even though he didn't like to think this way, had been her illness, and the fact that he might protect her, shelter her. She needed him, and that drove their love to a level that Cody hadn't known existed.

Elle wasn't sick with a deadly disease, but the damage to her heart was enough to cripple her for a lifetime. Working with people like her sister was enough for Elle. She was willing to put her own feelings on ice while she served others. Better that than to experience the pain and rejection that could come with falling in love.

And that made Cody want to shelter Elle, the same way once a lifetime ago he'd wanted to shelter Ali. He spotted a pair of deer in the distance. They stopped and looked his direction, and then ran off into the hills. Cody leaned back on the rock and thought about the hike.

When he stepped on Elle's feet, when she stumbled into his arms, he had the sudden urge to love away all the betrayal and rejection inside her, to protect her and care for her and teach her that love didn't have to hurt so bad. The strength of his feelings took his breath. Feelings he hadn't acknowledged until that instant.

He breathed in, and as always he felt his body stop short of a full breath, the way it had done since the transplant operation. The tangible reminder of Ali that he would always carry with him.

He looked at his wedding ring one more time. Then he stood and stared into the distance. "I know what I have to do, Ali. And I know somewhere in heaven you understand because . . . you made me promise."

His eyes were dry now, his thoughts more about Elle and the future than anything from the past. A sense of peace warmed him, the way it had earlier when he prayed. He hesitated a moment longer. He slid his hands into his pockets, took one last look at the sky, and then made his way back to his truck. On the way home, his jumbled thoughts all seemed to right themselves. And suddenly he knew exactly what he was supposed to do next.

When he walked in the door, his family was sitting at the dinner table, just about to eat. The smell of lasagna was thick in the air, and as Cody came closer, Carl Joseph's face burst into a grin. "Brother! You came back in time!"

Cody laughed. He loved the way Carl Joseph made dinnertime feel like a vacation to the Bahamas. "Yes, Buddy. I made it back."

He raised his fork in the air. "Brother's here for Mom's lasagna."

The celebration hung in the air for several minutes after Cody sat down. Only then did he notice the way his parents were looking at each other, as if they had something they could hardly wait to say.

Finally his dad set down his fork. "We talked to the doctor, the one Elle suggested."

"He called us here. On a Sunday." His mom's eyes grew damp, but the joy there was undeniable. "He told us about a new medication."

Cody was dizzy with anticipation. He looked from his mother to his father. "And?"

"I can't keep it, Mom!" Carl Joseph pushed back from the table and jumped up. He danced in a few circles and pumped his fists. "No more secrets! I can't wait!"

A tear spilled onto his mother's cheek, and she made a sound that was more laugh than cry. "Carl Joseph is going back to the center on Monday."

Cody felt his breath catch in his throat. He stood and studied his parents. "You're serious?"

"I can keep working for Goal Day, Brother!" Carl Joseph raised both fists in the air. " 'Cause better medicine now."

His mother folded her hands, and Cody noticed that her fingers were trembling. As Carl Joseph danced into the kitchen, she lowered her voice. "He had another seizure this morning." She swallowed, fighting her tears. "It was bad, Cody."

A sobering shadow fell over the moment. "When . . . when can he try the new medicine?"

"Monday afternoon." She found a shaky smile. "We're meeting with the new doctor then."

"We still aren't sure we're doing the safest thing." His dad crossed his arms. His chin quivered and he coughed, finding his own control. "But it's the right thing. We know that."

"The doctor was very encouraging."

Cody thought about Ali again. She would rather have raced horses for one year than spend ten years in the safety of a sterile room. It would be the same way for Carl Joseph. Suddenly the decisions that lay ahead for Cody were clearer than water.

Carl Joseph returned to the table out of breath. "My turn to pray!" His voice was louder than usual, and he caught himself. He covered his mouth and raised his eyebrows. "Sorry," he whispered. "'Cause it's my turn to pray."

"Go ahead, son." His father smiled at him.

Carl Joseph reached for his mother's hand and everyone closed their eyes. "Dear God, hi. Carl Joseph here." He stifled a quiet laugh. "Everything's perfect now, God. So thanks for the lasagna, and thanks for Mom and Dad and Brother and Teacher." He giggled again. "And Daisy. And medicine." He clapped his hands. "Now we can dig in!"

Cody opened his eyes, amazed. Hours ago Carl Joseph had been in the throes of a terrible seizure. But as far as he could tell, life was perfect. It was one more way Carl Joseph's faith stood as an example to the rest of them.

They let Carl Joseph talk for a while. He told them that he and Daisy had decided the next hike would be at Disneyland. "'Cause we have to get there first and we don't know the bus route."

"You'd probably have to fly." Their dad was finishing his dinner. He had an easy way with Carl Joseph, something Cody hadn't noticed in his hurry to blame his dad when he first returned from the rodeo circuit.

"Yeah." Carl Joseph looked out the window. He'd never been on an airplane, and his anxiety over the possibility was written in the lines on his forehead. "'Cause we could fly."

After a few minutes of talk about Disneyland, Carl Joseph stood and took his empty plate and cup to the kitchen. "I'll wash." He gave their mother a big smile and tapped their father's shoulder. "That would be good life skills."

Dad stood and joined Carl Joseph in the kitchen. "Let's do it together."

"Goodie." He clapped, sheer joy filling his tone.

Cody stood and joined his father and brother in the kitchen. Carl Joseph was relating a comical version of the hike, and how Cody and Elle had danced together.

"Brother is not a good dancer." Carl Joseph made a dramatic shake of his head, so dramatic that his glasses nearly fell to the floor. He caught them and set them back in place. Then he patted Cody's shoulder and gave him a rough embrace. "But he's a very, very good brother."

They played Uno that night, and Cody stayed up later than usual before returning across the ranch to his own house. He'd been anticipating this moment all day, and now—in a way he was helpless to stop—it was here. He stepped inside his front entrance, closed the door, and locked it.

What he had to do now, he would do alone—the same way he had handled the trip to the bluff earlier. He walked through his living room and stopped at the fireplace mantel. Perched on top of the polished piece of oak was his framed wedding picture. Ali and him, when the future still seemed possible. When a cure for cystic fibrosis was all that stood between that fleeting moment and forever.

He ran his thumb over the glass, over their faces, smiling and hopeful. "It's time, Ali." He smiled, even though somewhere inside him he could feel his heart breaking. He looked at her face, her eyes. "I know you'd tell me the same thing."

Then, feeling a hundred years old, he moved into his bedroom and opened the top drawer of his dresser. A small wicker basket sat near the back, a catch-all for things that didn't quite have a place. His old pocketknife from middle school and a pair of earplugs he wore when he ran the tractor out on the ranch. And next to that, on top of a mound of old quarters and nickels and dimes, were the two velvet boxes.

He took the pale pink one first. The hinges made a soft creaking sound as he opened it. The ring inside was still beautiful, mostly because seeing it reminded him of how it looked on Ali's finger. He took the ring from the box and brought the cool white gold close to his face.

Once in a while, holding her wedding ring this way made him feel as if he were holding her hand again. Her fingers tucked in his. But tonight it was only a cold, empty reminder of all that wasn't. All that would never be.

Cody placed the ring gently back in the velvet box

and closed the lid. Ali was not in the grave, and she was not in the small velvet box. She lived in his heart, in a back room where she had recently moved, one that would always belong to her. He lifted the other box, the dark one, and set it on the dresser top.

He'd never come even this close before, so every move was slow, painful. He opened the lid and then looked at his left hand. Ali had placed the ring there seven years ago, and it had stayed there every day since. But here, on a day when he had prayed for answers, he felt beyond certain that this was the next step, the move he absolutely had to make.

The wedding ring fit just as it had the day they were married. So it took only a few seconds to gently twist it up over his knuckle. The ache in his heart spread to his chest and up into his throat. Then, with a sharp breath, he did what he never thought he'd do.

He took off his ring and tenderly set it back in the box. For a few seconds he stared at it. The things he felt about the ring would always stay in his soul. But what it meant to the world was no longer true. He wasn't married, and after four years it was time to acknowledge that fact.

Even if doing so practically dropped him to his knees.

Cody closed the box and set it tenderly next to Ali's. Then he closed the drawer and moved to an old recliner he kept in his bedroom near the window. He sank into it and peered into the dark of the night. God was leading him; Cody could feel His guidance in every step. In the process he had let go of Ali, just enough to take one step forward. And now he was ready to face whatever came next. Because—whether he returned to the road or not—he had the one thing Elle had talked about, the thing he felt God urging him to have.

Empty hands.

Chapter Twenty-five

Elle was about to start class that Monday when the door opened and Cody and Carl Joseph stepped inside. A smile lit up Cody's face, and Elle knew the answer before a single word was spoken.

"Carl Joseph would like to come back to class," Cody said. He and his brother moved closer to Elle and the students.

Gus stood straight up. "You're back? You're really back?"

"I knew it." Sid high-fived the guy next to him. "I told you he'd be back!"

Daisy was on her feet. She tiptoed over to Carl Joseph and flung her arms around his neck. "You're home, CJ! Welcome home!"

Elle was grateful for her students and their loud celebration. Because she couldn't have talked if she wanted to. She stood and went to Cody. "Your parents talked to the new doctor?"

"Yes. I'll tell you about it later." He smiled, and for a long beat he held her eyes. "Whatever time Carl

Joseph has, he wants to live it." He turned toward his brother. "He can do that here."

Elle asked Cody to stay, but he shook his head. "I have things to do." He smiled, but there was something deeper in his expression, feelings he was maybe working through.

"Have you decided? About returning to the rodeo?"

"Not yet." He briefly touched her hand. "Let me know if he has any trouble." Cody told his brother good-bye, and he left.

Every day that week was the same, only a few words from Cody when he dropped off Carl Joseph or when he picked him up. Something was happening inside him, and Elle could do nothing but pray for him.

Once in a while he would look at her across the room or share a few words with her, and when he did there was a depth that was constant. A depth full of conflict and vulnerability, one that she didn't dare ask him about—not in what could only be a few minutes' conversation before class.

By Friday morning, Elle wasn't sure what to make of the change, but it scared her. Because she didn't know any way to undo feelings that had already taken root. Especially when she looked forward to seeing him every morning during drop-off time. She thought about asking Carl Joseph, but somehow the idea didn't sit well. If God wanted her to know what was different with Cody Gunner, the information would come to her some other way.

And it did.

It came Friday morning just before their field trip to a supermarket two miles away. Carl Joseph and Daisy were sitting together, waiting for the rest of the class to arrive. They were talking about shortcake and Disneyland and which pair of socks were their favorite if they got to hike the theme park.

Elle tuned out on their conversation for a few minutes. She was sorting through information packets for the students when she heard her sister's tone change.

"Why would he go on the road?" Daisy pulled her knees up and sat cross-legged, facing her friend.

"He wants to think." Carl Joseph tried to pull his legs up, but they were too short and stout to maneuver and he quickly gave up. He blinked as if he were trying to remember what he'd been saying. " 'Cause . . . Brother wants to think about things."

Daisy looked around the room, clearly confused. "He could think here, CJ." She pointed to the seat next to her on the classroom sofa. "Right here on this spot."

"He could think on top of Ace, the horse."

"Or on his bed." She put her pointer fingers together and made a careful heart in the air between them. "My bed has big hearts."

"My bed has Mickey Mouse." Carl Joseph put his fist in the air in a show of victory. "Mickey Mouse is the best bed."

Elle needed to be alone. She stepped into the break room, braced herself against the counter. Cody was leaving? After all the emotions she'd ridden because of him, he was taking off? *God, is that how this is going to end? You bring him into my life for what, so I can tell him good-bye before anything comes of all this and—*

Her self-pity fell off abruptly. What was she thinking? How shallow to consider that the only reason Cody Gunner had showed up at all was for her. The reason God had brought Cody into her life probably had nothing to do with her. She pictured Carl Joseph, giddy about today's field trip, already back in sync with his classmates and making progress toward independence. Carl Joseph was reason enough, even if she never saw Cody again.

A sense of futility came over her, and she was tempted to let the subject go, walk out of the break room and conduct the field trip and believe that one day in the not-too-distant future she'd forget about Cody. But her eyes fell on a sign posted near the coffeemaker.

Don't forget to pray! It's the most important life skill of all!

A lump formed in her throat, and she swallowed back her tears. *Forgive me, Lord. Even if Cody leaves, we can stay friends. But please . . . if it's Your will, convince Cody to stay. Convince him to work here at the center so we can share our love for people with Down Syndrome and maybe someday . . . something more. And if not, Lord . . . help me let him go.*

She collected herself and returned to the classroom. Most of the students were there, talking about how they would spend their imaginary hundred dollars.

She had arranged with the manager of the store that each student could have a cart and choose food within a budget, and then—so they would better understand the sections of a grocery store—they would return the food to the shelves.

And as they set out for the first bus stop half an hour later, she refused to think about Cody and whether he would stay or head back out on the road. God had all the details figured out. If he left, even in her sadness she would know that was God's will.

Even if she would remember for a lifetime how it felt to dance with him on a patch of clover halfway up a mountain trail on a sunny afternoon in June.

CODY KEPT HIS distance on purpose. He didn't want his feelings for Elle influencing his decision to stay or go. Because if he stayed, he wanted to go to her not only with empty hands, but with a full heart. Full of hope and promise and excitement for tomorrow and every day after it.

So that week he kept his distance from Elle and his parents, and in some ways even Carl Joseph. In the process, he took his brother's advice and prayed. He talked to God every chance he had. Should he go and spend a year sorting through his options, his feelings? Or should he stay, roll up his sleeves and work alongside a girl who filled his senses? Was he ready for that, or would he be better off by himself? Him and God.

The way he'd never really been even after Ali died. Until now, now that he'd let her go.

317

Day after day he prayed, stopping in each morning to take Carl Joseph to the center, and forcing himself to stay only a few minutes, so he wouldn't change his mind and stay all day. He was that drawn to Elle. In some ways, he expected the answer to come easily. Should he stay or go? Simple question, simple answer. But God didn't shout at him or whisper in his heart or make the answer clear in any way.

The answer came on Friday, after Carl Joseph's field trip.

Cody had ridden Ace that day, and he was in the barn brushing the horse down, patting his neck. He heard Carl Joseph tromping out to meet him long before his brother appeared at the door.

"Brother!" It was midafternoon, and the sun splashed rays on either side of Carl Joseph. "Supermarkets are fun!"

Cody set down the brush, dusted off his hands, and crossed the hay-covered floor to the door. He wiped his brow and smiled at his brother. "I hadn't noticed."

"What?" Carl Joseph didn't pick up on sarcasm. It was one more innocent way about him.

"Yes, Buddy." Cody patted his shoulder. "Supermarkets are a lot of fun."

"Yeah, and I picked out a melon and"—he held up two fingers—"a two-gallon milk and butter unsalted and wheat bread." He clapped his hands and laughed the way he did when he was practically overcome with joy.

"That's great, Buddy. I'm proud of you." He meant

it. Every field trip, every class session was another victory for Carl Joseph, another step closer to Goal Day.

Carl Joseph bounced a little, nodding and explaining in detail about the trip. But after a minute of talking, he stopped and his smile dropped off. He pushed his glasses up onto his nose and squinted at Cody. "Why, Brother?"

"Why what?"

"You didn't go. I like you to go, Brother. But maybe you don't like supermarkets?"

Cody stared at his brother, past the extra chromosome to the tender-hearted boy inside. A boy who had looked up to him and longed for his attention since he was old enough to talk. And there, in the guileless question from his only brother, Cody had the answer he was looking for.

Just as strongly as if God had walked into the barn and hand-delivered it.

CODY AND CARL Joseph walked into the center ten minutes late, but Elle was nowhere to be seen. Cody's heart pounded, but he expected that. He'd taken his answer back to God and prayed about it over the weekend. Time and again the feeling in his heart was the same.

Now it was time to act on it.

Carl Joseph didn't know what Cody was about to do or how today was different from any other day. He bounded into the classroom, stopped, and was about to give Cody a good-bye hug when Cody stopped him. "I'm staying, Buddy."

His brother's eyebrows lifted high up into his forehead. "You're staying?" He made a few disbelieving guffaws. "Really, Brother?"

"Really." Cody patted his brother's shoulder. "I'll sit here by the door. You go with your friends."

Carl Joseph ran to the group, waving his hands. He was just announcing, "Brother's staying! Brother's staying!" when Elle walked back in from the break room. She must've felt Cody watching her because she turned to him and their eyes met and held. They held while Daisy jumped to her feet and as she danced around Carl Joseph, celebrating the fact that his brother was staying.

Elle put her things down on her desk, turned, and slowly came to him. Her expression told him that she was confused, that she didn't understand whether he was staying for the day, visiting with Carl Joseph's class.

Or staying in Colorado Springs.

When she reached him, a hundred questions shone in her eyes. But she asked just one. "You're staying?"

He hated the way she looked nervous, Elle Dalton whose heart had been through enough. He stood and glanced at the class. The aide was working with several students. He searched her eyes again. "Can you step outside for a minute?" His pounding heart grew louder, so loud he could barely concentrate. He steadied himself. *Breathe, Gunner. Take a breath.* He could do this. God had made it clear.

Elle announced to the class that it was time for group discussion. She gave a knowing look to her aide and then smiled at her students. "Find your seats, please. I'll be right back."

She followed Cody outside, and a warm wind met them on the patio. He leaned against the cool brick wall and waited until she was a few feet in front of him. "I have a question."

"Okay." She ran her tongue along her lower lip. She looked nervous, no idea what was coming.

He smiled, and never broke eye contact. "Is that position still open? Running the fitness program here at the center?"

Surprise worked its way across her face, but it took only a few heartbeats before her eyes lit up. "Are you serious?"

Cody felt the anxiety leaving him. "On one condition." In this moment there was Elle, and only Elle.

A happy cry came from her. "What?"

"I want a dance studio."

Her reaction wasn't slow or measured or cautious. She threw her arms around his neck and hugged him, the sort of victory hug the moment demanded. But it demanded more than that.

He eased back just enough so he could see her, and slowly she took her arms from him. They stood there, inches from each other, and the mood between them changed with a sudden intensity. He crooked his finger and brushed it against her cheek. "You were right." He reminded himself to breathe again. "I feel it, too. I felt it then on the mountain." He moved closer, searching her eyes. "And I feel it now."

"Cody . . ." Fear shadowed her eyes, and she looked away. "I don't know."

"I won't hurt you, Elle." He took her hands in his. "I wouldn't be here if I hadn't thought this through."

When he rehearsed this moment in his mind, he hadn't been sure where exactly it would take place or how it would wind up. But he knew one thing. He wouldn't let her go until she was clear about his feelings. Only now, with her class waiting for her and doubt trying to distract her, he could think of just one way to convince her.

Gently, with a tenderness that he had learned a long time ago, he released her hands and worked his fingers along the sides of her face and into her soft brown hair. Then in a moment he was sure they would both remember forever, he leaned down and kissed her. It was not the kiss of passion and desire, even if those feelings were hidden inside him. Rather it was the kiss of everything new and tender and innocent. A tentative kiss that lasted only a few seconds.

When he straightened, he never took his eyes from hers. "Well." He hugged her again and whispered into her hair. "Do I get the job?"

She didn't answer him, and at first he wondered if she'd changed her mind. Not about him, but about the fitness program. But then he felt the trembling in her shoulders. She wasn't hesitant.

She was crying.

And for the first time in far too long, Cody savored the sound. Because this time Elle's tears did not come from a place of utter despair and heartbreak.

They came from pure, boundless joy.

ELLE SNIFFED AND wiped her tears. "Yes." She pressed her cheek against Cody's chest. "You can have the job."

He stroked her hair, and after a little while they moved apart and he took her hands again. "Good thing, because I don't exactly have a Plan B." He smiled. "Not anymore."

She was about to ask him what happened, how come he'd stayed away all week only to come here now with his mind made up. But with his fingers around hers, she suddenly noticed something.

He wasn't wearing his wedding ring.

"Cody"—she ran her thumb over the smooth indentation, the place where the ring had been just a week earlier. She looked at his finger and then back at him. "Why?"

"I wanted empty hands." Sadness touched his eyes, but only in a distant sort of way.

She could imagine how hard it must've been to make this move, to set aside his wedding ring. As much as she felt giddy and alive, as much as her head was spinning trying to believe what was happening, she couldn't have him doing this unless he was certain. She framed his face with her hands and looked deep into his eyes, all the way to his heart. "Are you sure?"

"Yes." His answer left no doubt, and his eyes told

her he wanted to kiss her again. But he resisted; they both did. This wasn't the time or place, and there would be no rushing whatever lay ahead. There were plenty of reasons to take things slowly.

He grinned, and his eyes danced. "So I was thinking that tonight, well, Carl Joseph and Daisy haven't seen each other outside of class for a long time."

"A week." She felt like shouting out loud. She felt that good.

"Right, a whole week." He gave a shake of his head as if to say a week was far too long. "So what about tonight the four of us go out for pizza?"

Elle tilted her head. She could feel the stars in her eyes. "That'd be amazing."

She soothed her fingertips over the empty place where his wedding ring had been. "What made you do it, Cody?"

"I took your advice." The laughter in his voice eased off a little, but the sorrow was gone.

"What advice was that?"

"I used a life skill." He was serious, even though the air between them was light.

"Oh, really?" Already she could see where this was going, how it would play out in the weeks and months ahead. God in all His glory was giving her a new beginning, the one her mother and sisters and even she had prayed for. The future suddenly had all the streaky pinks and blues of a brilliant sunrise and Elle could've shouted her thanks to heaven because she could hardly wait.

She wanted to know what he meant, and she caught his eyes once more as they headed back toward the classroom. She worked to focus, but her head was still spinning. "Which life skill?"

"Prayer." He smiled, and it gave her a window to his soul. "The one that matters most."

Chapter Twenty-six

SIX MONTHS LATER

Mary Gunner stood at the door of her house and waved good-bye. Cody and Carl Joseph were setting off to help move Daisy into her new apartment, the one she was sharing with Tammy, another student at the ILC.

Daisy had reached Goal Day the week before, and Mary and Mike had celebrated with Daisy and Elle's mother, and all the students and their families. She had a job now, taking tickets at a movie theater one mile down from her apartment.

"Just two bus stops," Daisy liked to say.

The moment was bittersweet for Mary. Spurred on by Daisy's efforts toward independence, Carl Joseph was making record progress toward his own Goal Day. His new medicine was working, but he still had terrible seizures every week or so. Mary sucked in a breath and held it. In four days Carl Joseph had a job interview at the western feed store—cleaning floors and stocking shelves. Elle had explained that she was fairly certain Carl Joseph would get the job. The manager understood about his potential for seizures. They didn't worry him.

Mary watched Cody pull out of the driveway and turn left toward the city. The two brothers were closer than ever. Mary smiled and felt all traces of sadness leave her. Yes, Carl Joseph would be leaving home soon. Cody and Elle had found a group home in the same complex where Daisy and Tammy lived. And that was the right thing for her son. She had believed it when they enrolled him at the center, and she believed it now. Even if once in a while her heart wavered.

Long after Cody's truck was no longer in sight, Mary stood there, pondering all that had happened. Elle had said they might be moving Carl Joseph into the group home in six to nine months. Already he had a roommate lined up—Gus. That way they could share the same independent-living coordinator, a social worker who would come once a week to make sure they were following their routines, remembering their medications.

She smiled. For all the amazing growth and change in Carl Joseph, the greatest change was in her older son.

Cody was in love. Deeply and completely, in a way Mary had thought would never happen again for him. Cody and Elle were inseparable, and already she'd heard mention of a wedding sometime in the near future. In a little more than a month, over Presidents'

Day weekend, the two of them were traveling with Daisy and Carl Joseph on a special trip. Something that had Carl Joseph literally counting down the days.

Mary leaned her head on the doorframe. Once, a lifetime ago, before she and Mike married, her mother told her something that stayed with her. She said, "A mother knows she's done a great job when she has an empty nest and a full heart."

She pictured Cody and Elle, lost in their own world, helping Daisy move into her apartment while Carl Joseph chattered on about his Goal Day. There were times in the last decade when she wondered if she was an absolute failure as a mother. Back when Cody wouldn't speak to her and anger was his only language, or when she realized that by not expecting more of Carl Joseph, she had nearly doomed him to a life of watching television from his spot on the living room sofa.

But here, with her empty nest right around the corner, and her heart so full it could burst, Mary could only hope that maybe her mother was right.

That maybe between her and God, she'd done something right, after all.

THE BIG DAY dawned beneath thick, dark clouds.

By the time they reached the airport, a steady rain was falling, and in the backseat Daisy had her head on Carl Joseph's shoulder. "I hate the rain."

"Don't hate, Daisy." Carl Joseph was talking a little more quietly lately. " 'Cause it's not nice to hate."

"Okay, I get scared in the rain." She rarely argued with Carl Joseph, rarely tried to be right the way she did with just about everyone else. Cody had noticed, and the fact made him smile.

As much as Cody and Elle were falling faster and deeper every day, Carl Joseph and Daisy were, too. Yes, their friendship was more complicated, but it wasn't impossible.

And Cody had decided if his brother wanted to get married someday, if he was well enough to handle the process, Cody would do whatever it took to help him. That way, the lessons Ali had taught him would live on in Carl Joseph.

Cody reached over and took hold of Elle's hand. "What time's the flight?"

"We have ninety minutes." Her face lit up the morning, in spite of the rain. "I can't wait."

"You?" He chuckled and kept his voice low. "This morning Carl Joseph showed up at the breakfast table wrapped in his Mickey Mouse bedspread. He wanted to wear it today, so everyone would know where he was going."

Elle smiled. "Daisy packed six colored pictures for Minnie. Three for each day we're there. So"—she raised an eyebrow—"I think we're about equal."

Cody kept his eyes on the road. The trip to Disneyland was Elle's idea, but he had been in favor of it from the beginning. They had purposely waited until just a week ago to tell Carl Joseph and Daisy. Otherwise the distraction could've messed up her Goal Day, leaving her too preoccupied to prove she was ready to live in an apartment.

He found a parking spot. "All I know is I wouldn't miss this for the world."

"I know." Elle smiled and it found its way to his soul. "My mom told me to fill a two-gig memory chip with their reactions, everything from start to finish."

"Well"—he looked back at his brother, still comforting Daisy—"let's get going. Disneyland's waiting!"

Once they were at the airport gate, they found a quiet corner where they could wait. The moment they were settled, Carl Joseph gasped and then caught himself. He uttered a softer breath this time and pointed at the ceiling. "Swing music!" He took hold of Cody's hand. "Come on, Brother. We can dance."

"Oh, no." Cody shook his head. He could feel Elle laughing at him from her seat beside him. "Not this time, okay?"

"Yeah, I'll need my feet for Disneyland." She whispered near the side of his face.

"Thanks." He squeezed her hand. "I told you, we have to take lessons. Real lessons."

A few feet away, Carl Joseph was undaunted. He took Daisy's hand instead.

She stood and did a graceful bow. Then they began dancing to the elevator music at Denver International, and with the bustle of activity along the concourse and near the gate attendant, only a few people noticed. But those who did walked away with a smile.

Elle had been teaching Daisy fear-management techniques and ways she could pray when the rain made her feel too afraid to move. Here, then, was progress. It was raining outside, but Daisy had found the courage to dance with Carl Joseph instead of cowering in his arms. Whatever Elle was doing, it was working.

"Did you work out the rooms?" Elle slid her fingers between his.

The closeness of her still took his breath. He loved everything about her, loved her in a way he never could have if not for Ali. He kissed her forehead. "You and Daisy across the hall from me and Carl Joseph."

"Perfect." She was about to settle into the chair when the gate attendant instructed their group to board.

Cody motioned to Carl Joseph and Daisy to get in line, and suddenly—as if she had just noticed it again—Daisy clung to Carl Joseph and started to whimper.

Immediately, Carl Joseph put his arm around her and patted her hair. "It's okay, Daisy. 'Cause you won't melt."

It was the same reassurance he always gave her, and it seemed to work. They inched their way past the gate and through the Jetway and onto the plane. It was the first time either Carl Joseph or Daisy had flown, so Cody and Elle had booked the seats with their siblings in the aisle seats. At least until they felt comfortable in the air. Then they could switch so Carl Joseph and Daisy could have window seats.

But as they walked toward the back of the plane and found their aisle, Daisy wouldn't let go of Carl Joseph's arm. Rather than make a scene, Cody sat by Elle so Daisy could sit by Carl Joseph.

"It's okay, Daisy. It's okay." His buddy patted Daisy's arm. "The rain won't melt you."

Carl Joseph comforted her throughout the safety announcements and as the plane lifted off. But then something almost magical happened. As the plane soared into the sky, it burst through the layer of clouds and into a brilliant blue sky.

Daisy sat up straight and looked out the window. "CJ, look!"

Cody leaned forward so he could hear them. Elle did the same.

Carl Joseph clapped his hands, not loudly and obnoxiously, the way he used to, but muffled and with a sense of wonder. He nodded fast and hard. "See, Daisy? I told you so. Sunshine . . . just beyond the clouds."

Her fear left instantly and she stared at the sky, clearly stunned by this new revelation. Carl Joseph did the same, as if he could hardly believe that all this time the words he had used to comfort Daisy had been right on.

Elle looked past him to their siblings. "Down Syndrome is nothing more than a layer of clouds, really. Clouds that cover up a very bright sunshine."

Cody leaned in and kissed her, the way he'd been longing to do since she climbed into his pickup that morning. Briefly, tenderly, and with all the feeling he held in his heart for her. They were still hiding their kisses from Carl Joseph and Daisy. No need to confuse them, or make them think they, too, should be kissing. Not yet, anyway.

"Good night." Elle closed her eyes. "See you in LA."

Cody settled in against the headrest.

He wasn't sure about the timing, but he wanted to spend the rest of his life with Elle Dalton. He was already looking at rings. He stared out the window at the vast and endless blue. He'd never thought about it that way, but Elle was right. Whether in a rainstorm or living with Down Syndrome, or trying to survive a loss so great it might've killed them, the sunshine had always been there. It always would be.

Just beyond the clouds.

Dear Friends,

Thanks for journeying with me through the pages of *Just Beyond the Clouds*. For a while now, I've wanted to go back to Cody Gunner, to find him in that place where I left him a few years ago—a place of heartache over losing Ali, his wife. But those of you who read *A Thousand Tomorrows* know that Cody wasn't only heartbroken over losing Ali. He was also changed forever by knowing her. For that reason, I was convinced the story wasn't finished.

After all, Ali made Cody promise one thing—that he would find love again.

And so this—like *A Thousand Tomorrows*—is a love story that made me smile as I wrote it. Like so many of my books, it played in my head and heart like a movie, and I had the simple and profound pleasure of capturing the story on the pages of this book for you.

I enjoyed very much writing more about Carl Joseph, Cody's brother. And I enjoyed delving into the world of Down Syndrome, where scientists are still learning so much about what is possible for these special people, and about how very high the bar should be raised for them.

One of the themes that runs through the book on a few different levels is the one represented in the title: *Just Beyond the Clouds*. Life has a way of sending in the clouds—not the clowns. That unexpected diagnosis, the pile of bills that won't go away, the empty mailbox, strained relationships. . . . But the truth is always what Carl Joseph tried to tell Daisy: There is sunshine just beyond the clouds.

Scripture tells us that God has good plans for us, and so He does. But sometimes it's a matter of holding onto that truth when the clouds come, when the sky is so dark that it's hard to believe there could really be sunshine on the other side. But there is, especially for those who believe.

Carl Joseph's faith is a simple one, and maybe one we can all learn a lot from. He doesn't process things the way most adults do. Rather, he thinks simply, like a child. He loves God, and so He gives God his best in every area. Sort of the way our kids do. If you've found hope in Jesus Christ for the first time while reading this book, then please know that I am praying for you. Your next step is to find a Bible-believing church in your area and get connected. Go to a Sunday service, take in a Bible class, attend a small group. And if reading Scripture is new to you and you can't afford a Bible, write to me with the words *New Life* in the subject line. I'll make sure my office sends you a Bible so you can get started on that new life in Christ.

I pray that this finds you well and walking in His truth and light. And most of all, I pray that you will join me in looking for the miracles around us and in celebrating life! Remember, sometimes His greatest messages come to us while we wait for the clouds to clear.

If you haven't been to my Web site for a while, stop by! My ongoing journal will give you a window into my personal and writing life, and you can connect with other readers in the Reader Room. Also, you can check out my latest contests and post a photo of someone you know who is serving our country. People all over the world are praying for the soldiers pictured on my Web site.

Also, pass this book on to someone who hasn't read it yet, and you can enter the Shared a Book contest. Just send an e-mail to Kingsburydesk@aol.com, and type "Shared a Book" in the subject line. In the e-mail, give me the first name of the person you shared with and why you shared it with them. At the end of every March, I will pick a winner. That person and a friend will win a trip to the Northwest to spend a day with me and my family. I hope to see you there!

By the way, I still love hearing from you! Your prayers and letters remain a very great encouragement to me as I write stories that God might use to change your life and mine.

Until next time . . . keep looking for the sunshine!

In His light,

Karen Kingsbury
www.KarenKingsbury.com

Center Point Publishing
600 Brooks Road ● PO Box 1
Thorndike ME 04986-0001 USA

(207) 568-3717

US & Canada:
1 800 929-9108
www.centerpointlargeprint.com